Leia Stone is the *USA Today* bestselling author of multiple bestselling series including Matefinder, Wolf Girl, Fallen Academy and Kings of Avalier. She's sold over three million books and her Fallen Academy series has been optioned for film. Her novels have been translated into five languages and she even dabbles in scriptwriting. Leia writes urban fantasy and paranormal romance with sassy kick-butt heroines and irresistible love interests. She lives in Spokane, WA with her husband and two children.

www.LeiaStone.com

Also by Leia Stone

The Kings of Avalier:
The Last Dragon King
The Broken Elf King
The Ruthless Fae King
The Forbidden Wolf King

Julie Hall is a *USA Today* bestselling, multiple award-winning author. Before diving into the world of publishing, she was publicist and marketer for Sony, Summit Entertainment, Paramount, The Weinstein Company, and the National Geographic Channel. Now, she crafts addictive action-packed fantasy stories that leave readers with epic book hangovers. Julie's books have been translated into four languages and won or were finalists in over twenty national and international awards.

Julie currently lives in Colorado with her four favourite people: her husband, daughter, and two fur babies.

www.JulieHallAuthor.com

T0371288

CURSED FAE BOOK THREE

BROKEN HEARTED

USA *TODAY* BESTSELLING AUTHORS

LEIA STONE
JULIE HALL

HQ

HQ
An imprint of HarperCollins*Publishers* Ltd
1 London Bridge Street
London SE1 9GF

www.harpercollins.co.uk

HarperCollins*Publishers*
Macken House, 39/40 Mayor Street Upper,
Dublin 1, D01 C9W8, Ireland

This edition 2025

1
First published in Great Britain by
HQ, an imprint of HarperCollins*Publishers* Ltd 2025

Initial cover design: Faye Lane
Map design: Brina Boyle
Character artwork: Anastasia Vasilevich

ISBN: 9780008706975

Set in 11.2/16 pt. Garamond by Type-it AS, Norway

Printed and bound in the UK using 100% Renewable
Electricity by CPI Group (UK) Ltd

For more information visit: www.harpercollins.co.uk/green

To our readers

ETHEREUM

NOREUM

MIDLANDS

WINDREUM

EASTERIA

SOLEUM

SOUTH ISLANDS

Chapter One

It was the night of the Winter Solstice. The portal was going to open, and I was about to either betray my people or my best friend. I was in an impossible position.

My mother smoothed down my long, dark hair, which mirrored her own. "You should have no fear. Even though you haven't trained for this your entire life like Dawn, you've done well these last months. We always knew it would be a possibility, even if a small one."

She was right. Every hundred years, the Summer princess, Faerie's champion, went through their portal and returned with the heart of an Ethereum lord, stopping the curse that threatened our realm. If she failed, the task fell to the next princess. But that had never happened before. So there had not been much reason to train me for a job that was unlikely to come my way.

Six months ago, the portal to Ethereum opened in the Summer Court, and Dawn had traveled to the mirror realm, but she never returned. Princess Aribella, the Fall princess, then became the champion and went with the same directive. But she, too, never returned.

As the Winter princess, I was third in line.

I peered down at my bag, packed with maps and rations. I was as ready as I'd ever be.

I'd been surprisingly calm after Dawn's ghostly apparition, along with Princess Aribella and the Ethereum lords, had come to see me. I knew Dawn at her core. She was not a woman easily fooled, and she would never give up on her people, so I had to believe that she had a plan to save us. I trusted her, which meant I could no longer trust Queen Liliana.

It had been hard to keep my questions buried deep inside over the past few months of training with the Summer queen. But I did. I trained with her, and I said *yes, ma'am* when she told me that I was Faerie's only hope and ordered me to cut out the heart of the first Ethereum lord I saw.

I told my mother I would do the same.

Only I knew I had been living a lie, and it was eating at me. Negative thoughts crept into my mind. What if Dawn was wrong? What if it hadn't been Dawn that visited me at all? What if it was someone pretending to be her in order to trick me?

But she knew about my birthmark and my first crush. Of course it was Dawnie.

I took a moment to really look at my mother. She was strong, emotionally and physically. She'd led our people well, with my father by her side, for twenty years. Until they ripped the illusion of a perfect marriage away from me and my sisters when I was fifteen by telling us they were divorcing.

Unhappy. Affair. I hate you. How could you? I'd heard my mother scream all of those things at my father one night when I was supposed to be sleeping. She wouldn't stand for the betrayal, and I didn't blame her. But I also still loved my father. It was a hard place to be: stuck between two people you loved. Now I felt that way again. Nineteen years old and I was torn again.

Between Dawn and all of Faerie.

"Your sisters want to say goodbye." My mother gestured to the door.

I turned to her. "If I don't make it back—"

"Nonsense."

"Mother, if I don't make it back in two days' time, take everyone to the Spring Court," I told her sternly.

She appeared a little shaken then, but the truth of the matter was that Dawn and Aribella had both been in my position and hadn't returned. The same could happen to me, especially if Dawn's plan to save Faerie was going to take a long time to execute. In that case, I wouldn't be returning right away.

"I will get the heart immediately, or something has gone wrong," I lied. I had no intention of killing one of those men. Not after Dawn claimed one was my mate.

Mate. That word was foreign to me, and I wanted nothing to do with it, but I recognized that I might have been lied to my entire life. That there was a chance the Ethereum lords weren't evil like we'd been told, but rather that they were just men with families and people who depended on them.

She nodded once, and we both left the room.

Seraphina, Elowen, Aria, Freya, Thalia, and Amara were waiting outside the door to my dressing room, standing stiffly with their arms at their sides. I knew they were trying to be brave, but their misty eyes and quivering lips betrayed how they really felt.

After me, Seraphina was the eldest at seventeen years old and the one I was closest to. The rest of my sisters were born two years apart. My mother planned her heirs perfectly, as she did everything else in her court.

I looked Seraphina in the eyes and grasped her shoulders. "Be strong."

For weeks, I'd agonized about whether or not to tell her about Dawn and what she'd said, but in the end, I decided it might endanger her life and my plan. So instead, I sent a letter to Lorelei, the Spring princess who was next in line to travel to Ethereum if I failed to destroy the curse. In the letter, I told her about Dawn and the Ethereum lords who had appeared in my bedroom. If I didn't return, she needed to know there might be another way to save our worlds that didn't involve carving a heart from someone's chest. Lorelei was the gentlest and most kind-hearted fae I'd ever met. Her gifts were rooted in bringing forth life, not ending it. Even with Queen Liliana's training, she wouldn't be able to kill an Ethereum lord. Of that, I was certain.

"Come back to us," Seraphina growled, and I grinned. There was the sassy sister I knew.

I pulled her into my arms, and then all the rest of my sisters pressed in around me, holding on to me and pushing me into the center of a giant sister hug.

Emotions clogged my throat, but I kept it together for them. When everyone pulled away, I was looking down at little seven-year-old Amara. She was missing one of her front teeth, and her hair had some streaks of red, like my father's. She was the sensitive one of us who had yet to fully control her power, which was evidenced by the snow now falling on my head even though we were still inside.

Reaching out, I brushed my fingertip along the falling tear on her cheek and froze it. She smiled, and it fell to the ground like a tiny shard of ice. Amara constantly asked me to freeze things. Fruit. Flowers. The annoying birds that chirped early on Sunday mornings. I, of course, ignored that last request, but she loved to see my power on display.

"You be good for Mother and Father, okay?"

She nodded and I gave her one final hug.

I had to leave before I lost my nerve.

I nodded that I was ready to Mother, who was patiently waiting for me to say goodbye to my sisters, and we continued down the hall to the throne room, stopping at the closed doors. My father stood there in his finest black velvet suit and gave my mother a nervous glance.

"Can I say goodbye?" he asked timidly.

Even after four years, he wasn't sure where things stood with her. She was the queen, and he was no longer the king consort now that they'd divorced. She'd allowed him residence on palace grounds in a guesthouse for the sake of my sisters and me, but it was a constant strain on our family when they were both in the same room.

"Of course. I'm not a monster, Leif," my mother said defensively.

"I never said you were," he added.

"Can we not?" I asked.

Always fighting. I'd vowed to never marry, just to avoid such a thing.

My father pulled me in for a hug. "Do what you have to in order to survive and come home," he whispered to me.

If only he knew. In order to do that, I'd have to slaughter Dawn's husband or one of the other handsome and seemingly kind men who had been present that night.

They weren't monsters. They were our mates, whatever that really meant.

It was a good thing the only one I'd truly been attracted to was already engaged. That would make all of this easier.

I hoped.

After my father released me, I took his hand and squeezed it. "I love you," I told him and pled with my eyes for him to get along with my mother while I was gone.

He must have learned to read minds because he nodded and said, "We'll be fine."

With a relieved sigh, I dropped his hand. My mother stepped up next to me, chin held high.

"Ready?" she asked.

I traced my fingers over the blue kyanite faestone dagger at my thigh and nodded.

Would I even use the weapon?

For a wild second, I had a dark thought. What was the heart of one man to save an entire kingdom? Even if he wasn't a monster, even if he was my mate, if he could save my people, maybe the sacrifice was worth it.

I'm pregnant. Dawn's words filtered back to me, and my heart pinched.

The princesses of Faerie were marrying the lords of Ethereum.

Having children with them. I couldn't just take one of their lives, not when there appeared to be another way. A way that wouldn't just delay the curse for a hundred years, but actually destroy it once and for all.

I strengthened my resolve. I'd already made my choice. And that was to trust Dawn.

The doors opened, and the cavernous throne room broke into applause as I smiled and waved, following my mother to the dais. Everyone who was anyone in the Winter Court was here.

My mother's most cherished advisors and courtiers stood around us, dressed in their finest attire. I nodded to the Honeyworths and then Mr. Thorpe before making my way past the Larkins. I'd grown up around these families, played with their children, and had dinner parties with them. It warmed my heart that they'd all come to wish me well.

We were Winter. We were resilient. We survived above all odds. This would not bring us down.

Suddenly, one of my mother's messengers ran forward, breaking through the crowd, alarm evident on his face. He was holding a scroll between his fingers.

A messenger would never interrupt my mother during a big event like this for something trivial. It must be urgent. She took the scroll with a smile, as if she'd expected it, and waved him off. Then she clutched it in her hand as we moved quickly around the room, thanking people for coming and accepting their well wishes.

Once we got to the stage, we stepped back into the small private alcove behind which was the ancient mirror portal. It was covered in dust yesterday, but now it shone.

Queen Liliana was there and greeted me as I gave her a small bow. My mother ripped the seal from the paper and scanned the message, her lips pursed as fear crossed over her face.

"What is it?" I asked.

She folded it and stuffed it into her pocket. "Nothing we can't handle. Let's get you off to the mirror world so that this entire nightmare can end."

Chills rose on my arms. I was a Winter fae, so that was saying something. "Mother, what does it say?"

I'd been preparing to take over from her for the past few years, she shared all matters of state with me.

Mother shared a look with Queen Liliana and cleared her throat. "The curse has started at the western edge of our lands. A deep freeze hit in the night and killed a dozen fae. They are frozen solid, and it comes this way."

I gasped. It was eerily similar to my power. Okay, it *was* my power, but without any intention behind it. It was just moving forward, killing everything in its path. It took a lot to freeze a Winter fae to death. This was frightening.

"It doesn't matter," Queen Liliana said. "You are about five minutes from stopping this curse and bringing harmony back to all of Faerie."

Right.

Crap.

I gave her a small smile, but I didn't like the way she scanned my face, as if trying to ferret out something I was hiding. Her gaze went to the dagger at my thigh, and I grabbed it, gripping it tightly like she taught me.

She relaxed a little then. "Remember, dear. Don't even let him speak. Get the heart, get home, and this is all over."

I nodded, my mind a whirlwind of anxious thoughts. What if that whole thing with Dawn was a trick? What if she'd lied to me? What if—

The mirror began to swirl in front of me.

"Okay, clear your mind. Just focus on the heart. The black heart of an Ethereum lord," she said.

I closed my eyes, taking in a deep breath, and doing as she said.

Black heart.

Black heart.

Tan skin, dark hair with honey-blond highlights, and bright teal eyes.

No. Don't think of the engaged guy, you idiot.

Black heart.

Before I lost my nerve, I opened my eyes and looked over at my mother.

"I love you. Forgive me," I said, and then jumped through the swirling portal before Queen Liliana could stop me, but the echoes of her furious screams followed.

Chapter Two

There was a tug at my navel as dizziness washed over me, and then my boots landed on white sand. I was temporarily blinded by the bright sun, something we barely saw in the Winter Court. My eyes adjusted and I gasped when I came face to face with a shirtless man. Beads of sweat rolled down his neck and onto his abs, cascading over each knot one by one.

Bless the stars.

I glanced up at his face and swallowed hard. It was him. Long hair. Honey-colored highlights. Engaged.

It was him.

We were on a sandy beach right in front of a giant castle as waves rolled in and out on the shore behind him. He had a basket full of fresh crabs at his feet.

For a moment, he looked as stunned as I felt, but then his eyes flared as they raked over me from head to toe and back up again. I reacted to that look like a physical touch and flushed under his inspection, but then his gaze caught on the blue faestone dagger clenched in my hand, and he seemed to come back to himself.

Taking a step backward, he held up his hands in defense. "Don't kill me, Isolde. Remember me? We've already met."

My heart did a somersault at the way he said my name. It was like there was music in his voice for a split second. Hearing and seeing him in real life was so much more potent than the ghostlike version of him that appeared in my room, and for a moment, it overwhelmed me. But then his gaze dropped to the faestone dagger again, reminding me of who he was and why I was here. And for a wild minute, I considered just killing him and going home, saving everyone. It was the easiest solution, even if perhaps not the moral one.

"Dawn said you might come. She sent a letter. It's inside," he said as he pointed to something behind me.

At the mention of Dawn, my murderous thoughts dissolved. She'd begged me not to hurt the Ethereum lords, and even though I didn't know this man's true character, I trusted Dawn. I couldn't kill this man. He was someone's family.

I sheathed the dagger, my hand slightly shaking with defeat. I was sweating gumdrops in my fur cloak, and I was pretty sure I would quickly get a sunburn from this mild exposure.

I peered over my shoulder at a giant white stone castle and then looked back at him.

"I'm Adrien," he said a little breathlessly and held out his hand. "This must be really weird for you."

I relaxed a little, realizing I hadn't spoken yet and probably seemed like a spooked animal. Or a rabid one, considering I'd just held a blade for half of our conversation.

"I'm Isolde," I said, even though he already knew that. When our fingers touched, a slight tingle went through my palm, and his brows drew together in confusion. His gaze then snaked slowly down my body, and my stomach heated.

"Adrien," a woman shrilled behind us. "Who's that?"

He yanked his hand away from me like he'd been burned.

"Elisana, darling," he laughed nervously. "Isolde has arrived, just like Dawn told us she might. We should give her Dawn's letter."

I spun and came face to face with a tall woman with long chestnut hair who did not look very pleased to see me. The fiancée. It had to be.

"Oh . . . interesting," she said, but her gaze was calculating. "Darling, why don't you put a shirt on and have your afternoon tea? I'll give her Dawn's letter."

"Yes, my love," Adrien said, and stepped away from me. I watched as he lugged the fresh crab basket up the beach and into the castle.

"Sorry about the intrusion." I gave a nervous laugh, expecting Elisana to tell me that it was no trouble, but instead she just stared at me with cold, unforgiving eyes.

I wanted to give Adrien's fiancée the benefit of the doubt. I didn't know her after all, but after only a few moments in her presence, I already greatly disliked her. Perhaps she was an acquired taste and would grow on me.

"This way," she said, leading me toward the castle and then through the same door Adrien had disappeared into moments before.

Despite everything, I found myself looking for him as soon as I crossed the threshold, but with a shake of my head, I forced my gaze forward as I followed Elisana through an open sitting room, down a hallway, and into what looked to be a kitchen.

The basket of crabs that Adrien had carried inside was sitting on a counter next to a portly woman who looked up from where she was filleting a large fish as we passed. Her eyes grew a little wide when she saw us. She dipped her head and murmured a quiet, "My lady," to Elisana, who breezed right by without acknowledging her at all. The chef's gaze shifted to me, and I gave her a warm smile that she returned before continuing with her task.

We exited the kitchen and passed a food storage room, before popping out into a large open foyer and taking a winding staircase up, up, and up. I tried to shrug off my heavy cloak, but Elisana wouldn't slow her steps as we ascended, and I didn't want to fall behind.

By the time we reached our destination, a small library on one of the upper floors, I was huffing and puffing and coated in sweat. I was sure my face was red, and after finally freeing myself of my cloak, I wiped the wetness off my brow with my sleeve. Unfortunately, taking off my cloak only offered a small measure of comfort, because my pants and long-sleeved tunic were both fur-lined. This served me well in the Winter Court, but here, which I assumed was the Southern Kingdom based on the map and journals from the previous champions that had been given to me, I was struggling with my wardrobe.

Without explaining herself, Elisana went over to a desk and pulled a key out of her pocket. Then she unlocked a drawer and pulled something out.

I was parched and swayed a little on my feet. I needed to get out of these clothes and into something lighter, if for no other reason than to be able to think straight again.

"Do you have anything more appropriate to the climate that I could wear?" I asked, feeling like I was standing inside a furnace.

Elisana turned, looking down her nose at me even though we were both around the same height. "No, my clothes would be *far* too small on you."

My mouth dropped open. Yes, Elisana was a slender woman, but from the disgusted look on her face, it was clear she was insinuating that I was twice her size, which I was not. I may have a few more curves than she did, but if she had a loose-fitting dress, I was certain it would fit me.

I was about to give her a piece of my mind when Adrien swept into the room, fully clothed this time. He'd pulled his shoulder-length hair back, and the sleeves on his shirt were rolled up to reveal strong forearms that I hadn't noticed before.

Much to my disappointment—or perhaps secret delight—covering up his chest did little to dampen his attractiveness. I was used to the pale complexions of the Winter fae in our realm, but I found Adrien's bronzed skin particularly appealing and had trouble tearing my gaze from him.

"You look like you are melting," Adrien said, snapping me out of my trance. "If you like, Elisana can get you something else to wear."

I shot him a look as I self-consciously pushed back the black hairs sticking to my forehead. Did he know his fiancée at all?

Elisana sauntered over to Adrien and slipped her arm through his. "I already informed her that there was no way any of my clothes would be large enough for her," she said as she stroked his arm, a small smirk on her mouth.

"Oh, well, I don't think that . . ." Adrien glanced back and forth between his fiancée and me, and even more warmth infused my already overheated cheeks.

It was one thing to insinuate I was large in private, but in front of someone else was a whole other matter. I didn't care that I'd only known her for less than an hour; I hated the woman and was already convinced that would never change.

Adrien cleared his throat. "I'll instruct my lead housemaid to find you something more comfortable to wear, Isolde. The Southern Kingdom's climate isn't for everyone, and coming from the Winter Court, I know this heat must be particularly uncomfortable."

The smirk quickly dropped from Elisana's face, and the sour look that replaced it brought a smile to my own.

"That would be greatly appreciated," I said sweetly, purposefully batting my lashes at Adrien to further infuriate his dreadful fiancée.

A look came upon Adrien's face as he stared at me, almost as if he was seeing me for the first time. It made me feel a little lightheaded, but maybe it was just the heat playing tricks on me.

"Darling," Elisana's shrill voice cut through the air as she tugged on his arm. "Have you had your tea yet?"

He shook his head, his gaze shifting to the woman at his side. "Oh, no, I was just about to do that, but I wanted to make sure Isolde had seen the letter."

"I have it right here," she said, holding up a piece of folded paper in her other hand that I hadn't noticed before. "Why don't you have your tea, and I promise I'll get this *issue* sorted out."

Issue? I was an issue now that needed to be sorted?

I brushed my fingers over my faestone dagger, imagining burying it in her instead of Adrien. The mental image was oddly comforting.

"And there is no need to alert Fiona, my love. I'll make sure to find Isolde something to wear," she went on. The evil smile on her face should have worried me, but at that point, I'd happily don a potato sack if it meant getting out of those sweaty clothes.

Adrien smiled down at the wench. "Thank you, my love."

My love? Please. I rolled my eyes as they stared at each other. How did he like this woman, let alone love her?

I couldn't fathom what he saw in her, but reminded myself that I didn't care who this Ethereum lord bound himself to. He could be engaged to a broomstick as far as I was concerned. I was here for one reason and one reason alone.

To end the curse and then go home.

Elisana finally released her grip on the lord when Adrien started to leave, but right before he left the room, he turned back. "Isolde, I'm glad you made it here safely. Dawn has been quite worried. I'll see you for dinner tonight?"

"Oh, no, darling," Elisana started. "I'm sure the princess would much rather eat alone in—"

"I'm looking forward to dinner with you *very* much," I said, cutting her off, which earned me a glare that gave me nothing but pleasure.

When Adrien was finally gone, Elisana thrust the folded letter at me, slamming it into my chest. I met her glare with one of my own and had to take several deep breaths to keep my cool. I peered down at the letter. Even though my name was scrawled across the front, the seal had already been broken. I ground my teeth at the invasion of privacy but pushed it from my mind when I saw Dawn's handwriting.

My dearest Izzy,

I'm so sorry that I can't be there to welcome you to Ethereum. I've missed you terribly, but the curse that plagues Faerie has also spilled into our kingdom in the northern section of Ethereum, and Zander and I are doing all we can to keep it from destroying the people and the land.

If you are reading this message, it means two things. First, that you have arrived in the Southern Kingdom rather than the Western Kingdom. For that, I am truly sorry, because I surmise that you won't get as warm of a welcome as you would have if you'd arrived in Zane's kingdom.

I glanced up at Elisana, who was impatiently watching me with her arms crossed over her chest and a frown pulling down her features. Dawn wasn't wrong about that. There's not much about my arrival that I'd call welcoming so far. Maybe except for Adrien.

As if to punctuate the point, a drop of sweat rolled off my forehead and landed on the page, smudging my name. I swiped the sweat away and continued to read.

Secondly, it means that you have chosen to trust me and haven't tried to kill Adrien. For that, I will be forever grateful. I want to assure you that I believe with my whole heart that we are doing the right thing and that we will succeed in destroying this curse on our lands once and for all.

In the letter, Dawn went on to describe a crystal called the Shadow Heart that Princess Aribella and her new husband, Stryker, the Ethereum lord of the Eastern Kingdom, had found. They all believed this Shadow Heart would play a part in destroying the curse, yet they didn't know how. She wrote that I needed to collect the Shadow Heart, which they'd given to Zane in the hopes that I'd arrive in his kingdom instead of here. Then I had to travel to see some sort of prophetic unseelie fae called the Wise Ones, who lived in the Northern Mountains near where Dawn now lived. She assured me they would set me on the right path toward ending the curse. The letter ended with . . .

As soon as we have things stabilized here in the Northern Kingdom, I will come to where you are. My thoughts are with you, but I know how strong you are and that you will be able to overcome anything in your path.

Your friend,
Dawnie

Refolding the note, I stored it in my bag. Elisana didn't bother pretending not to know what it said.

"We had hoped you'd appear in the Western Kingdom. Terrible timing that you are here because Adrien and I are set to marry in three weeks. We don't need the intrusion."

She paused, as if waiting for a reaction from me. But I didn't have one to give her. Besides the rudeness of the comment, what did I care that they were getting married? Better them than me.

"But I suppose there's nothing to be done about it now," she went on when it was clear I wasn't going to respond however she expected. "The important thing is to get you out of our kingdom as soon as possible. We'll send word to Lord Zane to let him know you are here, and then you can be off the moment he arrives to collect you."

"I'll *gladly* leave the second he gets here," I said, meaning it. I didn't want to spend any more time in this woman's presence than I had to.

"Then we agree," she said, her smile looking sickeningly sweet.

"In this, we do."

"Well, then, I'll show you where you can stay until I come get you for dinner."

And with that, I followed the wench out of the room, trying not to second-guess all of my decisions up to this moment. Killing the handsome Lord Adrien would have been easier.

Chapter Three

Elisana put me in a servant's room, of that I was certain. The only things in the room were a sleeping pallet in the corner and a chamber pot. There wasn't even a washbasin for me to clean up.

After two hours, a maid finally appeared with a dull brown dress so large I had to rip a strip off the bottom of the skirt to create a sash to keep it in place. It couldn't have been less flattering. I should have just gone ahead and asked for a potato sack because it would have had more shape. But at least it was light and flowy and allowed air to breeze through it.

The sun had set, offering a little bit of reprieve from the oppressive heat by the time Elisana showed up to bring me to dinner. We ignored each other as we walked the halls of the castle and toward the dining room. Not speaking to this woman was fine by me, but I was curious about her relationship with Adrien, especially since Dawn had hinted that the Ethereum lords were our 'mates'. I had already taken that to mean that this Zane fellow must be mine, but where did that leave Adrien? Where did that leave Lorelei, the Spring princess?

I shook my head to dislodge the thoughts. It didn't matter anyway. Even if Zane was my mate, there was zero chance I was ever getting married.

"How long have you known Adrien?" I asked her as we approached a set of open double doors that led to a dining table. I saw that Adrien was already seated with a lavish display of food out before him.

Elisana gave me an annoyed side glance. "A while," she said shortly and then stepped ahead of me to rush over to her fiancé.

"Sorry I'm late, my love. I had to look my best for you." She pulled her shoulders back, puffing up her cleavage and turning just so to show off her expertly done hair and make-up, but his gaze only rested on her for a second before it flicked past her to me.

I wore no make-up, my hair was messily tied back, and the dress was not flattering, yet the way he looked at me lit a fire inside of my chest that burned all the way to my belly. It felt like the air was sucked from the room as I was caught up in those blue-green eyes.

"Glazed pork," Elisana shrieked, and both Adrien and I jerked our heads in her direction.

"Darling, you know that's my favorite." Taking a seat next to him, she reached out and stroked his upper arm. And for some wild reason, I felt something ugly flare to life inside of me.

Calm down, Isolde. He's taken, and you've sworn off love.

Adrien sat at the head of the table with Elisana to his right, and so I took the seat to his left, which put me directly across from her. She kept her hand on his upper arm and gave me a glare, letting me know she was marking her territory.

Our meal server entered the room then, and I caught my breath as I stared at the small horns protruding from his forehead.

Unseelie.

I didn't want to be rude, but I couldn't stop staring. I'd never seen an unseelie before, obviously, and even knowing this world was filled with the fae folk, I still wasn't prepared.

The fae came over, poured me a glass of wine and gave me a kind smile. "Enjoy your meal, my lady."

"Thank you." I returned the smile, hoping my interest in him wasn't obvious, as I had no desire to offend him.

When he left the room, we began to eat, and Adrien directed a question at me. "Is it true in Faerie that there are only seelie fae?"

So he had noticed.

I nodded. "It's true. Our land seems set up similar to yours but instead of north, south, east, and west, we have summer, spring, fall, and," I pointed to myself, "winter."

He returned my smile with ease. "I'd like to see Faerie one day."

I opened my mouth to respond, when Elisana interrupted.

"Darling, did you hear the dreadful news that the floral designer is ill? Could we send the royal healer over to her to make sure she's ready for our big day?"

He smiled fondly at Elisana. "Of course."

Then he looked back at me. "May I ask what your powers are? I've always wondered—"

"Darling," Elisana said with a sharpness in her tone, and for the first time, I saw a flash of annoyance appear on Adrien's face as he glanced over at her.

"Yes?" He asked her with the same sharpness.

Her mouth popped open in shock as if he'd slapped her. "Did you have your tea?" she asked in a tone that made the hair on my arms raise.

What was with this tea? Was he ill? Maybe it was medicinal.

The realization shone on his face, and he laughed. "I totally forgot."

She relaxed, rolling her eyes. "You are so bad. I'll just have to make it for you so my love stays healthy for our big day." She stood, and leaning forward, she planted a slow kiss on his lips.

Nausea roiled in my gut as I watched them. My fingers curled around the meat knife I held, and I envisioned driving it right into her eye.

What was going on with me? Why was I acting like this?

I forced myself to release the knife and looked away to give them privacy.

When they finally broke apart, Elisana sauntered from the room, her hips swaying seductively with every step. Just before leaving, she cast a glance over her shoulder at me, a sly smile curving her lips.

I cast my gaze to Adrien. "So this tea sounds pretty important."

Something was not right here. It was weird, but I couldn't put my finger on it.

Adrien nodded. "Elisana has been a lifesaver. I was sleeping horribly and dealing with a lot of stress. I would toss and turn, grinding my teeth, and not even the royal healer could help me relax on a nightly basis. Elisana is from the Northern Mountains and grew up learning about herbs and tinctures. She's studying to be a herbalist. She created a tea that's taken away all of my symptoms."

I relaxed a little after hearing that. Okay, so this tea *was* important, and it made sense, but I still didn't like her.

"That's nice," I said just as Elisana appeared with a steaming mug of tea. The scent hit me, and I inhaled. Notes of rose petals and jasmine tickled my nose. "Oh, that smells lovely. Can I have some? I often have trouble sleeping, too." And since I was in a foreign land, it would be nice to have some help.

She glared at me. "Sorry, fresh out of this batch, and by the time I make another, you'll be long gone. So sad," she mock pouted.

I ate the rest of my meal in silence, shooting eye daggers across the table at Elisana.

* * *

My sleep was fitful, I was nervous about meeting Zane and this whole Shadow Heart thing, and I couldn't stop thinking about those blue-green eyes and how they bore into mine. It was good that I was leaving soon. Staying here might get me into trouble with Adrien. Or more correctly, Elisana.

After rising, I ate a quick breakfast alone, as Elisana had it delivered to my room and did not invite me to eat with her and Adrien. Even though it might take days for Zane to get to the Southern Kingdom from the Western, I was still ready with my bag packed, hopeful I wouldn't have to remain in Adrien's castle for very much longer. After my morning meal, I waited for hours before Elisana finally sent a maid with a note. Apparently, Adrien had somehow contacted his brother directly through some magical means after dinner the night before. Zane was coming down from the Western Kingdom to pick me up but wouldn't arrive until after nightfall.

I had no idea how Adrien had been able to talk to his brother from a long distance, but maybe that was how the Ethereum lords' magic worked? In Faerie we didn't have the means to communicate across long distances besides sending ravens or messengers, but however it was done, apparently, it left Adrien drained. In her note, Elisana complained about the strain, blaming me for Adrien having to recover all day. She said that it would be bothersome for me to be wandering about the castle, and so I should stay in my room for the day.

I prickled at the authoritative tone in her note. I was a princess of Faerie: who was she to order me to stay in my room? But on the other hand, I had no desire to run into her and be forced to endure her sour presence any more than necessary. So I spent the day in the tiny room, pacing the floors until my feet hurt, my mind swirling with thoughts of Zane and Adrien and the curse.

No one had come out and said it, but it was clear the assumption was that Zane was my mate. I could claim I didn't believe in mates as much as I wanted, but what if it were true? What did that mean? Was I going to be expected to marry him? Because if that was what he thought, he was going to be in for a surprise. I was happy for Dawn and Aribella. They seemed content with their new lives, but I wasn't going to just shack up with the first Ethereum lord who paid a little extra attention to me because we were supposed "mates". Especially not after seeing what my own mother and father went through.

Mate or not, my mind was made up. I was only here to help

end the curse, then I was going to do everything to get home to my parents and sisters. My life was in the Winter Court, not this foreign land with one of its dark lords.

A knock at the door ripped me from my thoughts.

"Isolde, Zane is here," Elisana's annoying voice called from the other side of the door.

I took a deep breath and grabbed my bag, slinging it over my shoulder. I was wearing the same baggy dress with ripped sash from yesterday because Elisana hadn't brought me anything else, but at least I'd had a bath this morning in the bathroom shared with the maids.

When I stepped out into the foyer, Elisana and Adrien were talking to a handsome man that stood a good three or four inches over Adrien, who was already tall himself. He had brownish auburn hair that was shaved on the sides and longer on top. When his gaze met mine, I noticed there was something different about his eyes. They were dark blue with a splash of brown in one of them. Unusual, yet interesting.

Stepping forward, Zane broke out into a grin. "Isolde. It's so lovely to officially meet you." He bowed his head a little, which was very sweet considering he was on the same level as I was royalty wise, if not one notch above since he was acting lord where in the Winter Court my mother was still queen.

"Hello, Zane." I gave him a sheepish smile.

Even though I'd sworn off love I had half expected sparks when I met Zane, but so far there was nothing. He was undoubtedly handsome and seemingly kind, but I didn't feel any fireworks, as my mother called them.

Good. I didn't want them.

"Well, you better get going if you want to make good time." Elisana opened the front door wide, and Zane frowned. "Oh. I thought we might have dinner together or—"

"Oh, we'd love to. Another time though, we're planning the wedding, remember?" Elisana reminded Zane. "So much to do. And I'm sure you're eager to get Isolde back to your kingdom."

Zane glanced at his brother Adrien, who stood still as a statue as Elisana clung to his arm and nodded. "Right. The wedding. I'm excited for that. We won't bother you then," Zane said.

Adrien frowned. "You're not a bother. If my brother wants to stay for dinner before his journey, he stays for dinner." He yanked his arm out of Elisana's grip, and Zane and I shared an awkward look.

"You know. I think heading out is probably best," I added, giving Zane a wide-eyed look. I didn't want to stay in this house one more minute than I had to.

Zane seemed to catch my meaning. "Right. We should go. Dinner next time, brother. Perhaps when we return for the wedding."

We? I didn't think so. I had no desire to ever come back to this castle, let alone watch Adrien and Elisana marry. But I didn't bother to correct Zane. It wasn't worth it.

Reaching out, Zane pulled Adrien in for a hug, and all the while Elisana just fixed me with a glare.

When they broke apart, Zane held the door for me. I passed Adrien and curtsied to him. "It was nice meeting you. I wish you well with your wedding and everything," I finished lamely.

His face fell for a second, like he just realized he'd probably never see me again. "It was nice meeting you too, Isolde."

I tried to look away then, but suddenly, there was something tangible in the air, something I couldn't explain. It made it hard to breathe as I was held captive by his gaze. I glanced at his full lips, not able to stop myself from wondering what they might be like to kiss, when Elisana stepped right in front of me and broke our connection.

"Bye," she said flatly.

It was like someone had doused me in cold water. I turned and fled out of the castle as fast as my feet could carry me. Zane jogged to catch up. There was a carriage up ahead with half a dozen guards on horseback around it.

"She's horrible," Zane said behind me, and I couldn't help but pop a grin.

"The worst. And you almost made us have dinner with her," I scolded him.

His smile matched my own. "My mistake. It will never happen again."

He opened the carriage door for me and took the bag off my shoulder. "This is light. Have you no more clothes?" He eyed my baggy dress.

I shook my head. "I'm from the Winter Court, and everything I wore was too warm for this land. I didn't pack extra clothes because it was assumed that I wouldn't be staying here long," I said.

He nodded. "You get the heart and get out."

My eyes widened at his blunt description. I mean, he wasn't wrong.

"Sorry, that was a joke." He gave a nervous laugh, which I matched. He was adorable, and sweet.

He looked at the driver of the carriage. "Take us to the shops and then the train station."

My eyebrows shot up. "You have trains?"

We had a small train in the Winter Court that went through the ice mountains and carried coal from the mines, but it was rudimentary and not fit for passengers.

I stepped inside the luxurious carriage, and Zane climbed in after me.

"The railroad is what my land is known for. That and coal mining. I've been working with my brothers to extend my railroad through all of Ethereum so we can travel with ease. We're not there yet, but we are getting close. We haven't connected the tracks all the way to Easteria, the capital of the Eastern Kingdom yet. It will take several more years to finish the big plan of having train stops in every major city, but we have gotten far. It will be nice to leave something behind that the people can benefit from." He smiled. "We've just finished connecting Windreum, the capital of the Western Kingdom where I live, to Soleum, here in the Southern Kingdom. It should cut our trip time by seventy-five percent."

"It sounds fun. I've never ridden on a train." I told him.

We made small talk then as the carriage took us into the heart of Soleum and stopped at a women's dress shop.

"Let's get you at least two weeks' worth of new clothes," he declared.

He was taking me shopping? That was so kind and thoughtful.

"You don't have to do that," I told him.

He nodded. "I want to."

It was late, but Zane was able to convince the proprietor to open the store just for us. As she showed me the latest fashions, Zane arranged for food to be brought to me so I wouldn't go hungry. His care and concern were such a change from how Elisana treated me, that I couldn't help but warm toward him.

After a couple of hours, I left the shop with a full belly and an entire new wardrobe. Even though I'd told Zane I only needed a couple of staple items, he wouldn't hear of it and now I had enough clothes to last me a very long time. Four full trunks to be exact. Zane had to hire an extra carriage just to get them to the train. It was a mix of dresses, pants, cloaks, and shoes for both warm and cold climates. He'd essentially bought out the entire store in my size, and as we departed, the owners were close to tears, thanking him profusely and telling us to return anytime.

And on top of that, Zane also assured me that he'd have a seamstress fit me for custom gowns when we returned to his kingdom. I told him that wasn't necessary; I only had plans to stay in Ethereum as long as it took to break the curse and then I would find a way to return to my home in Faerie, but he only smiled and said that it was no trouble.

By the time the carriage brought us to what I assumed was the train station that Zane had told me about, it was well into the evening and my eyelids were heavy with exhaustion. Who knew shopping could be so tiring?

Zane had told me that the trip from Soleum back to his castle in Windreum would take twelve hours, so we could sleep overnight and would arrive in his kingdom in the morning. I marveled at how quickly we would get to his homeland, considering the distance. I'd studied the map of Ethereum before traveling here. It would easily take at least three days of horseback riding, if not more, to travel that far. This train of his was truly a marvel, and he seemed very proud of it.

The train station was a beautiful large brick building that when you stepped inside brought you to a platform that held a gorgeous red train with over twenty cars all linked together. It was nothing like the dinky coal train I'd seen in Faerie. This was brand new, still smelling of fresh paint and varnish. I couldn't wait to see what it looked like inside.

Zane reached forward and put a steadying hand on my elbow to help me up the steps that led into the train car.

"Thank you," I told him, and he released me when I reached the top.

I found myself wondering if Zane acted this way to every woman or if he was treating me differently because he believed we were mates. I hoped it was the former because if he expected anything romantic from me, he was going to be disappointed. Which, strangely enough considering I'd just met him, made me feel a little bad for him. He was so attuned to my needs, he'd spent the last few hours making sure I had proper clothing and feeding me, and now he was taking care that I didn't trip on the steps. If I were to marry anyone, Zane was the kind of partner my mother would dream of me having. He was the biggest sweetheart in the world, but when I looked into his eyes . . . I felt nothing.

No fire. No zest. No oomph, as Seraphina would call it.

Not even an inkling of what I felt when I looked at his brother Adrien. The engaged one.

Stop. I scolded myself and forced my brain to think of other things.

Zane smiled at me warmly. "You must be exhausted. Let me show you to your room in the sleeping car."

"Sleeping car?" I asked, and he nodded.

"We have several small rooms on the train set up for overnight travel." He gestured for me to move deeper into the car we stood in just as the train started to move.

There were windows on either side and rows of padded seats where fae could sit. As we walked down the aisle and through a few more cars, opening and closing doors between each, Zane explained the name and purpose of each of them.

Besides the sleeping car we were headed toward, the train also had several coach cars to carry passengers, a dining car to eat in, and even an observation car with lots of windows so passengers could enjoy the view. He told me that the train also had storage cars and flatcars to transport materials as well.

Zane's train was impressive, to say the least, and seemed like a wonderful way to travel. I wished we had something like it in Faerie. Maybe someday we could build a train this grand in my court as well.

When we finally reached the sleeping car, Zane paused in front of an open compartment. Inside was a narrow bed with thick blankets and linens, as well as a towel and basin of water sitting atop a small nightstand for washing up.

The space was lavishly decorated with thick drapes that were currently pulled down over the window for privacy. The walls were lined with rich, dark green fabric, and a black and gold patterned rug covered the floor.

"I know the space is rather small," Zane said with a wince. "But I hope it will be okay for just tonight."

"This is perfect. Thank you," I said, meaning it. Despite the size, it was definitely a step up from the room Eliana had stuck me in at Adrien's castle.

"Do you need anything before retiring for the night?" he asked, and I shook my head.

"I'm fine, really. I expect to be asleep the second my head touches the pillow."

He smiled. "Good. Then I'll leave you alone." He pointed further down the car. "My room is the last one on the left. If you need anything, anything at all, please don't hesitate to get me."

When he'd left I fell into the bed with my oversized clothes still on, and within minutes the rocking of the train lulled me to sleep.

Chapter Four

The next morning I woke to a soft knocking. My eyes popped open, and it took a couple of seconds to remember where I was. When I did, I jumped out of bed and took two short steps to the door, unlocked it, and peered out. A kind-looking fae with dark blue skin and two leathery wings folded behind her smiled back at me.

I took a half step back before stopping myself. We had always been taught that the unseelie were as evil as the Ethereum lords who ruled this land. If we were wrong about the Ethereum lords, I assumed we were about the unseelie as well, but it was going to take a little more time for me to get used to seeing unseelie and not reacting.

"Oh, hello," I said, trying not to focus on her wings.

"I'm Greta. Lord Zane wanted you to have something fresh to wear this morning," she said, and then handed me a small bundle of clothes in her hands that I'd been too distracted to notice before.

"Thank you," I said, returning her smile and accepting the clothes.

"Will you need help putting them on?" she asked, and seeing

that it was a fairly simple dress with the typical underclothes, I shook my head. "Very well then," she said. "We're still a couple hours out from Windreum, so just come out when you're ready and I'll show you to the dining car where you can have breakfast with Lord Zane."

I thanked her again and shut the door, quickly changing out of the frumpy dress Elisana had given me and into one of the cotton gowns that Zane had purchased the night before. It was burgundy and fit like a glove.

I wasn't particularly vain, but it felt incredible to be wearing something that finally fit and was appropriate for the climate. Zane had told me that his kingdom wasn't as warm as the Southern one, and thank goodness for that. He said that the days were comfortably warm, and the evenings had a slight chill. The dress Greta picked out was lightweight, but had sleeves that went down to my wrists, appropriate for the weather Zane had described.

When I was dressed and ready, Greta was waiting outside my door with another smile. "This way," she said.

I followed behind her, my eyes catching details I was too tired to pick up on last night. The gilded sconce lanterns lining the walls, the polished wood floors, the fabric-covered ceilings. The train truly spoke of luxury and refinement, yet Zane had told me last night that he intended it for all his people, not just the wealthy. It was a testament to his character that he didn't think luxury like this should be hoarded for only the rich to enjoy but that he wanted to share it with everyone. He was a thoughtful and kind fae, and I was finding it impossible not to like him.

When we walked through the observation car on the way to

meet Zane, my mouth dropped open. We must have crossed into the Western Kingdom because the scenery had changed drastically. The train was passing through a forested area, and the trees were a kaleidoscope of colors. Burned oranges, bright sienna tones, rich reds, deep purples, and cheerful, buttery yellows.

It reminded me of the time I visited the Fall Court on official business with my mother, but admittedly, the vibrancy and depth of the colors even put the Fall Court to shame. I didn't know what exactly I expected of Ethereum, but it wasn't that it would be this beautiful.

Zane rose from his seat when I entered the dining car, a smile on his face. He looked handsome, with his hair braided back into a tight plait and dressed formally in a royal blue jacket and matching dark pants, but my stomach didn't flip when I laid eyes on him or even when his gaze rolled over me from head to toe and back up again.

"Did you sleep well?" he asked as he pulled out a seat opposite him.

"I did, thank you," I said, and joined him. There was a delicious spread of fruit, scrambled eggs, and charred meat which I helped myself to and then Zane pulled out a black leather pouch and handed it to me.

"From Dawn. It's the Shadow Heart," he said, keeping his gaze on me.

"Oh." I set my fork down and pulled open the flap. I don't know what I expected, but a heart made of black stone kind of made sense considering its name. "Do we know what I'm supposed to do with this? Maybe we should go see Dawn?"

"We can if you want to, but Dawn left me a note stating that they are dealing with a crisis at the moment, and if I could help you with this and accompany you to the Wise Ones it would be preferred. But if you're not comfortable—"

"That's fine," I told him. Poor Dawnie. "In her letter to me, she said that the Northern Kingdom where she lives is cursed too."

He nodded. "It's like a plague. Started by making the unseelie sick and now it's bled into the land. We need to see the Wise Ones so they can tell you what your part in all of this is."

"Okay, let's go see the Wise Ones then," I agreed. The sooner I could do my part and figure out a way to get back home to my family, the better. Already, I'd been two nights without my little sisters. I bet they were worried sick.

"Perfect. Just a quick stop in my capital, if you don't mind. I have some urgent matters to deal with, and then we can leave tomorrow morning for the Northern Mountains. That's where the Wise Ones live."

I nodded. "Sounds good."

He heaved a book out from under the table. It was all tabbed up and underlined. "In the meantime, Aribella sent this."

I laughed. Book-loving Aribella *would* send me something like this.

I stroked my fingers along the title. "*Magic of Old.*"

My curiosity was piqued, and I started thumbing through the tabbed pages. There was interesting information about Ethereum's magic, particularly how it was passed down from one lord to the next, but I didn't find anything that would help me defeat the curse.

When the train pulled into the station of Windreum we stepped off the platform to a gathered crowd of cheering fae. They clearly loved their lord, and threw flower petals at us while Zane waved to them as we stepped into his awaiting carriage.

"Somebody is well-liked by their people," I said playfully as I clutched the black leather bag containing the Shadow Heart and Aribella's book to my chest. I planned to read as much of it as I could today while Zane had matters to attend to.

Zane ducked his head. "Well, it's not just that . . ." He eyed me shyly. "They think . . . well, they heard that the princesses of Faerie come and then the lord gets married, and they assume . . ." He trailed off, and dread sank into my gut.

"Oh," I said. "They think we will be married?"

He nodded, looking hopeful but also unsure.

"Listen, Zane—"

He waved me off. "Of course it's too soon to know any of that," he said, almost as if he already knew what I was about to tell him and didn't want to hear it.

"Of course," I told him, not ready to have that awkward conversation right now.

Just because Dawn and Aribella claimed to have met and married their mates didn't mean Zane or Adrien was mine. Perhaps it was just a coincidence that Dawn and Aribella fell in love with the two brothers, and they were reading too much into the situation? Maybe I was destined to be a lonely spinster with twenty cats. I wasn't even mad about the idea.

After taking a carriage ride through his beautiful capital, we stopped at a hillside mine on the outskirts of Windreum. The mountain had been half carved out with rich black coal hidden inside, but I could see from my place inside the carriage that something had gone wrong. The entrance was half caved in. They'd had a mine collapse. I knew how dangerous those were. I overheard my mother talking about one just last month in the Winter Court. It had killed a dozen miners.

"I have to deal with this. You're welcome to stay in the carriage and read your book or walk around. This part of the city is safe, and the people are very friendly," he assured me.

The area was very quaint. The thatched roofs and bright red- and orange-colored buildings had a vibrant air to them, but I needed to focus on my task. End this curse and go home.

"I'll read my book in here. Thank you," I said, with a smile.

Over the next few hours, I tried to read but kept losing concentration by the grunting and yelling of the men at the mine entrance. I bent the corner of the page I was on and closed it. Maybe it was time to see if there was any way I could help.

After exiting the carriage, I took the small pathway to the mine entrance at the base of the mountain. When I got there, I saw that Zane was shirtless, which was a sight to behold. The man was all muscle.

I felt my eyes widen when black bolts of lightning shot from the tips of his fingers, blasting the rock blocking the entrance. The boulders exploded, creating an opening for half a second, only for it to collapse again. Men stood to the left and right with thick beams of wood and rushed forward when he'd created an opening, only to run back as it collapsed. It seemed they were trying to clear the debris and create a new opening.

Zane and his men repeated this process again and again with the same results before I finally stepped forward.

"Need help?" I asked as Zane groaned for the fiftieth time.

"Is there any way you can keep the mine entrance open while my men repair the opening?" he asked me, with slight sarcasm in his tone.

I grinned. "Yes, I can. Do you have water? I can pull it from the air or a person's body in an emergency, but filled buckets would be better. Six should do it."

Zane's mouth popped open as if he didn't expect that response and then he looked at two of the men who were standing by. "Go fetch the water," he called to them.

They ran off and returned quickly. When we had the six buckets sitting at the base of the collapsed entrance, I looked at Zane. "Have them pour three of the buckets onto the fallen dirt mound."

Zane ordered the men to do just that, something I didn't feel comfortable doing since they weren't my men. They did as they were asked, and I felt my palms tingle with the anticipation of using my power.

"Stand back," I told the group of men, Zane included. They took several steps back, and I inhaled deeply, calling on my power.

I could feel the moisture in the air, the moisture in the men's bodies and on their breath and the wetness of the dirt. I exhaled and a chill formed in the air, causing the men to look around in surprise. Using my power I froze the wet dirt and then levitated it up into the caved-in ceiling.

Once it was held above where it should be, I pulled the water from the buckets, forcing it upwards and freezing it so that it would hold the dirt in place even when I pulled my power back. By the time I was done, the opening of the mine had been restored, and the men were able to rush forward to install the new beams and create a sturdy entrance.

I looked over at Zane to see him grinning ear to ear. "You watched me struggle for over an hour when you could have done that the entire time?"

I laughed. "I thought you had it handled."

He stepped closer to me, hope in his eyes. "We make a good team. Don't you think?"

We did. But did that really mean anything significant? I made a good team with my sisters as well as my tutors, trainers, and even Dawn, yet none of them were my mate.

His face fell when I waited too long to respond, and he turned to the men and gave them some instructions for finishing the job before he spun back to me.

"Shall we head back to the carriage?" he asked, his voice betraying the hurt he was feeling.

I hated this. I hated how much love, or even the prospect of love, could hurt you and let you down. It was very clear to me now that he was hoping I might be his mate.

After tugging his shirt back on, Zane walked over to the carriage and stepped inside, and I followed after him, feeling like a total jerk. The trip from the mine to his castle was mostly silent, with the occasional interruption when Zane pointed out something of interest in the city. I didn't get the impression that Zane was angry with me, but rather that he was disappointed and sad. And that, in turn, made me feel melancholy as well. I wished we could just put this whole mate issue aside because I really just wanted to focus on saving my people.

When we finally pulled up in front of Zane's castle, his smile as he helped me from the carriage didn't reach his eyes, but I could tell he was trying.

"Welcome to my home," he said proudly as I looked up, up, and up at the soaring castle in front of us.

The red stone structure was as beautiful as it was impressive. It was taller than our palace in the Winter Court, with multiple terraces, flying buttresses, and giant spires reaching high into the sky.

When I looked back at Zane, I was sure he could see the awe on my face, and his smile finally rang true. "It's lovely," I said honestly.

"Thank you," Zane said and then motioned me forward, up the steps to the front door.

When we entered the castle, the interior was no less remarkable than the façade. The foyer was three stories high. In front of us was a set of curved staircases leading to the upper floors. Rich tapestries of fall hues hung from the walls, a chandelier dripped with crystals that sent a kaleidoscope of colors across the space, and thick rugs lined the stone floors.

A far cry from the stark shades and clean lines in the Winter palace, but Zane's home was somehow warm, yet still grand. It was so different from what I was used to, but not unappealing, and just for a moment, I wondered if this was somewhere I could live.

"Greta will see you to your room so that you can freshen up," Zane said, interrupting my thoughts as he nodded toward the familiar unseelie who was walking toward us. She must have come from the train with the rest of his staff.

Just as I was turning to leave, Zane blurted out, "I was hoping you'd have dinner with me this evening."

Stopping, I turned back to him. He was standing tall, and there was a confidence about him. Confidence was attractive in my book.

"Yes, of course I'll have dinner with you," I said with a smile, and he visibly relaxed. Just because I didn't want a mate didn't mean I couldn't have dinner with the guy. I just feared breaking his heart if he thought I was about to marry him.

"Then I'll let you get some rest and freshen up beforehand. I'm going to get a little more work done in preparation to depart again in the morning, so I'll see you later."

When I nodded, he tipped his head to me in acknowledgment and then headed in the other direction. I followed Greta up one of the sets of stairs, and she led me to the second floor. We then traversed down a long corridor lined with oil paintings of what I assumed were the previous Western lords and ladies. Stopping in front of one of the last doors, she opened it for me and then stood back for me to enter.

The room was lovely. Decorated in soft lavenders and grays, it had a definite feminine touch. There was a huge four-poster bed against one wall, and beside it, a matching nightstand. A small settee was placed in front of a fireplace on the opposite wall. And directly in front of me was an open set of French doors that led to a terrace.

"Will this do, my lady?" Greta asked, silently closing the door behind us.

"It will more than do," I told her with a smile. It was lovely.

Seeing the sincerity on my face, she released a relieved sigh.

"Oh, I'm so glad. The lord asked for our finest room to be made up for you, and to let him know if anything wasn't to your liking. He wants to make sure you feel at home here."

My smile wobbled a little, but I didn't think Greta noticed because she was already moving to the clothing cabinet.

Home. This wasn't my home. My home was in the Winter Court. Back with my sisters and parents and my people. I still couldn't fully comprehend how Dawn and Aribella had just left everyone to die . . . okay, that wasn't completely fair. They believed there was a way to end the curse for us and future generations and chose not to murder someone to temporarily stop it, which I respected. But to marry and settle down here when our people were drowning in black waters or freezing solid. I could never.

Greta flitted around the room, picking out an evening dress for me to wear, completely oblivious to my inner turmoil. Now that I'd been reminded of home, I couldn't stop the concern for my family and people from intruding on my thoughts.

Was the curse still freezing my lands and people? Had it reached the palace? Had everyone already given up hope on me, and were they fleeing to the Spring Court, the last untouched part of Faerie?

Even after Greta laid out a dress and left to let me wash up and rest, my mind wouldn't quiet, so I used the time before dinner to continue reading the book Aribella had sent me. But I grew frustrated when there weren't any obvious answers in the tome. A growing urgency to see these Wise Ones started to take over, and I wished we didn't have to waste a night here in Windreum.

Greta came back after some time to help me get ready for dinner. She helped me into the dark purple gown that she'd picked out for me earlier, claiming it flattered my complexion and dark hair. She also insisted on doing my hair and light make-up.

As Greta led me through Zane's massive castle to the dining room, I tried to get my head in a better place. Zane was helping me and he was a kind and good man. I was determined to have a good evening with him, and at the very least, find out a little more about him and his family. My best friend Dawn had married one of his brothers. I, at least, wanted to know more about that.

Zane was waiting for me when I arrived. He'd swept his hair up in a knot at the back of his head, and it appeared that he had even shaved. As my gaze ran over him, I had to appreciate how handsome he was in his dark green coat and matching waistcoat. The cut emphasized his tall and muscular physique while still looking fashionable. As we stared at each other for a moment, I waited to have a deeper reaction to the Ethereum lord, but there was nothing there. Again.

"You look breathtaking," Zane said, taking long strides until he was standing in front of me.

"Thank you. You look very handsome yourself," I said truthfully, which made Zane's smile widen.

"Come, sit," he said, tucking my hand in the crook of his arm as he led me toward the table.

Pulling out a chair for me, I took the seat he offered before he sat next to me at the head of the table. Almost immediately, servers started bringing out platters of food. The table we sat at could easily fit a dozen fae, and Zane's staff delivered tray after tray of food until the entire table was covered. There was roast beef and quail and pork. Shrimp and crab and lobster. Mashed potatoes, honeyed yams, roasted vegetables, beet salad, fresh fruit, nuts, cheeses, and the dishes went on and on.

When the last platter was placed on the table and the servers disappeared, I looked up at Zane in shock. "Are we expecting other dinner guests?" I asked.

Zane laughed, and a touch of color appeared on his cheeks. "No. This is all for us. I just didn't know what you preferred, so I asked the kitchen staff for a variety."

"They certainly took you seriously," I told him with a light laugh myself. "But this is so much. We won't even make a dent."

"Don't worry, whatever we don't eat won't be wasted. It will go to the castle staff and the orphanage downtown immediately after we finish." He leaned toward me with a glint in his eye. "I have to admit, I asked for the four-tier chocolate cake because I know several of the children at the orphanage love it."

He takes care of his staff and orphans, too? Could he be any more perfect? The only thing was, I wasn't sure he was perfect for *me*.

"Well, in that case, I'll have some of the berry pie instead," I told him with a wink.

After that, Zane grabbed my plate and insisted on serving me. He went around the table asking what I'd like and then brought my plate back to me when it was brimming with more food than I had a hope of eating. After he returned with his own overfull plate, we both dug in.

The conversation flowed easily enough, but I wanted to take the opportunity to learn more about my mission here.

"What can you tell me about these Wise Ones?" I asked after taking a drink of some type of sweet fruit puree. "Dawn's letter wasn't very descriptive. What are they like?"

"Well," Zane began, "I haven't actually ever met them myself."

"You haven't?" I asked with raised eyebrows.

He shook his head. "No. You already know they live in the Northern Mountains," he said, and I nodded, taking a bite of the most succulent piece of smoked pork I'd ever had. "They never leave."

"Then how do they even know what's going on in Ethereum, let alone how to end a curse, if they stay isolated?" I asked.

"They're prophetic," he explained. "Unseelie, and very powerful. They're gifted with the power of future sight and will allow anyone who journeys to see them to ask one question, and one question only. So you'll have to be very intentional about how you choose your words because you won't get a second chance."

"Why have you never been to see them?"

Zane shrugged. "There was never anything important enough that I needed to know. But my brother, Zander, did visit them before Dawn arrived. There was a time when Zander's kingdom was taken over by an evil being. The rondak. Zander was desperate, so he went to the Wise Ones and asked them how he could save his kingdom from the creature."

"And what did they tell him?" I asked, intrigued.

"Nothing," Zane said.

"Nothing?" I asked, frowning. "They didn't say anything? But I thought they would answer one question."

"No, they literally said, 'Nothing.' As you can imagine, that was extremely frustrating to Zander."

I snorted a half laugh. "I'll bet it was."

"But the thing is, they were right. Zander couldn't do anything because it was Dawn who defeated the rondak. She was the one who ultimately won Zander's kingdom back for him, so they were right when they said that there was nothing *he* could do."

Pride for my friend swelled in my chest. "That's my Dawnie," I said with a grin.

Zane smiled as well. "I'm quite fond of her as well. She's perfect for my brother. Zander was always a notorious flirt. There was a time when I had doubts that he'd ever settle down, but seeing the two of them together, it's obvious how in love they are."

I thought back to when Dawn and the others appeared in my room back in the Winter Court. The way that Dawn had looked at her husband, I'd never seen her look at someone like that before. And there was a softness to her she hadn't had since we were children, before her mother trained it out of her.

Zane didn't need to convince me. Even that short interaction made me believe that they were in love. That Dawn was happy with Zander. Which was wild because I always imagined Dawn would marry for political reasons, not for love.

If love had changed Dawn's mind, maybe it could change mine, too? That thought was equal parts exciting and terrifying.

"Tell me of your brothers," I said, changing the subject before it went too much into the territory of love and mates, which I wasn't yet ready to broach with Zane. "Who's the oldest?"

"That would be Stryker," he said, leaning back in his chair, but then added, "only by a few minutes, so the rest of us don't really count it."

"Only a few minutes? Then that makes you twins?"

He shook his head. "Quadruplets, actually."

49

"Really?" My eyes widened as I imagined carrying four babies at once. Ouch. "Are you close?" I asked, and Zane's smile slipped a little.

"We used to be," he admitted. "And we're getting back to that place. For a long time there was a rift between Stryker and the rest of us. But we're working on healing it now. Aribella has helped in that regard."

"I can see that. Aribella has always been known to be wise as well as kind-hearted. A natural-born peacemaker."

We spent the rest of the meal trading stories of our families. Zane told me of the times he and his brothers played pranks on their parents. Apparently, the quads had given their mother and father a run for their money and his stories were hilarious.

I told him all about my sisters, and how close I was to them, especially Seraphina. There was a small ache in my chest when I spoke about them because even though I'd only been gone a short time, I still missed them terribly.

At the end of the night, I had to admit to myself that the meal was delicious, and the company was even better. Zane was amazing. He was everything someone would desire in a mate or a husband, yet whenever he told a story about his childhood I found myself hanging on to the information about Adrien. I wanted to know what he was like as a child and adolescent. I wanted to know more about the fae who was engaged to that horrible woman.

I repeatedly forced my mind away from Adrien, only to have my thoughts drift back to him again and again. And that was concerning on a number of levels. If anyone was my mate, it was supposed to be Zane, not Adrien, so I needed to banish him from my mind. Besides, Adrien was already as good as married, and I was no homewrecker.

By the time we said our goodnights, I had to force my smile, and I worried that Zane could tell. It wasn't anything he'd said or done. He was practically perfect. It was that I couldn't chase thoughts of his brother from my mind through the latter half of our evening, and that frustrated and confused me.

I wanted to get a good night's sleep. I didn't know what the upcoming days would bring and couldn't help feeling like this was the calm before the storm. But sleep didn't come easily, and when it did, the eyes in my dreams weren't dark blue with a speck of brown, they were teal, like the shallow coastal waters of the sea.

Chapter Five

Adrien

I closed my eyes, letting the evening sun warm my face as the ocean breeze ran cool fingers over my exposed skin. Inhaling, salty air filled my lungs, making me feel alive and rejuvenated.

I was made for the sea. I always felt that was true. I loved the sound of the gulls calling overhead and the waves as the surf rolled in. I loved the feeling of wet sand beneath my bare feet and the smell of brine. There was nowhere else in all of Ethereum that I felt as at home, as myself, as the shores of my kingdom, or when I was at the bow of my ship, cutting through crystal clear surf.

A smile bloomed on my face as I felt a presence come up behind me.

She was here.

A delicate hand appeared on my shoulder, and a moment later, her fingers caressed the side of my throat. I tilted my head, giving her more access to the sensitive skin. When she placed a barely there kiss on the back of my neck, delicious awareness ran down my spine, and need formed in my gut.

Reaching up, I grabbed hold of my fiancée's hand and turned, ready to take her in my arms, but when I looked into her eyes, they were ice blue instead of brown, and her hair was raven feather black instead of chestnut.

A bolt of pure adrenaline shot through my system, and I took a half step back.

Isolde?

I must have said her name out loud because the beauty in front of me nodded and smiled. Like the lure of a siren's call, my eyes were drawn to her lush, berry-red lips. The urge to taste them was intense, overpowering my common sense, and so I stepped forward, tugging her to me at the same time.

As her body pressed against mine, a sense of rightness settled on me, wiping traces of any other woman from my thoughts.

Isolde was in my arms, right where she belonged. No one else existed but her. No one else mattered but her.

I let my gaze drift over her features, as if drinking them in for the first time. Her high cheekbones, her straight and small nose. Her delicately pointed ears. The dark eyebrows and inky lashes that framed her striking pale blue eyes.

She was beautiful beyond compare, and a possessiveness that I'd never felt before swelled in my chest as I gazed at her.

Reaching up, I traced a finger around the shell of her ear, and her slight shiver brought a lazy smile to my mouth. I dragged my finger from her ear to her cheek and down to her chin, and then gently tipped her head back, aligning that irresistible mouth with mine.

I'd held myself back long enough. I didn't just *want* to feel her mouth pressed against my own— I *needed* it.

I leaned down, anticipation humming through my veins stronger and more palpable than even my magic. Deep inside I knew what would happen when our lips touched, what it would mean, and I welcomed the revelation.

Just as my mouth pressed against her own, putting an end to the sweet torture, I awoke with a start.

A fine layer of moisture coated my skin as I blinked against the morning sun, trying to make sense of what had just happened.

A dream. It was just a dream.

But it had felt so real. I hadn't dreamed in forever. Since before I started taking Elisana's tea.

I closed my eyes, trying to remember the details of the vision, but they'd already started to slip away from me like sand through an hourglass.

Isolde. The beach. An almost kiss.

I shook my head and reopened my eyes. The coastal breeze blowing through the windows did nothing to cool me, and I tossed the thin blanket off and got to my feet. I was grateful at that moment that Elisana was waiting to share a bed with me until we were married. I wasn't sure I could look her in the eye right now. Lumbering to the bathroom, my mind was still half in a haze as I splashed cold water on my face.

When I looked up at myself in the mirror, my eyes had a feverish look in them, and my skin was flushed. Even as the dream was fading from memory I could somehow still feel the press of Isolde's body against mine, the softness of her skin beneath my fingertip. Her scent, freshly fallen snow mixed with mulled spices, still tickled my nose.

"What are you doing, Adrien?" I asked my reflection.

Groaning, I pressed the heels of my hands against my eyes, trying to banish thoughts of the black-haired beauty from my mind and replace them with Elisana, my fiancée, my love. But that didn't work, so I filled the clawfoot tub up with cold water and submerged myself in an icy bath, hoping to shock Isolde from my system. I forced myself to stay in the tub until thoughts of the Winter princess had faded to the recesses of my mind where they belonged.

I didn't have any official duties to attend to today, so after I bathed, I threw on a casual linen shirt and breeches and then went down to the breakfast room where Elisana and I ate most mornings.

When I arrived, she was already there, seated at her usual place to the right of the head of the table, waiting for me. Spotting me, she got to her feet and rushed over, throwing herself at me. Bringing my arms up and around her, I held her tightly, doing my best not to think about how different she felt in them than Isolde had in my dream.

Perhaps I hadn't stayed in the tub long enough after all?

Going up on her tiptoes, Elisana gave me a quick kiss, and I ignored the acid feeling that churned in my gut. It was probably just because my stomach was empty.

"What are your plans today, my love?" I asked as we both settled into our seats.

"Well," she said with a smile. "I'm working on more wedding planning. I'm determined to make sure this wedding is the largest and most extravagant that Etherum has ever seen. At least twice as large as Dawn and Zander's."

Something twisted in my gut. "Does it really matter how large or lavish the wedding is?" I asked, uncomfortable that it sounded like she was trying to one-up my brother and his wife. If it were up to me, we would just marry on the beach with only the officiant and the two of us. I had no need for such pomp and circumstance.

Elisana frowned, a sour look settling on her face. "Yes, it matters," she snapped, and it startled me, but she immediately wiped the look away and smiled demurely as she reached forward and took my hand. "The size of the wedding, darling, should mirror the love and devotion we have toward one another. Are you saying that your love for me isn't very big?"

"Of course that's not what I'm saying," I said, feeling a pinprick of annoyance rise up inside. But then I took a calming breath.

What did it matter if she wanted a large wedding or not? I was in the position to provide her with what she desired, and if it made her happy to invite half of Ethereum to witness our joining, then why stand in the way?

I lifted her hand and kissed the back of it. "If you want a large wedding, then that's what you shall have," I said, and her smile grew.

Releasing her hand, I picked up my fork and speared a strawberry. "Has there been any news from my brother?"

Elisana's brows bunched together in confusion. "Your brother?" she asked with a head tilt.

"Zane," I clarified. "I just wanted to know how things are going with him." *And Isolde.* "If he and Isolde have made any progress with the Shadow Heart. I very much want to see this curse ended before it reaches our shores."

Elisana's face pinched at the mention of the Winter princess. It didn't escape my notice that Elisana was the jealous sort. A flash of guilt went through me when I recalled my dream, but I shook it off.

It was just a dream. Not something I had control over. I had never been unfaithful in a relationship and would never be. She had nothing to worry about.

"No. I don't believe we've received any word from Zane," she said. "Don't you think he and Isolde will make the most perfect couple, though?"

The acid in my gut roiled more aggressively. Glancing up, I caught Elisana watching me carefully, so I forced a smile and nodded. "Yes. I'm happy for my brother. Out of all of us, he's desired love the most. He deserves happiness." But to be honest, I didn't think he and Isolde would make the perfect couple. I always pictured Zane with someone soft-tempered, and I didn't get the impression that was Isolde. Perhaps that wasn't fair since I didn't really know her, but in my gut, she just didn't seem to be his match. I'd never tell my fiancée that though: she was short-tempered herself and might not take it well.

Elisana's gaze turned shrewd, and she asked abruptly, "Did you drink your tea last night, darling?"

I shook my head. "No, but I had no trouble sleeping," I said, willing my mind not to go back to my dream. It was only fragments now, but the emotions I felt still rushed to the surface, heating my blood. I cleared my throat. "I don't think that I need that concoction anymore. Perhaps you've cured me, my love?"

Alarm flashed across Elisana's features, but she quickly covered it with a smile and a light laugh. "Don't be silly. Remember how troubled your nights were before you started taking the tonic? One night's sleep does not erase the problem." Pushing back from her seat, she rose. "I'll go make you a cup since you missed your last dose. Then you can take a nice afternoon nap." And she breezed out of the room before I had a chance to argue.

I glanced out the windows as I waited for Elisana to return, absently taking bites of my eggs and toast. I was restless, but I didn't know why.

Perhaps it was the curse slowly working its way through our world that weighed heavily on my mind. It was certainly cause for concern. Both Zander and Stryker had sent reports of the curse's destruction in their kingdoms. Zander and his people were even getting ready to take refuge in our kingdom.

Despite their best efforts, neither of my brothers had been able to find a way to cure the unseelie afflicted with the magic illness, and now the curse was spreading through their land as well. Blackening their harvests and turning the fresh water to sludge and their crops to ash. If it wasn't stopped, it was only a matter of time before it descended on the Southern Kingdom as well.

But as disturbing as the curse was, it felt like there was something else causing me unease. Something sinister that was hidden from me, which nagged at my subconscious. If I were being honest with myself, it had been bothering me for a while. Deep inside, my instincts screamed at me to run, but I hadn't been able to figure out why and from what.

Elisana returned with a smile and a cup cradled between her hands. "Here you go," she said as she placed the cup in front of me before returning to her seat. "You'll feel much better after you've finished this." Her expectant gaze stayed fastened to my face as she waited for me to drink.

I frowned at it. Tea for sleep in the morning? Did that make sense? I usually had a cup in the late afternoon and another before bedtime, but never in the morning.

My mind felt a little foggy. Elisana reached out and stroked my cheek, and the fog cleared. I would drink this tea and all would be well.

Picking up the cup, I gave her my thanks and then took a sip of the warm liquid, trying not to wince. I didn't want to hurt her feelings, but it tasted awful. Bitter, no matter how much honey was added to sweeten it, and there were even times I wasn't sure I could keep it down.

As the tea slid down my throat and into my stomach, a familiar hazy feeling overcame me. The next sip wasn't so bad, and when I looked over at Elisana, a rush of love for her started to flow through me.

"Darling," Elisana started, and I hung on her every word. "I was thinking. Perhaps we should move the wedding up. I don't know if I can wait a whole three weeks to be with you."

Her eyes were so beautiful in the morning light. Her hair, so soft and glossy. When she smiled, it was as if the sun itself shone on me.

I found myself nodding, not even remembering what her question was, but knowing that I needed to make her happy. When a grin lifted the corners of her mouth, I knew I'd done just that.

Chapter Six

Isolde

The train car rocked back and forth in a slow, rhythmic motion as I played cards with Zane. The train ride wasn't quite as long as the one we took from Soleum to Windreum, but it still took most of the day. We'd boarded the train together early in the morning, just after breakfast and after two more meals, a nap, and some time reading, we were now playing cards to pass the last few moments of the long trip to the Northern Kingdom where we would search for the Wise Ones.

"Random question," Zane asked.

I peered up at him, fully comfortable in his presence now.

"Ask away," I said and took a card, shuffling them into my deck to arrange them how I wanted.

"What if the Wise Ones said you had to kill a tiny puppy to save your people? Would you?"

"Zane! Why would you even ask that? Puppies are off limits."

Zane grinned. "My apologies. This long train ride has caused my mind to go dark with boredom."

I returned his smile but couldn't help the unease in my stomach.

He liked me. It was so obvious, and yet . . . the feeling was unrequited. It made me wonder; did he *really* like me? Or was he just forcing the issue because when Dawn's ghostly form had visited me, she'd told the entire room that the princesses of Faerie were sent to hunt their mates, who were the Ethereum lords.

I wasn't yet sure if I bought into the whole mate concept, but it was clear he did. If I allowed this to go on much longer, this was not going to end well for sweet Zane's heart.

"Zane?" I asked just as the door to the train car opened, and a messenger came in with a black raven on his shoulder and a rolled up note in his hand.

When the messenger handed the note to Zane I shifted to the edge of my seat as he read it.

Was it from Adrien? Was he asking how I was? Or maybe it was from Dawn or Aribella? I'd do anything to hear from one of them right now.

Zane glanced over the top of the page with a downcast expression, and my stomach sank.

"Is everything all right?"

He sighed. "I sent word to Dawn that I was coming to collect you and intended to take you to the Wise Ones. She's written back to let me know that both roads to the mountain the Wise Ones live on are . . . impassable, and we may need to find another way forward or go back to studying the books as an option solving what the Shadow Heart does."

"Impassable? What happened?" I sat up straighter.

"The curse has gotten worse in the Northern Kingdom, and

they're thinking about evacuating. Black water has flooded the entire northeast border." Zane seemed shocked, and my heart pinched for Dawn and her people.

"That's how it is in our world, too. Displaced refugees, crops dying, blackened water. It's awful," I told him. "But we must find a way through. Because if the Wise Ones have the answer to end this curse, I have to see them."

There was a reason Queen Liliana left Aribella before her training was finished and came for me. I could be ruthless and unforgiving when needed, kind of like winter itself. I would not give up on this quest to end the curse, and if finding my way across diseased, blackened waters was how I did that, then so be it.

Zane appraised me with respect. "You want to press on? Even though it's dangerous."

I tipped my head back and laughed. "Oh, Zane, you truly do not know me yet. I'm the eldest of seven sisters. A princess of the Winter Court, the most perilous court in all of Faerie. Danger doesn't scare me."

He nodded. "Then we find a way."

"If it's dangerous, you don't have to come. I'm so appreciative for how—"

"I'm coming," he declared in a no-nonsense tone that told me that was the end of that.

Truth be told, I was in a foreign land and so I was grateful for the company. "Okay," I said, not fighting him on it.

I felt the train slow as I peered out the windows, and pure joy flooded through my body at the sight of the white fluff falling from the sky.

"Snow!" I shouted, like a five-year-old kid, and leaned against the window. My hot breath caused fog to flood the glass and momentarily obscure my view.

Zane chuckled beside me. "I didn't tell you? The Northern Kingdom is much like your Winter Court."

Bless the stars for that. Since I'd walked into the portal and landed in this strange place, I finally felt at home. Nothing could beat this moment, a small reprieve from a stressful few days.

"You did not," I told him. He said the climate would be chilly, but he didn't say there would be snow. What a lovely surprise.

"Did I also mention that Dawn said she would try to meet us at the train station, even if only for a short while, to see you?" Zane teased.

I spun around with wide eyes. "Are you serious?"

He handed me the letter and pointed to the very bottom.

I read the line as tears clouded my eyes and nearly spilled over onto my cheeks.

P.S. Please tell Isolde I'm going to try to meet you at the train station. I don't want her feeling alone in this place like I did for so long. Even if it's only for a hug, I will try to make it.

The train whistled as it came to a stop, and Zane tapped the glass. I followed his gaze to see a beautiful blonde woman sitting atop a black horse. She wore a light blue wool cloak pulled up over her head, and there were a dozen royal guards behind her.

Dawn.

Not caring about decorum at that moment, I burst forward and yanked open the train door. Leaping onto the platform, I smiled as the frigid, snowy wind slapped against my skin.

I bolted around the train car and jumped over the connecting point, grateful I was wearing pants.

"Dawn!" I shouted as I approached her.

She grinned and slipped down from her horse slowly, awkwardly, and it was at that moment that I remembered why. When she turned to face me, her swollen pregnant belly protruded out from the slit in her cloak.

My dearest friend, married and with child. It felt like a dream.

She opened her arms and smiled at me. "I'm pregnant, not contagious. You can hug me."

With a laugh, I fell into her arms, careful not to press against her belly.

She squeezed me hard.

"I didn't realize you were so far along," I said with a giggle when she finally let me go.

She pressed her hand to her stomach and shook her head. "I'm not, but my husband's family has a history of multiples, so we think that's why I'm carrying so big. I'm sure you know by now all the Ethereum lords are quads."

My eyes widened. "Oh, no, Dawn. How many are in there?"

She shrugged as if the thought of having a bunch of babies at once didn't horrify her and gave a nervous laugh. "I don't know. But I'm hoping for no more than two." She waved a hand through the air and changed the subject. "Thank you for not hurting Adrien when you first saw him. They are all such good men. My mother lied to us, Izzy. Thank you for believing me."

I nodded. "I know. Zane is . . ." I peered back at the train platform where he was directing his men to unload our bags and put them on horseback. "Wonderful."

Dawn smiled and wagged her eyebrows a little. "How wonderful?"

I rolled my eyes. "Listen, I'm happy for you and Aribella, but that's not how this is going for me." I pointed to her belly and then her wedding ring.

She frowned, looking back at Zane as if she were sure some magic would have had me confessing he was my mate.

"And forget all that. How are things going here? Zane said you are thinking of evacuating?" I asked.

Dawn's face instantly changed, as if I'd just snapped her back to reality, and she cradled her belly, nodding.

"This land is no longer sustainable. We sent word to Adrien, and he's agreed to allow our people to stay there in the villages surrounding Soleum, though I sensed some reluctance from his fiancée." She rolled her eyes then.

"What do you mean?" I asked, curious about her reaction.

"We were told not to have any refugees visible during the wedding."

I growled. "She's awful. Why don't you ask Zane if you can go to Windreum? I'm sure he would be more than happy to take your people in. Then you don't need to worry about Elisana."

Dawn shook her head at my response. "We speculate that's where the curse will hit next. So we intend to get our people as far away as we can."

Oh. Because she thought Zane was my mate, and the curse always hits in the princess's mate's kingdom. At least that's what Zane told me.

"Well, good luck with Elisana. Not sure what that wench did to deserve Adrien."

She perked up at my response. "I heard you came out of the portal directly before Adrien and not Zane. That's interesting."

I frowned, shifting on my feet. "Interesting how? Those mirror portals can't be controlled, you know that."

"Do I?" she said. "I thought I did . . . but now I'm not sure."

Okay . . . whatever that meant.

I peered around the frigid landscape and smiled a little. "The Summer princess living here? You must hate it."

Dawn gave me a soft smile. "It's grown on me . . . but now it doesn't matter," she finished, the smile slipping from her face.

I reached for her arm. "Oh, I'm sorry. I didn't mean to upset you."

She squeezed my hand. "I know. I just . . . I did fall in love with this land and its people and now if you don't find a way to get to the Wise Ones, I fear it might all be lost. Including those I love back home."

The Summer Court was certainly lost, but I wasn't about to tell her that. There was no use. Her people were safe in my court for the time being, and that was all that mattered.

"I promise I'll find a way to them," I vowed and dropped her hand. "Go evacuate your people. I'm sure Zane will let you use his train. We can manage on our own."

"Of course you can use the train." Zane's strong voice came from behind me and I turned. "Where is my brother?" he asked.

"On his way with the most fragile from our castle," Dawn said.

We gave each other one last hug and then she shouted something at her guards. They moved out of the way then, and a horde of people I hadn't noticed, who must have been hiding behind the line of a dozen guards on horseback, began to move forward toward the train.

We stepped back as seelie all but dragged sickly looking unseelie toward the train platform. Black veins grew along their skin, and they limped along if conscious or were carried on a stretcher if not.

"Dawn," I breathed, emotion clogging my throat.

She tipped her chin high, her bottom lip unwavering. "No pressure, but we're all really counting on you."

An unseelie fae with green skin passed by on a stretcher, and Dawn's eyes lingered on her as if she truly cared.

"I won't let you down," I said.

It was in that moment that I realized I was no longer doing this for Faerie alone; I was doing it for Ethereum, too.

Patting the Shadow Heart at my hip, where it sat safely in the satchel, I readied myself for a rough night and day ahead.

* * *

We didn't get much time to visit, but I briefly got to meet Dawn's husband, Zander, in real life when he arrived with more refugees. Apparently, his official name was Lord Roan, but his closest friends and family referred to him by his middle name, Zander, instead. Like his brothers, Zander was a handsome man, and even though it was a short introduction, it was enough to convince me of his love and affection for my friend. The way he looked at her, as if she was his whole world, even made my icy heart melt a little. All too soon, though, I had to say goodbye to Dawn and watched glumly as she led a long line of refugees onto Zane's train.

Dawn gave us a detailed map, but assured me it was impassable with waters as high as a horse.

"You may be able to cross it using your powers, Izzy, but even then . . . it would take a lot out of you," she'd told me.

I'd balked at that. Take a lot out of me? In order to tire me, I'd have to freeze half the world. I assured her I'd be fine.

After she was out of sight, Zane and I headed for the mountains where the Wise Ones lived. We only rode for a few hours before it was too dark to travel any longer and so we stayed at an inn that Dawn recommended just outside Noreum, the Northern Kingdom capital. The next morning, after a light breakfast, we were off again for our true full day of travel.

We were well into that tiring day of travel with nighttime approaching, when a man rushed up to us. He had blackened stains up his legs all the way to his hips.

"Go no further," the fae warned, and I stared at the little serrated points on the tips of his ears and the black horns on his forehead.

I followed the man's gaze to a sheet of black water that crept forward through what looked like some old farm-lands in the valley in front of us. Trees and cottages were halfway submerged in the dark liquid. It was hard to tell from here exactly how deep it was, but the waters were definitely rising and would eventually reach the high ground where we were.

Zane looked at me in alarm, and I pulled my horse to a stop. The man was traveling with his wife and a small child. The child clung to the arms of his mother, and I noticed that the woman was also covered in the same stains up to her waist. Whatever was in this water, it wasn't good.

I slid off my horse. "Please take my horse. It's a day's ride to the train station in Noreum, but from there, everyone is heading south for safety."

They wouldn't be able to make it before dark, because the sun was already low in the sky, but if they were careful and rode through the night, they could reach the station by morning.

The fae man looked at me like I'd grown two heads. "We couldn't possibly deprive you of your horse, my lady."

I handed him the reins. "Nonsense. I will ride with my friend. Please make good time so that the waters do not hurt you."

"And what about you, my lady? Are you heading back to the train station?" he asked me.

"I am not," I said flatly, hoping he didn't ask any more questions.

The wife took the reins from me and bowed deeply. "Thank you for this kindness, my lady. We shall not easily forget it. We'll leave the horse at The Winterside Inn's stables for you, back in Noreum."

I unslung my pack and looked up at Zane, wondering if this was all okay with him. It was his horse after all, but he was smiling sweetly at me.

"That's fine," he told them.

After the man, woman, and child climbed onto the horse and left, Zane looked down at me. "That was incredibly kind of you," he told me.

I shrugged. "I have my moments. If my little sisters were here we would be at each other's throats, so it evens out." I winked.

Talking with Zane was easy. He was incredibly laid-back and

we got along so well. But now I had to share one horse with him and that felt slightly awkward. Why? I had no idea. Was it because I'd sworn off love after my parents' divorce and now everyone was telling me this guy should be my mate? It wasn't because of his looks, that was for sure. He was as handsome as they came . . . and sweet as pie.

But then I had a fleeting thought that I'd rather be trapped on a horse with his brother, and I realized in that moment that was what bothered me about Zane. He looked so much like Adrien. Which made sense, they *were* brothers. Thinking of Adrien caused my heart to race, my stomach to knot, and guilt to worm its way into me. But he was engaged. And Zane probably believed I was his mate.

Why was this all so complicated? I didn't want to deal with handsome Ethereum lords who may or may not be my mate. I just wanted to do my part in ending this curse and then return home. Was that really too much to ask?

"If we share this horse, are you going to be a gentleman?" I asked him with a mock glare.

He grinned. "Probably."

I burst out laughing and then he laughed too.

"Of course I will, Isolde," he said more seriously. "We have all the time in the world to . . . get to know each other."

I was grateful he hadn't said the M word. *Mates.* I was going to avoid that subject for as long as possible.

After strapping my pack to his horse, he reached out an arm and pulled me up in front of him. He immediately scooched back as far as he could so that we weren't pressed too tightly against

LEIA STONE & JULIE HALL

each other, which I thought was very sweet, and he even handed me the reins.

"I assume we are not going to expect the horse to swim?" he asked, eyeing the black water in the distance. "It would be a lot for her with both of us on her back."

I chuckled. "We are not."

Nudging the horse slightly with my heels, the mare took off, and Zane had to reach out and grasp my shoulders to steady himself for a second before mumbling an apology.

I brought the horse right up to the edge of the black water when she began to whinny.

"Whoa." I pulled the reins and took in a deep breath.

This was it. The survival of both of our worlds depended on my getting to see these Wise Ones, so that's what I was going to do.

"Head in that direction," Zane said, pointing toward the mountain jutting high into the sky in the distance. "That's where we are headed."

"Okay. Pull up your hood because it's about to get cold," I told Zane.

"Colder than it already is?" he asked.

"Yes."

I was wearing a thin cloak. As a Winter princess, the cold didn't bother me like it did others, and I'd discovered that I couldn't freeze to death. Seraphina and I had got in a huge fight once when I was fifteen and she tried to freeze me with her powers, and I turned out to be impervious to such things.

Once I saw that Zane had bundled himself up, I pulled on my power. It was so easy here, since the climate was so similar to the

Winter Court. It wasn't snowing anymore, but the air was crisp and full of humidity.

Aiming my right hand at the black waters before us, I expelled some of my power and watched as the stirring waters stopped and began to ice over.

Zane gasped behind me as the black water froze, creating intricate snowflake designs in the ice as it continued to grow outward. He'd already seen me display my power at the mine, but I guess this was a little different. This was more—

"Beautiful," he said, finishing my thought.

A frozen pathway grew out before us just as snow began to fall from the sky, and I lightly kicked the mare to get her going. She was hesitant at first, but then started to walk.

Her hoofs clacked against the ice I'd created, but it held, and I heard Zane give a sigh of relief behind me.

I had to concentrate then, using my power to freeze the walkway before us as we moved toward the mountain ahead. The blackened waters were rising higher and higher. Many of the trees were now almost completely submerged, and our journey became all the more challenging as the sun set, and we were left with only moonlight to lead the way. Our horse was navigating the ice path trail so far, and for that I was thankful.

"Once we reach the mountain, we can make camp and then hike to see the Wise Ones in the morning," Zane told me.

I nodded, grateful for the prospect of some rest. It wasn't much longer before we reached the base of the mountain, and then I shepherded the mare onto the steep path leading upwards. It was slow going and steep, but we eventually reached a bit of a plateau with a cave well above the water that felt safe to camp in.

Zane slipped off the horse first and then helped me down. My legs were stiff and my fingers ached from holding the reins tightly.

Zane shivered. "I'm going to build a fire," he said.

I nodded. I wasn't that cold, but I felt bad that he was.

After the fire was lit, he fed the horse, and then we sat next to each other and shared a loaf of herb bread, some meat and dried fruits. "What do you think the Wise Ones will say?" I asked Zane, beginning to feel nervous.

He considered the question, the firelight casting shadows across his face. "Probably something to do with the Shadow Heart." He pointed to my satchel.

I nodded. "Probably. But what if they tell me I have to kill you?" I kept my face straight.

He froze, a hand holding some dried fruit halfway to his mouth.

"Would you?" he asked seriously, and I could no longer keep up the ruse. I burst into laughter, and Zane heaved a sigh of relief. "Well, thanks, Isolde. Now I won't be sleeping tonight."

My laughter only grew at that. "I'm not killing anyone," I told him. "I had my chance with Adrien and didn't take it. I won't hurt you either. I'm not a monster."

He shrugged his shoulders as if he didn't fully agree with that assessment. I reached out and smacked his arm, and he grinned, but then the smile faltered. "You know I've been wondering . . . why did you arrive in front of my brother and not me? When you go through your portal, is it random, or . . .?"

I stiffened. "It's random," I said quickly. Of course it was. It had to be. I hadn't meant to plop myself in front of the tanned, shirtless Ethereum lord. It just happened.

Zane nodded, but stayed quiet and fatigue weighed down my limbs. I yawned and pulled out my bedroll from my pack. "I think I'm going to try to get some sleep," I told him and pointed to the cave.

He nodded. "All right. Good night, Isolde."

"Good night, Zane," I told him, and stepped into the mouth of the cave.

It was shallow, and we'd already checked it for animals so I laid out my bedroll and slid inside. With the train ride yesterday and seeing Dawn and her poor people forced to flee to safety in the south, it was an emotionally taxing journey.

I wondered what Queen Liliana and my mother thought now that I hadn't come back and if the curse was no doubt wreaking havoc on my land back home.

But just as my eyelids closed, I wondered something else. I wondered what Adrien was doing right now and if he really wanted to marry that hag, Elisana. Something wasn't right there, but I couldn't put my finger on what.

Chapter Seven

I awoke to Zane shaking my shoulders. My eyelids snapped open, and I gasped.

Black water lapped at our feet.

I shot out of my bedroll so fast I got dizzy as I threw my hands out and pushed the water back out of the cave, freezing it as I did so that it created a wall.

The mare, who I'd learned was named Orchid, was still with us, thank the stars, but was whinnying nervously.

"That was close." Zane brushed a hand through his hair.

"We should hurry, or by the time I see these Wise Ones won't be able to get back," I said. It had to be early in the morning because the sky was only starting to lighten, but we didn't have any time to waste.

Zane nodded, grabbing his now soaking pack, and called the mare over with a click of his tongue.

After grabbing Orchid's bridle, we began a steep trek up the side of the mountain.

"According to the map, this isn't the usual path to get to the Wise Ones. It's longer, but it will have to do."

I nodded, still in shock at how much of the land the water had eaten up. Poor Dawnie. All of these people . . . their livelihoods. Gone.

We rode on for hours and hours, but eventually, the path became too narrow and we had no option but to leave Orchid while we continued on foot. My legs burned, but I didn't complain as we walked slowly in a zigzag pattern up the mountain path.

We traveled for most of the day and I was about to ask for another break when Zane stopped before an open cave. When I peeked inside, I couldn't see a thing. It was pitch-black.

"We're here," he said.

Oh, thank the stars. I wanted to get this over with and get out of this flooding kingdom. I moved to step inside when Zane hooked me by the arm. "Remember—"

"One question. Asked perfectly. I know," I said.

He'd told me all about the Wise Ones, and Dawn explained a little bit about what this would be like. A disorienting darkness and then voices that come from their minds.

I was ready.

* * *

I had not been ready.

Even after the voices faded and light appeared behind my closed eyelids, I stayed hunched on the ground with my hands over my ears, and my eyes squeezed tightly shut. In the sudden silence, I could hear the blood rushing through my veins with every fast beat of my heart. My ragged breaths sounded like the banging of drums.

I had never been called a coward, but in that moment, I felt like one because I couldn't force myself to open my eyelids and face the Wise Ones. And it wasn't just because walking through the black void with disembodied voices ringing in my head had been terrifying. It was because when I picked up some of their whispers, they'd known things.

Not just my name, but my fears as well. It was as if they'd cracked open my head, dug through my mind, and then whispered my fears back to me.

"Worried she'll never be loved."

"Afraid to believe mates are real."

"Doesn't want to end up like her parents."

My darkest thoughts still bounced around in my head, even though the Wise Ones' voices had long since gone silent.

"Princess Isolde of the Winter Court. Daughter of broken vows, child of ice, spell breaker. You have nothing to fear here. Rise and face us," a voice commanded.

I didn't want to. If these unseelie knew my deepest fears and secrets, what other fragmented pieces of myself had they seen? I felt stripped bare, raw and exposed, but even so, I knew I had no choice. I had to face them. For Faerie, for Ethereum, and for myself.

Sucking in a fortifying breath, I forced myself to lower my hands from my ears and open my eyes. In a semicircle in front of me were four beings. Male, with pale white skin, who looked seelie except for the two small horns upon each of their heads. They were unnaturally still, and their neutral facial expressions made it impossible for me to gauge their thoughts, which was unsettling.

The Wise Ones were short in stature, but their height wasn't an indication of their power. I could feel their magic. It filled every corner of the candlelit room and pressed up against me, even as they sat on their stone thrones, looking down on me with their cloudy eyes.

Gathering my courage, I rose to my full height. "Wise Ones," I started. "I'm here to ask my question."

"*We know why you are here*," one of them said.

None of their mouths moved, but I somehow knew it was the one on the far left who had spoken. "*The Fall princess succeeded in finding the Shadow Heart*."

"She has," I said, even though it was a statement rather than a question. I reached into my satchel and dug out the crystal. "I brought it with me," I said, holding it up for them to see.

For the first time, I saw some hint of life in the beings' milky eyes, and one even went so far as to lean forward.

"I don't know what we are supposed to do with it," I said, taking a step forward as I held the crystal out in front of me toward them.

"*Put it away!*" The voice of the Wise One in front of me cracked sharply, startling me. His fingers wrapped around the arms of his throne and tightened until I heard the stone crack beneath his hand. He shifted forward, and it seemed like his grip on his throne was the only thing keeping him from leaping at me.

I quickly shoved the crystal back into my satchel, and it felt like the Wise Ones let out a collective sigh of relief.

What just happened?

"*The crystal carries more power than you can imagine*," another Wise One said. This time, the one who was seated on the far right. "*Its magic is . . . tempting*," he said, by way of an explanation.

"Oh, sorry. I didn't realize," I said, not knowing how else to respond. I looked down at my satchel, where the Shadow Heart was now hidden from view. I knew that it was supposed to be powerful. I'd learned that much from the book Zane had given me, but I hadn't felt anything from the crystal myself.

"*The magic inside the crystal is concealed,*" he replied. "*Not very many fae would recognize its power.*"

But they had.

A shiver ran down my spine. Just how powerful were these unseelie? I'd always been told the queens of the courts of Faerie and the Ethereum lords were the most powerful fae alive, but standing in front of these four had me questioning that.

"*You have come to us for a purpose,*" the Wise One in front of me prompted. The one who almost flew out of his seat at me before. He wasn't my favorite, even though looking at him now, his stance and facial expression were identical to the others.

"Right, yes," I said, and then cleared my throat. This was it. This was my one question. So much was riding on this single sentence that my voice shook a little as I asked, "What do I need to do in order to destroy the curse that is affecting both Ethereum and Faerie?"

The Wise Ones nodded as if pleased with my question.

"*The Shadow Heart's magic must be unlocked in order for it to be used to destroy the curse.*"

This thing in my bag right now was what could destroy the curse? I was about to ask how to unlock it, when another spoke up.

"*To unlock the Shadow Heart, you need to take it to the belly of the sea and combine your magic with your mate's.*"

The breath stilled in my lungs and when no one else spoke after that, I started to panic a little.

Take it to the belly of the sea. What did *that* mean? And combine my magic with my *mate's* magic? How was I supposed to do that? And then what was I supposed to do with the crystal after?

It felt like I had more questions than answers, but that might be all they were going to tell me since I'd just used my one question.

Maybe, hopefully, Zane knew what they meant by 'the belly of the sea'. That would at least give us a place to start.

Zane. My heart dropped into my gut. I'd had doubts that he was my mate since the beginning. And now if he wasn't, we wouldn't be able to unlock the Shadow Heart. I had to know if he was the one.

"We don't have mates in Faerie, but I know you do here in Ethereum, so when you say, 'my mate', you mean Zane, right?" I asked, praying they would answer. If they would just tell me who they thought my mate was, this would be so clear.

"We've already answered your one question," the Wise One stated, and disappointment flooded me. Then he added, *"But if you look inside your heart, you already know the answer to your second."*

A nervous laugh bubbled up in my throat. "Umm, no. I can assure you I don't know."

The Wise Ones just stared back at me, unblinking.

"Please," I begged. "You have to give me more information. If Zane isn't my mate, then I will fail."

"*We've given you all the information we are going to,*" the Wise One on the left said. "*We will not see you again.*"

And then the room went pitch-black, and they were gone.

*　*　*

"Isolde," Zane called the moment I emerged from the cave and then rushed to my side. "What did they say?"

I quickly told him everything the Wise Ones had said. "Do you know where the belly of the sea is?" I asked, and he looked thoughtful.

He shook his head. "I don't. But we should send a message to Adrien. No one knows the seas better than my brother."

A little jolt of something shot through my body at the thought of Adrien. A trickle of unease ran through me. I hadn't told Zane that I questioned the Wise Ones about who my mate was, but I knew I couldn't put off this conversation any longer.

"Look Zane . . . this whole mate thing is new to me. We don't have mates where we come from. And my parents are divorced, so love . . . isn't really something I'm looking for."

His face fell, but he nodded. "Okay," he said. "I can understand that mates are a foreign concept for you. That's why I haven't been pushing anything on you."

I nodded. "Yes, and I truly appreciate that," I said truthfully. "But . . ."

His eyebrows pinched, and I could tell he didn't know where I was going with this. I had to just lay it out there.

"I think you are amazing," I started. "One of the most genuine men I've ever met. Kind, thoughtful, strong, and handsome. You make me laugh, and I feel so comfortable around you. Any woman would be so fortunate to be mated to you."

"I can't help but feel there is another *but* coming," he said with a frown.

I gave him a small smile. Zane wasn't stupid. "But if mates are real and if I need one to unlock the Shadow Heart . . . I'm not sure it's you. It just feels like there's something missing."

The moment the words were out of my mouth hurt flashed across Zane's face, but closely after that, a completely different expression appeared. One I had a hard time interpreting. Relief?

"I asked the Wise Ones if you were my mate," I plowed forward before Zane could say anything. "But they wouldn't tell me. I just wish there was a way to know for sure. Especially since, according to them, I have to combine my power with my mate's to unlock the Shadow Heart and end the curse. I know you think it's you but . . . I'm sorry, I just . . . I'm not sure. What if we go to the belly of the sea and combine our magic, only to find out we're not really mates? The curse will then eventually overtake not only Faerie, but Ethereum as well. All will be lost."

Zane seemed slightly distressed, but I could tell he was hearing what I was saying and taking me seriously. Another way he was proving he was the perfect guy. But the nagging feeling that he wasn't *my* perfect guy still wouldn't leave me.

"There *is* a way to determine whether or not we are mates," he confessed.

"There is?" I asked, my back straightening.

Zane cleared his throat, suddenly looking slightly uncomfortable. "A kiss."

I froze at that. "What do you mean?"

His eyes bore into mine. "When we kiss our mate, we know. There's a magical reaction. Undeniable physical proof."

My heart hammered in my chest, and I knew what needed to be done.

"Okay. Then kiss me."

Zane looked shocked at my forwardness; he peered at the path leading down the mountain as if he wanted to run away.

I couldn't help but laugh. "We need to see if you're my mate. So kiss me. A small chaste kiss should prove your theory, correct?"

He seemed unsure now. "You are beautiful. Funny. Kind."

It was like he felt deep inside that I wasn't the one for him either, but he was trying to convince himself I was.

"Thank you. Now kiss me to prove whether we are or are not mates." I stepped forward, pursed my lips and closed my eyes. Best to just get this over with right away. We didn't have time to waste.

I felt Zane move closer. He took my face gently between his hands right before he leaned down and pressed his lips against mine. We stayed like that for a good five seconds. It reminded me of when I was younger and would kiss my mom and dad on the lips.

But nothing more.

No spark, no heat, nothing close to what I read about in the romance novels. I popped one eye open just as he did the same. He peered at the space around us as if expecting to see something and then pulled away from me frowning.

"You're not . . . but . . . what does that mean?" He sounded fragile, so I didn't want to kick him while he was down.

Reaching out, I took his hand in mine. "It means, if Dawn's

theory is right, that the Ethereum lords and Faerie princesses are mates, Princess Lorelei of the Spring Court is your mate. Not me."

What that also meant was that if Zane wasn't my mate, then Adrien was, and that felt . . . surprisingly right.

But Adrien was engaged. And that didn't feel good at all.

A barrage of emotions suddenly slammed into me. Fear. Excitement. Dread. Joy. It took a moment, but I wrestled all my feelings into submission, cramming them deep down inside until I had the luxury of examining them.

The important thing was that now I knew Zane and I weren't mates. All the friendship vibes I felt around him made sense. We needed to move forward from this and focus on what needed to be done to end the curse.

Looking up at Zane, he still seemed a little lost, but at least he wasn't arguing with me.

"Lorelei is amazing," I said. "I can already picture the two of you together."

He started to relax a little at that, as if not having a mate at all would have sent him into a spiral, but hearing that he'd just gotten stuck with the wrong one for a bit was okay.

"That means Adrien is yours," he said, and we both just let the giant unsaid words linger in the air.

And he's engaged to marry someone else.

"That kiss was mortifying," he graciously changed the subject. "We never speak of it again."

I laughed. "Like pecking my mother."

"Hey," he scolded. "I'm an amazing kisser, given better circumstances."

I grinned at him. "I'll bet you are. With Lorelei."

He shook his head, a look of chagrin on his face.

"We should go," I said. "I have to figure out not only how to get to the belly of the sea, but convince Adrien to come with me."

I turned to leave, but Zane stayed rooted in place, his gaze fixed on the dark cave opening.

"Zane?" I asked, and he glanced over at me.

"I need to know something," he said. "Will you wait here for me?"

"You want to see the Wise Ones?" I asked.

He nodded. "I'm here. And you're not my mate. I need to ask them—" He cut himself off before revealing what his question was. I wanted to know what he felt he needed to ask the Wise Ones, but it wasn't my place. And I think I already knew . . .

"Yes. Of course I'll wait," I said.

With a grim but determined look on his face, Zane turned and walked into the cave. He was swallowed by darkness immediately. A chill ran over me when he disappeared so suddenly from view, but I hoped that whatever Zane felt like he needed to know, the Wise Ones would tell him.

Chapter Eight

I was sitting on a stone, tossing pebbles into a circle I'd etched in the dirt to pass the time, when Zane all but stumbled from the cave. His face was pale, and he wore a dazed expression. I imagined I looked similar when I emerged as well.

Popping up to my feet, I hurried over to him. "Are you all right?" I asked when his gaze didn't seem like it was focusing on anything.

Zane gave his head a small shake and looked at me. "Sorry," he said and then ran a hand through the long strands of his hair on the top of his head. "That was just . . . a lot."

"Did you get the answer you were looking for?"

He let out a shaky half-laugh that I didn't know how to interpret. "I got an answer," he said. "But it wasn't exactly the one I was looking for."

"I'm so sorry, Zane," I told him, my heart aching for the kind lord.

"Don't be," he said as he straightened his shoulders, shaking off the last vestiges of fog from his mind. "I now know what I have to do."

"And what do you have to do?" I asked, not able to keep my curiosity in check.

When he turned to me, there was a fire in his eyes I'd not seen from him before. Determination was etched on every sharp angle and curve of his face. "I have to go to Faerie and get my mate. Together, we will destroy the curse."

* * *

By the time Zane and I started our trek back down the mountain, night had fallen. Zane told me more of the mission he said the Wise Ones had given him as we walked in the moonlight. After I unlocked the crystal, he was tasked with taking it to Lorelei in Faerie, and then both of them needed to bring it to the place where the curse was born and destroy it.

I'd asked how they were supposed to use the crystal to destroy the curse, and he said he didn't know. When I questioned him about how he was supposed to get back to Faerie when the only way we knew to get there was through using the faestone dagger to cut out an Ethereum lord's heart, he said he didn't know that either.

On the one hand I was glad we knew the final step that needed to be taken to end this curse forever, but on the other hand, it was incredibly frustrating that it seemed like we still had more questions than answers.

We didn't waste time sleeping but instead spent the night making our way back down the mountain, finding Orchid safely where we'd left her on the way. The sun was just starting to rise when we made it to the black water.

From there, it took us a full day to get back to the train station in Noreum. The water level was even higher than before, so I used far more power to get us back than I had to travel to the Wise Ones. I was already exhausted without sleep and doing this put me over the edge.

As far as I could tell, the ominous black water was slowly making its way to the capital city. When we finally arrived, I was shocked to see that even though it had been days since we left the train station, refugees were still piling on to make their way south. We caught the last two seats and collapsed into exhaustion the moment the train took off.

We had a loose plan. I wanted to travel to Soleum and see Adrien, and Zane had some books back in Windreum that he thought might help him get to Faerie. Since Windreum was on the way and the next train stop, we would part ways there. If Adrien was in fact my mate, I needed his help in unlocking the crystal, and I was sure Elisana was going to be a problem. But after using so much of my power to freeze the black waters, I was just too tired to figure out what to do with her. I would beg him to help me solve this puzzle to save all of our people. After that we could go our separate ways. Mates or not. It didn't matter to me.

I set my head back for just a second and dozed off quickly.

The train jerked to a stop, and my eyelids snapped open. Had we reached Windreum already? The sun wasn't yet out, but it looked like the sky was beginning to lighten.

Zane sat next to me as people stood and gathered their things.

"What are you going to tell Adrien when you see him?" Zane asked.

I opened my mouth to tell him I wasn't exactly sure when someone cut me off.

"Your brother, Lord Adrien of Soleum?" a lanky female seelie asked beside us. She looked well-off, dripping with fine jewelry, and had light blonde hair curled and pinned up.

"Yes," Zane told her.

She smiled. "Oh, you must be heading to his wedding, Lord Zane. How lovely. We are all so happy for him. Though moving up the date screams of a pregnancy to me," she winked.

My stomach bottomed out. "Moved up the wedding?" I asked. Why did my voice shake? Why did I care?

The woman smiled as the train doors opened. "Yes, it's tomorrow night. Have fun. You will just make it in time." She waved as she exited the train with most of the people in the car.

The thought of Adrien marrying Elisana made me want to punch someone in the face. Anger and red-hot jealousy roiled through me.

"You have to stop it," Zane said, bringing me back to myself.

I looked up at him. "What?"

"You can't let my brother marry her. Not when he's your mate," he said in a lowered voice.

I swallowed hard, not sure how to tell him that whether Adrien was my mate or not didn't matter. I still didn't plan to marry. But without having to utter the words, Zane seemed to know what I was thinking and reached across the seat and grasped my hand. "Regardless of how you feel right now about being mates, please stop my brother from making a huge mistake. Something isn't right there. No one can understand why he's with a woman like that."

His words lit a fire under me because it was true, and I was the only one who could save him right now.

"Now I kind of wish you were coming with me . . ." I said.

He chewed his lip. "I will if you need me too, but I have some books on portals back home . . ."

I nodded. "No, it's fine. That's more important." Maybe he could figure out a way to make a portal back to Faerie without having to cut out his or one of his brothers' hearts with a faestone dagger.

He stood, eyeing the open door of the train that was likely going to shut soon and head for Soleum.

"You are sure you're okay alone?" He peered around the car, worried. It had always been the plan that I go on to Soleum alone, but now that there was a wedding to break up, that task felt monumental.

I chuckled. "I have my powers. I'll be fine. Go, together we can end all of this." I motioned around at the refugees clinging to their belongings in the car.

He reached into his coat and deposited a small sack of coins in my hand. "If you run into any trouble, just use my name, and that should get you out of it. I'll also take care of any bills that come up."

"You are incredibly kind," I told him and I meant it.

He nodded and then headed for the open doors. Taking one last look at me, he gave me a radiant smile. "Adrien is a lucky guy."

I blushed, taking the compliment to heart. "So is Lorelei."

Zane seemed like he'd been looking for love for a long time and Lorelei was such a perfect match for him. Sweet yet strong, loyal to her people and humble.

He stepped onto the platform just as the doors closed and I exhaled a deep breath.

I was on my own now.

I had twelve hours to figure out how to stop the wedding and convince Adrien he needed to help me.

Stars be my guide.

Chapter Nine

I stayed awake for the entire rest of the day, filling myself up on caffeinated tea and snacks. I was practically buzzing by the time the train got to the station and had zero clever plans on how to stop Adrien and Elisana's wedding.

The way I saw it, I had two options.

1. Just walk up and kiss the guy, either proving all of this to be a farce or convincing him and myself that mates were real.
2. Knock Elisana over the head with a frying pan, grab the groom, and run for the mountains.

I burst out into a snort laugh, which drew the looks of a few random passengers, so I turned it into a cough.

No, there had to be a third option. Pull Adrien into a room and prove to him how wrong they were for each other. Yes. That was the plan. Make the man see reason.

I exhaled a calming breath. I could do this.

The second the train stopped and the doors opened, I flew out of them. Any lingering doubt about mates being real was beaten back because, with every passing moment, the thought of Adrien marrying that hag caused untold amounts of rage to swell inside of me.

She'd better not be pregnant.

I paid a man to borrow his horse and took off for the giant white castle that faced the sea. As I got closer, the streets became more congested. I looked up at the sun and noticed it was about to set. A sunset wedding on the beach? That only made my jealousy grow.

"Get your flower crowns!" Someone held out a beautiful ring of flowers, and I peered around to see that everyone was wearing them as they walked toward the castle.

Sliding off my horse, I grabbed a purple flower crown from her arm and tossed her a coin.

"Thank you kindly, milady," she said as I slipped the crown on my head and pulled my horse over to the barn, where an attendant was tying them up. After checking the mare in with the attendant, I began to make my way through the crowd.

There were hundreds of people. This wedding was going to be huge, which only made my nerves increase.

Moving with the flow of the people, I wound around the back of the castle where the guests were flocking and skittered to a stop. The beach was teeming with beautiful white chairs, each covered with a purple silk bow. An aisle had been erected in the middle and was covered with small white shells. It was absolutely incredible.

"Take your seats," an attendant cried, and I spurred into action.

Breaking away from the group, I slipped inside the back door of the castle and made my way through the open sitting room and down the hallway toward the kitchen that Elisana brought me through the first day I arrived in Ethereum.

It was total chaos. Household staff scurried about, grabbing trays of food and floral arrangements.

"Hurry!" Elisana yelled from somewhere deeper in the kitchen.

The kitchen door was propped open with a stack of books, and I peered into it from my place a few feet away. I should avoid Elisana completely, but a small part of me wanted to see her dress. I bet it was beautiful.

The door swung open wider as a chef ran out carrying a small stack of chocolate cakes, and I spotted Elisana standing with her back to the rest of the room. She was all alone now and what I witnessed then stole my breath.

She was holding a cup of tea, and she'd just *breathed* purple magic over it.

I ducked out of the way just as her gaze shifted to the doorway, and my heart pounded frantically in my chest.

The tea.

The cursed tea!

I knew from reading past champion's journals that this realm had witches, but I never thought Elisana could be one. I suspected something was up, but I'd certainly not imagined her to be giving him enchanted tea.

So that's why he was so gaga over her. It was a love potion.

Spinning in the other direction, I bolted for the stairs, the hair on the back of my neck rising as I went up to the next floor and then turned the corner and ran right into the chest of the very man I was looking for.

For a beautiful moment, it was like time stopped. All the oxygen felt like it had been sucked from the room, and I was lost in those teal eyes. Adrien had reached out to steady himself and his fingers were still on my upper arms. He wore a white jacket with a powder blue shirt underneath, and I'd never seen him look more handsome.

"Isolde?" He seemed confused, but pleased to see me.

"My love? I have your tea," Elisana called out from deep in the castle and panic rose up inside me.

I shoved Adrien backward until he hit a door, and then I shoved us both through, only to find out that we were in a storage closet. The light was on in the cramped space and it smelled of musty linens.

"What are you doing?" he asked, shocked.

I swallowed hard. "I'm saving you from marrying the wrong person."

His brows knotted. "What?"

"Adrien?" Elisana sounded panicked.

My chest heaved. "Elisana is a witch. She's got you under some love spell. I'm . . . I need your help."

"A witch? There's no way that can be true." He looked at me like I had sprouted two heads. She must have already given him the tea, and this was a double dose to ensure he would marry her.

"What do you like about Elisana?" I whispered because her voice was getting closer.

Adrien looked flustered. "She's . . . pretty . . . ish and she's . . ." His mouth opened and closed like a fish, but no words came out. "I love her!" he finally yelled, and I winced at how loud it was.

"Adrien? Are you down here?" Elisana was too close, and he was too far under her spell for me to reach him right now.

New plan.

"I'm sorry," I whispered and grabbed the heavy metal cast-iron chamber pot on the shelf next to me and cracked him over the side of the head with it.

He went down quickly, and I used my one free arm to keep him from falling too badly or making too much noise. I coaxed him onto a tall stack of linens where he slumped over.

I'd just knocked out the groom. This was officially going down as the craziest thing I'd ever done.

"Darling," Elisana's voice was just outside the door, and I froze.

Please, no. I was prepared to attack her if necessary, but to be totally honest, I had never fought a witch and didn't know what it would entail.

Footsteps faded and I breathed a sigh of relief.

My next act was painfully clear. I needed to get Adrien out of there and wean him off of this tea.

I cracked open the storage closet door and came face to face with a portly woman carrying a giant stack of linens she couldn't see over.

"Oh," I said, surprised. "I'll take those from you," I told her and moved to grab them, positioning my body so that she couldn't see Adrien behind me.

She handed them off to me without a second glance. "See that this and the rest in the closet make it down the laundry chute." She jerked her head to a giant rectangular trapdoor on the wall a little way down the hall, and a wild idea came to me.

Dropping the linens the moment she turned the corner, I rushed over to the trapdoor, opening it and peering down. A smile lifted the corners of my mouth because when I looked down, I could see that there was a large pile of linens and towels only about ten feet below us. Thank the stars we were only one floor up from the laundry room because that made the fall somewhat safe.

I ran back to the closet and maneuvered Adrien's body until I could grab him under the armpits. Once I had a good grip, I dragged him across the hall to the trapdoor.

I huffed and puffed, and somehow wrangled part of him into the chute, feet first because that felt safer even though he was landing in a pile of sheets and towels. The man was heavier than a load of bricks, so I had to use some of my magic to help prop him up on a sheet of ice. When he was mostly in, he pitched downward and then dropped into the center of the pile. His body flopped and then rolled to the side.

I winced, hoping he was okay.

It was a small miracle I managed the task, let alone got away with it without anyone seeing us. My heart was racing the entire time, terrified that Elisana or even one of the castle staff would come around the corner any minute and see me struggling to stuff him in the chute.

I didn't waste time climbing in after Adrien. I leaped into the chute, and although I landed upright, my knees buckled on impact and I tipped over, falling onto Adrien's hard body. My face planted right in his chest.

Mmmm. He smells good, I thought and glanced up at his handsome face.

His full lips caught my attention and my head went a little fuzzy. Without even intending to, I reached up and ran a finger over his bottom lip. A delicious shiver ran through me at the contact. It was so soft.

Elisana's shrill voice sounded above me. "What do you mean, you don't know where he is?" she screeched, shocking me back to my senses.

We had to get as far away from this place as possible. And fast.

I jumped to my feet and scanned the room. It was filled with large water basins for washing and was blessedly empty.

I was searching for something, anything, that could help me sneak a muscular six-foot fae out of the castle undetected when my gaze landed on a laundry cart.

Yes, that would work.

Grabbing the cart, I rolled it over to Adrien. I was half worried, half thankful that he remained unconscious while I fought to hoist his considerable form up and into it. Sweat ran down my face and back when I finally got him in and then I covered him with a sheet, taking care not to smother him. Sucking in a deep breath, I schooled my features and pushed the cart with Adrien hidden in it, out of the room.

Most of the activity for the wedding seemed to be going on above us, and so I managed to get us outside the castle without much notice. Fae were nearly frantic as they raced to complete the set up, so anyone who passed us didn't bother to question why there was a girl pushing a laundry cart down the halls or out of the castle.

I had no idea how long Adrien would remain unconscious, but I knew that I had to get him as far away from that witch as possible.

And that meant I needed to find a horse or a carriage quickly. The more distance between Elisana and Adrien, the better.

Panic nipped at my heels, but I shoved it down through will-power alone.

I was Princess Isolde of the Winter Court. I could do this. I could steal a prince and convince him to help me.

I rounded a corner of the castle and spotted my escape in the form of a covered wagon. Wine sellers were just rolling their last barrel off the ramp attached to the wooden bed when someone came running from the other direction, yelling at them to hurry. They rushed off to deliver their goods, leaving the ramp attached to the back of the bed unattended.

Ignoring the guilt that wanted to rise up in me for what I was about to do to the poor wine sellers, I ran toward the covered wagon, building up as much speed as possible. I would need the momentum to get the laundry cart with Adrien up the steep ramp and into the bed of the wagon. I used all my physical strength, and managed to push it into the wagon with a grunt.

With Adrien still stowed in the laundry cart, but now hidden under the wagon's covering, I sprinted to the front of the wagon and jumped into the seat.

Grabbing the reins, I flicked them, and the two horses tethered to the wagon started forward. I wanted to sigh in relief, but we weren't safe yet.

It was slow going as we left the castle grounds, dodging both wedding attendees and merchants. At any moment I expected to either hear the outraged shouts of the poor fae whom I'd stolen the wagon from, or the shrill screams of Adrien's fiancée.

My heartbeat didn't calm its furious cadence until I'd cleared the wedding congestion and was on the outskirts of Soleum. Only then did I let myself dwell on the truth.

I'd just kidnapped a lord of Ethereum, and I had no idea what to do with him.

Chapter Ten

I traveled two hours outside of Soleum before stopping at an inn
in a small village. When we'd arrived, I'd told the innkeeper
Adrien was my husband and that he'd drunk too much, and
so I needed help getting him inside. The innkeeper had given me
a look that said he absolutely didn't believe me when I led him to
the bed of the wagon where Adrien was sprawled out. And I hadn't
blamed him.

Worried that someone would recognize their lord, I'd stopped
on the side of the road before then and smeared mud on his face
to conceal his features. I'd taken Adrien's fancy jacket off earlier,
and dirtied his pants and clothes as well. There was no way the
innkeeper had believed my story, but when I'd offered him extra
coin, he'd only shrugged before hefting Adrien on his shoulder
and carrying him up to our room for me.

Now I chewed on my bottom lip as I stared at Adrien's prone
form, worried I'd hit him too hard because it'd been hours since
I smuggled him out of Soleum, and he was still unconscious. Maybe
it was something in the concoction that Elisana had been forcing
down his throat for so long that slowed his natural healing or made

it hard for him to wake? I didn't know. If his chest hadn't been steadily rising and falling I'd have thought he was dead.

At first, I thought it was good luck he wasn't waking, but now . . . I was concerned.

My stomach was in knots as I stood and walked closer to where he lay, pausing at the side of the bed to look down at him.

I hadn't wanted to restrain him, but the tea that Adrien had been drinking was clearly some potion that Elisana had used to brainwash him, so there was no telling what he would do until it was out of his system. So after the innkeeper had set him on the bed and left, I tore one of the bedsheets into strips and tied Adrien's arms to the metal bed frame.

I cocked my head as I stared down at him, a little put out that even covered in mud I found him attractive.

He was going to be mad when he woke.

If he wakes, my mind whispered, and a bolt of fear shot through me.

No, not *if*, *when*. He was going to be fine.

Turning, I grabbed a rag and dipped it in a deep bowl of water intended for hand washing. The least I could do for him was wipe the mud off his face so he was clean when he regained consciousness.

After I had wrung the excess water out of the towel, I twisted back toward Adrien to find a pair of angry, teal eyes staring back at me.

Yelping in surprise, I dropped the rag, and it hit the floor with a splat.

"Adrien," I said, pressing a hand against my furiously pounding heart. "You're awake." Sweet relief rushed me, overshadowing the angry glower on his face.

"Why am I tied to this bed?" he asked, each word clipped and laced with ice. "And *why* does it feel like a horse sat on my head?"

"Right, that," I said, wringing my hands. "Well, it's kind of a long story . . ." Where did I even begin?

Suddenly, a wall of shadows appeared to my left and right, boxing me in place, and I shrieked in surprise.

Was this his power?

"Start talking," he growled.

I pulled the moisture from the bowl of water I'd dipped the towel in and created a long thin sword, pointing it at his neck. As it suspended in midair, I expected to see anger in his gaze, but I only saw mirth and a flash of respect. Like he enjoyed a worthy opponent.

"I'll speak when I feel safe," I told him and gestured to the walls of shadows pressing into my shoulders.

He sighed, and the shadows dissipated. I tossed my ice sword to the floor, and it shattered into a dozen pieces.

"Okay, Isolde. Why did you steal me away *from my wedding* and tie me to the bedpost?" he asked with one eyebrow raised.

When he put it that way, it sounded awful.

I gave a nervous laugh. "Well, I went to see the Wise Ones and they told me what I needed to do in order to end this curse. But I'll need your help."

His brows drew together. "I will gladly help you. But why couldn't you at least have waited until after my wedding to my beloved?"

On second thought, tying him up did seem a bit excessive now. But hearing the words "my beloved" caused a sharp pain to form in my chest.

"She's not your beloved," I spat with more anger than I should have had. "She's a witch. I caught her doing a spell over your precious *tea*."

A dark look overtook Adrien's face, transforming his handsome features. "Liar. You're here to carve out my heart!" He bucked against the restraints and the shadows were back, pressing in on me. I re-created my ice sword and pressed it against his throat.

"Adrien, I don't know you very well, but you seem like an intelligent man. Why do you think she pushed you to drink your tea every day?"

He frowned. "Because she loves me. She cares about my health. Besides, I haven't had the tea in a few days. I tossed it out because my sleep had improved."

"*No*, because she was drugging you with some love potion," I told him.

"Elisana is not a witch. She's my future wife." The dark walls pressed closer into me, and even though they were made of shadows, they began to crush me like a boulder, squeezing the air from my lungs.

I moved the tip of my ice sword to his neck until a single drop of blood formed. He eased the shadows off, which allowed me to breathe and have some limited range of motion.

We were in a standoff. I'd forgotten he was an Ethereum lord, and therefore powerful.

Plan B.

"I'm not here to kill you, okay? In order to do that, I would need this." I pulled my faestone blade from its sheath and then held it out with the handle facing him. "Here, you can have it. As a show of good faith."

I walked slowly toward him, the shadows moving with me as I reached out to lay the blade by his head.

He tracked me with his eyes, and I could see a cloudiness there. The tea was still at work, and I would need to detox it from his system before he saw reason.

As his attention was engrossed with the faestone dagger beside him, I sent a hunk of blunt ice from the floor into his temple, knocking him out cold.

Again.

The shadows fell away, and I sighed.

This was not how I had planned for this to go.

* * *

After paying the innkeeper nearly all of my coin, he procured a fae with a dampener rune wand and the ability to use it. I needed Adrien's powers neutralized for the next few days, and that was the only way I could think to do it.

When the fae arrived, I was a little surprised at his elegant appearance. In his early thirties with a neatly trimmed beard and mustache, he strode confidently into the room with a bowler hat and three-piece suit, but there was a conniving look in his eye that made my skin crawl.

"You can dampen his powers?" I asked.

He just nodded, walking over to the bed without sparing me a second glance. Opening Adrien's shirt, he drew the rune onto his naked chest with his wand.

His nostrils flared as he sniffed the air. "Love potion. Interesting. No judgment," he told me with a smirk.

"It's not mine," I protested.

He could smell it? Did that make him a witch too? I swallowed hard.

He raised one eyebrow. "Well, if he's coming down from it, you are in for a rough few days."

I frowned. "What do you mean?"

He held out his hand as if to say that his knowledge cost money. I'd already paid him for the rune.

With a growl, I dropped two coins in his palm.

"Depending how long he's been ingesting it, he'll get sick after a few days and then the potion will try to make him cling to thoughts of whoever it was focused on. It's ugly."

My heart hammered in my chest at the thought of it. I felt so bad for Adrien and even more furious at Elisana. If this fae was right, we were both in for a rough few days. If he'd already stopped drinking the tea, then he would probably start getting sick soon. But what I was really dreading was having to endure listening to him cling to Elisana for who knows how long after that.

"How do I get the rune off when I don't need it anymore?" I asked the man as he glanced at Adrien in bed. Dispelling runes was no doubt part of Dawn's training to be a champion, but I'd only had time for a crash course before coming to Ethereum.

His gaze fell to the blue faestone dagger on the pillow beside

Adrien's head. Desire flashed in his eyes and I snaked my hand out and sheathed the weapon back at my hip.

"One touch of that blade will do," the fae said. "Unless you want to sell it to me."

"No chance. Thank you for your time." It was a goodbye, and my tone was firm. He got the point and with a little hesitation, he left.

It only took about ten more minutes for Adrien to rustle awake. He was out for a much shorter time than before, which I was going to take as a good sign. But when he glanced down at the rune on his chest, he growled and then bucked like a maniac in the bed.

"Shhh, calm down," I told him. Running to his side, I tried to soothe him. "You'll hurt yourself."

His gaze flew to mine. "You dampened my power? You *are* trying to kill me." Fear flashed in his eyes, and I splayed my hand out on top of the rune across his chest. His heart fluttered wildly against my palm, and my gaze fell to his lips.

"I would *never* hurt you, Adrien." The honest admission shocked me, and for a wild second I considered kissing him to prove we were mates.

"I need Elisana. I need my love," he begged, and it was like ice-cold water down my veins. I retracted my hand as if I'd been burned.

"She's a witch," I reminded him.

His face contorted. "Don't speak about her like that," he yelled, his eyes wild and unfocused. A thin sheen of sweat beaded his brow, and he looked a little ashen.

I glanced at the door. Was it safe to stay here for a few days? I doubted it.

I thought of the way the fae had stared at my dagger. He wanted to steal it, I was sure of it. And the innkeeper knew I had a man up here against his will. How long before the fae either returned for the dagger or the innkeeper sold me out?

I grasped the sides of Adrien's face, my gaze boring into his. "Adrien, I need you to trust me. You're going to have a rough few days as the love potion Elisana force-fed you wears off, and then, when you are feeling better, we can talk about how you can help me. But first we need to get out of here. It will be easier if you work with me. I don't want to knock you unconscious again."

He yanked his head out of my grasp and turned away from me, vomiting all over the side of the bed.

My stomach roiled at the sight. I'd taken care of my little sisters when they were sick many times, but I didn't enjoy it.

I ran over to where there was a bucket sitting in the corner of the room, catching a slow drip from a roof leak, and snatched it. Holding the bucket under Adrien's face as best as I could, he threw up again. I felt bad that he was vomiting with his hands tied, so I unknotted the strips of cloth and he sat up and grasped the bucket, heaving into it over and over again. He barely had time to breathe between retches. It was awful.

If he tried to hurt me, I'd use my powers on him, but with the dampener rune on his chest I felt confident he wouldn't be a danger to me.

When he finally seemed to have nothing left in his belly he slumped back in bed with a groan. "We need to move to another town. We are too exposed," I told him and then leaning forward, I hooked my head under his left armpit.

He moaned as I forced him to stand and his legs nearly buckled. Poor guy. Since it was well into the night, I was hoping that everyone was already abed at the inn and we wouldn't draw much attention as we left.

I was wrong. Despite the late hour, the inn's tavern was still crowded and we garnered multiple stares as we stumbled downstairs and out the door, the bucket still clenched in my free hand just in case.

"Too much mead," I laughed nervously, and clutched Adrien's unbuttoned shirt closed over the rune to cover it. When we got to our wagon I tossed the contents of the bucket into a bush and lay Adrien in the back with it.

"I'm dying," he said between heaves.

"No, you aren't. You're purging Elisana's poison." Hadn't the fae said something about the duration of the sickness depending on how long he'd been enchanted?

"How long were you and Elisana together?" I asked, but then amended the question. "Or rather, how long has Elisana been making your tea?"

"Almost." He heaved. "A year." And then he threw up again.

I sighed. It was going to be a long night.

Leaving Adrien in the back of the wagon, I climbed up onto the front bench. Clicking my tongue, I pointed us in the direction of some lights in the distance, and steeled myself for no rest.

We passed a small town in the dead of night. My eyelids kept closing: it had been days now since I'd had a decent night's sleep, but I knew just one town over from where we were last seen was the first place anyone would look for us. I imagined by now Elisana would be scouring the kingdom for Adrien. So once the lights from the town were far enough behind us, I pulled the horses off on a dirt path that headed east into some sparsely wooded forest.

The moonlight illuminated the path, but just barely. My intention was to pull the wagon into the woods and sleep for a few hours, but at the end of the path was a tiny cabin with no lights on. I wondered if someone lived there or if it was one of those seasonal cabins people used for hunting or fishing trips like we did in winter.

Adrien's sickness had slowed, but he still moaned between retches, and my heart ached for him. I pulled the wagon right up to the small house, deciding if someone was there, I'd tell them I was lost or offer coin for lodging.

I knocked on the door, quite loudly since it was the middle of the night and I wanted to wake whoever lived there.

Then I waited. One minute. Two.

I knocked again, swaying on my feet with exhaustion just as Adrien got sick in the wagon for the hundredth time.

Finally, feeling bold, I tried the handle.

Locked.

"Forgive me." I used my power to throw a ball of ice at the small window next to the knob, and the sound of crashing glass filled the space.

I winced, but there were no shouts of alarm. I thought we were safe, so I reached in and twisted the lock, throwing the door wide open.

"Hello," I called, but there was no answer.

My shoulders sagged in relief. I'd leave coin for the broken window, but I really needed sleep.

I went back to the wagon and hoisted Adrien against my side.

"Why are you trying to kill me?" he asked. "I want Elisana. I love her. That soft skin, those brown eyes. I *need* her."

I wanted to tell him to shut up, but I knew it was just the effects of the potion leaving his system and took his renewed obsession with her as a good sign.

"She's on her way," I lied. He was delirious at this point.

"She is?" He perked up a little. "My love?" He stumbled into the cabin, his boots crunching the broken glass as he walked, before collapsing onto the couch. One more heave into the bucket I'd had the sense to grab from the wagon and then he was lights out.

The living room, kitchen, and dining area were all in one main room. The space was sparsely furnished, but looked to have everything necessary for a hunting cabin. There was a narrow hallway at the back that might have led to a bedroom, but I didn't have the energy to search for it, let alone try to get Adrien up and moving again. I went back and shut the door, and then fell onto the bearskin rug in front of the couch. I just needed a few hours of sleep.

* * *

Sunlight danced across my skin and my eyelids flew open. My gaze shot frantically to the couch where Adrien was shivering, a waxy pale ghost.

Oh, stars!

I sat up, rushing to feel his head and pulled my hand back with a hiss.

Fever. This evil hag had such a grip on him that her spell wouldn't leave him without a fever.

"I'll kill her," I vowed.

"Elisana," he mumbled in his delirium. Even in his darkest hour, he wanted her. I hated her even more for that.

Was it because I wanted *my* name mumbled on his lips?

I shook myself, pushing those thoughts out of my head. Then I got to work. I did everything Mother did for us when we were sick. I rinsed the bucket in the stream and fetched water with a clean pail they had in the kitchen. I swept the glass from the entry and left the coins on the table with a note so I wouldn't forget.

Then I got a cool bucket of water to give Adrien a sponge bath. Wrestling him out of his shirt and shoes and pants. He lay there in his under garment and I couldn't help but stare. He was all muscle, toned in every area, and deeply tanned all the way down to right above his hips.

Clearing my throat and focusing on the task at hand, I brushed his teeth as he mumbled Elisana's name and spit into a cup for me. Then I ran the cool cloth along his face, his cheek, and his neck, cleaning off the remnants of the mud I'd smeared on him the day before. I dipped it back in the bucket and brought it to his forehead, and he moaned.

His face felt a bit cooler, but when I touched his stomach it was scorching. After rinsing the cloth in the bucket again, I ran it along his abdomen, my cheeks heating with a blush I was sure was redder than a tomato. I leaned forward and blew across his now wet skin like our mother did, and he sighed.

"I love you," he whispered, and I froze.

The shock of those three words, even if they were not aimed at me but his fever dream, hit me hard. It was something my mother and father had said to each other countless times. I love you. In the end, the I love yous meant nothing.

I tossed the rag in the bucket and stood, working to clean up the space a bit more and hunt for food in the cupboard. After finding some dried meat and canned fruits, I fed myself and poured some of the fruit syrup into Adrien's mouth.

By the time night fell again, I was exhausted. Adrien's fever was still high and I'd given him three sponge washes. I was starting to worry this love spell detox might kill him. If he wasn't better by morning I'd have to leave and search for a healer, risking Elisana finding him. I lay on the floor next to the couch where Adrien slept fitfully and ran the cool rag over his face as long as I could before sleep took me.

Chapter Eleven

Adrien

I wasn't dead, but my body hurt so bad I almost wished I was.

I could only open my eyelids to slits, and even that was brutal. My abdominal muscles ached, and the light streaming in from the windows felt like it was stabbing me in the head.

I forced myself to glance around the unfamiliar room, but there wasn't much to see from my reclined position on the lumpy couch. I didn't know where I was, and I didn't remember much from the last couple of days, but I distinctly remember thinking that I was dying.

I tried to sit up, but a weight on my chest kept me in place. Glancing down, a shock ran through me.

Isolde.

The Winter princess was fast asleep with her head resting on my stomach, her legs curled under her on the floor next to the couch. Her dark lashes cast crescent shadows under her eyes as she took in slow and easy breaths. One of her arms was wrapped over my waist, and the other rested against my ribs, a damp cloth clenched in her hand.

Something green caught my eye, and I looked down at my chest to see a dampener rune there. As I stared at it, bits and pieces of the last couple of days started to filter back to me. The most recent memories came back first.

I'd been sicker than I ever had before in my life. Violent shudders had racked me as a fever ravaged my body.

And Isolde had been there the whole time. Talking softly to me. Cleaning the sickness and sweat from me with cool rags. Urging me to drink what I could.

My mind started to drift further back, to before the sickness took hold. My brows furrowed as I tried to make sense of it.

I'd woken up tethered to a bed. Isolde had done it. I'd been furious and attacked her with my magic when she tried to tell me something I didn't want to hear. What, I couldn't yet remember. I'd thought she was going to kill me, cut out my heart and take it back to Faerie, but rather than plunging her blade into my chest, she'd laid her faestone dagger on the bed next to me, surrendering it.

I squeezed my eyes shut, willing myself to remember more, and it finally came to me with a silent gasp.

The wedding!

It had been my wedding day. Isolde had appeared out of nowhere and dragged me into the linen closet. Those moments started to replay in my mind as if they'd just happened.

She'd been sure Elisana was a witch. I hadn't believed her, but now that the potion had been detoxed from my body, I could see it all so clearly.

I didn't love Elisana. I never had. Over the year that I'd known her she'd practically force-fed me that tea at times, and now I knew why.

Isolde had saved me.

Looking down at her now, I knew I should wake her to let her know that I was free of the spell, but I couldn't bring myself to move. And it wasn't the aches and pains in my body that stopped me—although those were starting to dissipate—it was that I couldn't tear my gaze from her.

My eyes were greedy for her. For details I hadn't noticed or remembered from the day we'd met. The faint smattering of freckles over the bridge of her nose. The graceful slope of her cheek. The silkiness of the strands of her long raven hair that were splayed out over her back and shoulders. Even her long fingers fascinated me.

Knowing that my dreams of her hadn't done her justice, I drank her in like a man dying of thirst. Every one of her features was like a drop of crystal-clear water, rejuvenating my mind, body, and soul.

And it wasn't the foggy obsession like I'd had with Elisana. No, my mind was clear, a complete contrast to how I'd always felt with my fiancée.

My ex-fiancée.

Thinking of Elisana brought a wave of rage to the surface so potent that I tensed involuntarily, jostling Isolde. The movement woke her, and her eyes blinked open. The ice-blue orbs had me catching my breath.

"You're awake," she said, her voice husky with sleep, and something stirred deep in my chest.

I nodded. "Yes. And clearheaded for the first time in a long time."

She started to smile, but it froze on her face when she realized she was half sprawled over me. Jolting back, her cheeks turned the most lovely shade of pink that only darkened further when she glanced over my body.

I arched a brow at her when I saw that I was nearly naked, and she jerked her gaze from me, stumbling to her feet. Without another word, she rushed from the room and as I pushed myself to a seated position with a groan, I found myself wondering where my brother Zane was and why he would leave his mate alone to tend to me.

Thinking of Isolde as my brother's mate caused an unexpected pain to slice through my chest. It didn't feel any more right now than it had the first time I'd seen them together, but there was nothing I could do about it, so I pushed the thought from my mind, with effort.

I was just shifting so my feet were on the floor when Isolde hurried back into the room and flung a thin blanket at me. It smacked me in the face, surprising me.

"Oh, sorry," she said as I rearranged the blanket over my lower half, covering me from the waist down.

I had to cover my smile. I didn't mind my state of undress. I'd gone fishing on my boat in similar attire when the sun was particularly hot, but clearly she did.

"I had to take off your clothes because they were covered in mud and vomit," she explained as she stood in front of me. "And you had a fever."

I winced. The state I'd been in the last couple of days wasn't one I'd want anyone to see me in, let alone a princess of Faerie.

Let alone this *princess of Faerie,* my mind whispered.

"I washed them in the creek yesterday though," Isolde went on, her voice a nervous chatter. "They're hanging on the line outside, but I'm sure they are dry by now. I can grab them for you if you want to dress."

I waved her off and then ran a hand through my hair, feeling it catch on snarls and tangles. I needed a proper bath, but we had important things to discuss first.

"I'm good for now," I told her and then crossed my arms over my chest. I didn't miss how her eyes followed the motion and then slowly moved from my arms to my chest and stuck there. This time, I couldn't hold back the smile. She liked what she saw, I could tell. And I liked that.

"Yes, well . . ." she cleared her throat and averted her gaze. "Now that you're awake, and the fever seems to have broken, would you like some water?"

My throat was parched, but it could wait as well. Reaching forward, I laid a gentle hand on her arm, pausing until she looked back at me to speak.

"Thank you," I said. "If it weren't for you—" I suppressed a shudder instead of going down that road.

She shifted a step back, and I dropped my hand, but I noticed that she ran her fingers over the place that I touched. I don't think she was aware that she was doing it though.

"It was nothing," she told me, downplaying her heroic actions. "Anyone else would have done the same."

I shook my head and rose to my feet, keeping a hand on the blanket so it didn't slip off me. My muscles protested, but I remained steady.

"No, don't do that," I said as she glanced up at me with those clear blue eyes. "It wasn't nothing. What you did took courage.

Kidnapping an Ethereum lord and helping break the spell I was under." I had to chuckle at that. I don't even know if my brothers would have dared to do what she had. But then I sobered. "I don't know very many fae who would risk themselves like you did. I could have hurt you badly."

She shook her head, but I knew it was true. I wanted to believe I never would have hurt her, but I was so far under Elisana's love spell that I would have done anything to get back to her.

A toxic mixture of shame and fury began to rush through my veins, but I grit my teeth and forced myself to relax. My anger was for Elisana, and Elisana alone. I would deal with my ex-fiancée and her treachery soon enough, but now wasn't the time for that. Now was the time for apologies.

"It's true," I said with a frown. "I even used my powers against you." A pang of remorse for what I'd done to her hit me as I indicated the rune on my chest.

I wasn't upset that she'd put it there. I was glad she'd done it to protect herself from me. I just wished it hadn't been necessary.

Isolde's eyes widened as she focused on the glowing green mark.

"Oh, right," she said, and before I had a chance to stop her, she pulled her dagger and swiped the tip through the rune. She didn't so much as nick my skin, but the faestone dagger coming that close to my heart still caused it to beat furiously.

The rune dissipated immediately, but my heart rate took longer to slow. I felt my powers surge forward as they were unlocked inside of me.

"Thank you again," I said, rubbing my chest where it had been. "But next time, give me a little warning before waving that thing so close to me." I nodded toward her faestone dagger and chuckled. "That's one blade every Ethereum lord has nightmares about getting too close to their heart."

She looked down at her hand, and her eyes widened when she realized what she'd done. "Sorry," she said, sheathing the blade at her waist.

"Don't apologize. You've done me a service. I don't even know how to start to repay you."

"I do," she told me, and my eyebrows lifted.

"You do?" I asked, and she nodded. "Well, then tell me. If it's in my power to grant, I'll do or give you anything you ask."

"I was hoping you'd say that," she said. "Because I need you to take me to the belly of the sea."

Chapter Twelve

Isolde

Now that Adrien was awake and no longer under Elisana's love spell, I could sense a change between us. He kept sneaking glances at me, and I was trying not to stare at his chiseled abs. *Put a shirt on already!*

I'd spent the last ten minutes briefing him on what the Wise Ones said, but no matter how many times I tried I couldn't bring myself to tell him about the mates part. I was still on the fence about it all. Zane and I had kissed and nothing happened. Perhaps the same would happen if Adrien and I kissed as well. But even if Adrien was my mate, it didn't mean anything. I was not going to end up like my parents.

My goals were simple now. Travel to the belly of the sea, unlock the Shadow Heart, and get back to Faerie. With any luck, Zane would find a way back to Faerie quickly, and before the end of the fortnight, I'd be back in my beloved land, telling my sisters all about my adventures.

As I told Adrien what needed to be done, he listened intently.

"There is a lot of lore about the 'belly of the sea'. Some say it's an island, others say it's a sunken ship, but me and my fellow sailors think differently."

Great. We had a couple of leads. "Do you know where it might be?" I asked.

He nodded. "I have an idea. There's a place we all avoid because it messes with our navigation. It's garnered many names over the years and the belly of the sea is one of them because it eats any ship that tries to pass through it, never to be seen again."

Interesting. Not exactly ideal. "Sounds like a good place to start," I told him. I wasn't letting some local lore scare me off my task. My family, my people, my whole realm was depending on me.

Adrien, still shirtless, eyed the cabin door. "Zane went with you to the Wise Ones?" he asked.

I nodded. "He was a great help."

Adrien frowned. "Where is my brother now?"

"Oh, right. He had a meeting with the Wise Ones too and they sent him on his own mission of sorts."

Adrien's frown deepened. "My brother let his mate go off on a mission alone to save me from a witch? Doesn't sound like him."

"Oh." He thought Zane and I were mates. "About that." I fidgeted with the cuff of my shirt, uncomfortable with this conversation, but knowing it had to be said. "Zane and I aren't mates."

Adrien's eyes flared. Was that relief in his gaze?

"How can you be sure?" he pressed.

I shrugged nonchalantly. "We kissed. Nothing happened."

"You kissed my brother?" Adrien shouted, jealousy laced through his voice.

He jolted a little after his outburst, seemingly as surprised by the intensity of his reaction as I was. Clearing his throat, he glanced away, but I still caught the faint hint of color that appeared high on his cheeks.

I couldn't help but grin a little. That was an interesting reaction. "I did. No sparkles or whatever he was expecting. Shall we get back to Soleum? I'm sure your staff is worried about you."

And please put on a shirt before I reach out and stroke those pecks, just to see if they are as hard as they look.

* * *

Adrien finally dressed—thank the stars—and we rode together back toward Soleum in the wagon I'd stolen from his wedding. Once we reached the nearest village, Adrien sent a raven ahead of us to tell his castle staff and army to detain Elisana and await his arrival.

As we journeyed back down south, he asked me things about my life in Faerie, my family, my hopes, and dreams. He was as easy to get along with as Zane. Telling him things I wouldn't normally tell someone I didn't know well, just came naturally.

"So women rule in Faerie, I hear?" he asked as we passed a small village on our left. By my calculations, we were almost back to his castle. Adrien sat next to me on the open bench seat behind the horses with the riding crop in his hand.

I nodded. "My mother is the Queen, and when my father was married to her he was king consort."

Adrien frowned at my wording. "Was married?"

LEIA STONE & JULIE HALL

"They divorced when I was fifteen."

His frown turned to understanding. "I'm sorry to hear that."

I gave him a polite smile and tried to think of something to change the subject, before he asked another question about it, but my mind came up blank.

"That must have been really hard on you," he said.

I swallowed hard. "It's fine. I had six younger sisters to be strong for." I tilted my chin up high.

He was staring at me with his teal eyes like he could see right through me, like he saw the little battered and bloodied fifteen-year-old inside of me that was still healing from the pain my parents caused.

"Oh, look, your castle," I blurted out and pointed at the white stone structure in the distance.

He nodded calmly, unsurprised, which he probably wasn't since he knew exactly where we were. It was his realm after all.

"Do you want marriage for yourself one day?" he asked suddenly.

Why was he going so deep? We didn't know each other well and it was a huge question to ask. Maybe not for other women, but it was for me.

"No," I answered honestly, and his head reeled back a little in shock.

"Why not?" He sounded hurt for some reason, like my answer had personally offended him.

I peered over at him, catching his gaze and holding it. "Because if I don't get married, I never have to worry about divorce."

Turning away from him, I gave him my back, sending a clear

130

message that this questioning was over. He was quiet for the rest of the ride.

When we arrived at his castle there was a flurry of activity. We learned that Elisana had fled after she realized Adrien had been taken and wasn't going to marry her. She had probably put two and two together and realized she was caught and that her time was up.

"I want every inch of this realm scoured until you bring her to me for justice," Adrien told one of his spies.

According to Zane, Adrien had a network of spies who were some of the best in the realm, who worked to not only ferret out information but also were among his most elite warriors. In some ways, Adrien's spies were like a small army themselves.

"Yes, sir," the man said and then left with a bow, disappearing into the hallway.

Adrien then turned to his head housemaid. "Please collect every article of clothing and personal belonging of hers and burn it. Let's not forget she was a witch and we don't know what other traps might lie in wait in my very own home."

Underneath the anger, he sounded vulnerable and hurt, and he had every right to be.

"Yes, my lord." She rested a comforting hand on his shoulder before leaving the room.

Night was falling, and it was well past dinner and as much as I wanted to just go out there and unlock this crystal, a yawn escaped me.

"I'm tired, too." Adrien rubbed his face. "Shall we have dinner and then get some sleep? Leave first thing in the morning?"

I agreed, and Adrien led me down to the kitchen. I expected

him to instruct the chef to feed us, but instead he told his kitchen staff they could take the rest of the night off.

"Would you like a melted cheese and tomato sandwich?" he asked me.

"Sure, that sounds great," I told him.

He looked relieved. "Good. Because that's the only thing I know how to make."

I laughed and pulled a milk crate over to the counter and sat down. As he sliced the tomato, bread, and cheese, he told me all about his childhood and what it was like to grow up with so many brothers.

"You've heard about my ton of sisters, so I totally know what you mean," I said.

"Chaos, all the time," he agreed.

I found myself enjoying the conversation and couldn't help comparing it to my talks with Zane. I liked both brothers, they were good fae and easy to get along with. But why did my eyes linger on Adrien's biceps as he cut the bread, watching his muscles flex? And why did my stomach turn over when he handed me my sandwich and winked when I said thank you?

I wanted to feel nothing for Adrien, just like when I'd thought about kissing Zane. But the mere thought of getting close to Adrien, of pressing my lips against his, caused a full-body flush to come over me.

"Is the food okay?" Adrien asked, his gaze studying me in a way that only made my blood heat further.

I gave a nervous laugh. "It's wonderful, thank you," I answered and took another bite of the warm cheesy goodness.

He watched me, his eyes going to my lips, and I wondered what he was thinking. Then he hung his head a little and shook it.

"What's wrong?" I asked.

He sucked in a deep breath and then exhaled, staring at his sandwich as if it held a secret.

"I can't believe I almost married her."

My heart ached for him. He was still processing Elisana's betrayal. Reaching out, I placed my hand over his, and he looked up at me.

"Take it as a compliment. You're so powerful and handsome that a witch wanted to enchant you to love her forever."

A lopsided grin graced his face, and my stomach bottomed out.

"You think I'm handsome?"

I burst into nervous laughter and pulled my hand back.

"No, please, Isolde, tell me more about that," Adrien pressed, and I just laughed harder, blushing red as a sunset.

"Stop. You know you're good-looking. All of you Ethereum lords are."

His face darkened a little, and I suspected he was thinking of me kissing Zane.

I swallowed hard and put the last piece of sandwich into my mouth, chewing.

"Well, I'm exhausted," I told him. "Thank you for the dinner."

I stood, and he followed suit.

"Let me show you to the guest quarters," he said.

I waved him off. "I know where they are. I've stayed here before."

His cheeks pinked. "Those were *not* the guest quarters. Those are for servants. I'm sorry I didn't stand up to Elisana. I . . . couldn't at the time."

"It's okay," I told him.

"It is not," he said, his face darkening for a moment.

It wasn't just that his face changed, but that the shadows in the room seemed to shift and press in closer.

I drew in a quick breath of air in surprise, and it snapped Adrien out of it. He drew in a slow lungful of air and the shadows retreated, returning to their proper place.

"My apologies," he said, running a hand through his hair, drawing my attention to his long, sun-kissed hair. "I lost myself for a moment. I'm just so angry with Elisana."

I told him it was okay again, because it truly was. What Elisana had done to him was beyond deplorable. She'd taken away his free will. I didn't expect him to recover overnight.

He gave me a pinched smile and then led me to a lavish two-room suite with a claw-foot tub bathroom and sitting area. It was plush with light-blue and sand-colored linens that reminded me of the sea, and a thousand miles from the chamber I'd stayed in before.

He lingered at the door. "Goodnight, Isolde."

"Goodnight, Adrien," I said, and for a wild second I considered kissing him, just to see if it was like kissing Zane, but I lost my nerve and shut the door.

Besides. Who said he'd want to kiss me back?

Chapter Thirteen

The next morning, we were up bright and early and took a carriage to the wharf where Adrien's ship was moored. It was a short ride down the coast from the castle, but as soon as we arrived I could tell it was the true heart of Soleum. The wharf was teeming with life. Fae rushed back and forth as they shuttled supplies to outgoing ships and brought in crates of goods from ones recently returned. There was a bustling market set up along the docks in front of where the smaller boats were docked. The larger ships were anchored out in the harbor. The way that it was set up was that we had to walk through the market to get to the docks where the boats were tied up, but I didn't mind. It was beautiful and lively. It reminded me of the market in Winter Court right before the solstice.

Adrien got out of the carriage in front of me and then held his hand out to help me down. Rather than releasing me when I reached the ground, he tucked my hand into the crook of his arm and led me toward the market. I told myself that it meant nothing, but couldn't ignore the thrill that went through me.

When we reached the market stalls, merchants were selling

everything from flowers to homemade cakes, to seafood fresh off the boats bobbing in the harbor. Sellers called out to us as we passed.

"Free samples. The best beignets in the Southern Kingdom."

"Handmade silk. The finest in all of Ethereum!"

"Tinctures to cure any ailment!"

"Perfumes from the Southern Isles' flowers!"

There were so many different items, I almost didn't know where to look first. A few of the merchants called out to Adrien by name, offering him hellos and well wishes He smiled and waved back at them, but didn't stop until a sailor jumped out in front of us.

The fae was a short man whose skin was overly tanned and leathery. He had pants on that were frayed at the ankles, and a faded striped shirt. He pulled off his hat and started twisting it in his hands. It was clear the fae was agitated about something. "Beggin' yer pardon, m'lord," he said, ducking his head. "But I need to be havin' a word with ya."

Adrien shifted slightly so that his body was protecting me. It was unnecessary. I was a powerful princess who could take care of herself, but the gesture was undeniably sweet.

"Can it wait?" Adrien asked. "We're to set sail this morning."

He shook his head. "I sorry to be interrupting ya, but this canna wait. It's urgent." The man's gaze shifted to me and I felt Adrien stiffen. "Perhaps we should talk in private," the tanned fae suggested.

Adrien glanced down at me with a frown, and then back up at the weathered sailor. With a resigned sigh, he nodded. "This will just take a moment," he told me.

"It's okay," I said, not put off by the interruption because it meant I could look around the market.

"I'll just be over there," Adrien pointed to an area off to the side where he could speak with the sailor but still stay in view.

I nodded, and Adrien and the fae stepped out of the main thoroughfare. I couldn't hear what the fae was saying anymore, but he was talking adamantly, waving his arms and making big gestures. Adrien's face intensified, and I wondered what they were speaking of when I felt a light touch on my arm.

Glancing over, and then down, I saw there was a young fae standing beside me. She was probably no older than six or seven and was holding out a blue shawl. She had round cheeks and the cutest pair of pearlescent horns peeking out from her head of blonde corkscrew curls.

"This one matches your eyes, milady," she said, and when she grinned up at me I could see a tiny pair of fangs. I didn't know what type of unseelie she was, but she was adorable.

I crouched down to her level and inspected the shawl she was holding. It was a beautifully embroidered piece of light-blue silk. And she was right, the color did resemble my eyes.

"This is so pretty," I said with a smile.

She pointed to the stall several feet behind her where there were a variety of different-colored fabrics on display, and then tugged my sleeve, trying to get me over there. I straightened with a chuckle and followed her over to where a woman a few years younger than my own mother stood behind a table covered in skirts, talking to another customer.

The little girl stayed by my side, showing me various embroidered clothes and fabrics. Even though she was young, she was a good sales-person. The quality of the work was exceptional, but my interest kept returning to the first shawl she'd brought to me.

"I think I'd like to get this," I told her and asked the price.

It was fair and there was no way I was going to haggle with a child, so I dug into my coin purse only to realize I was out of money. Zane had given me a decent amount, but I'd spent most of it on the innkeeper and the fae who had put the rune on Adrien for me, and then left what I had remaining for whoever owned the cabin we'd broken into.

"I'm sorry," I told her with a frown and the little girl's face fell. "It's beautiful, but I'm afraid I'm out of money."

"Oh," she said.

"There you are," came a voice behind me and I twisted to watch Adrien join me.

His gaze dropped to the shawl in my hand. "It reminds me of your eyes," he said, and a warm feeling bloomed in my chest.

"That's what I said," the little girl piped up and Adrien smiled back at her.

"Well, then she must have it," Adrien reached into his own pocket for the coin.

I was about to stop him when the woman behind the table finally finished with her customer and turned to us. Her eyes grew large when she spotted Adrien. "My lord," she said, dropping into a curtsey.

Adrien went to hand her the money for the shawl, but she tried to wave him off. "If you like it, it's yours," she said.

Adrien shook his head and then reached into his pocket and

pulled out a few extra coins. "Nonsense," he told her. "I can tell the superiority of the work. Whoever embroidered this is very talented."

"My momma has the best needlework in all of Soleum," the little girl said seriously.

The woman blushed, ducking her head to try to cover the coloring of her cheeks. "Thank you, my lord," she said, finally accepting Adrien's money.

Gently taking the fabric from my hands, he draped it over my shoulders. From behind me, Adrien leaned forward and spoke in my ear. "It can get chilly at night on the ship," he said. His breath brushed against my neck as he spoke, sending delicious shivers to dance down my spine.

I smiled up at him. "Thank you for the gift," I said.

His gaze locked with my own and then dipped to my mouth. Feeling suddenly dry, I swiped my tongue over my bottom lip to wet it, and Adrien's teal eyes darkened. "Entirely my pleasure," he said, his voice husky.

"Don't you want a skirt to go with it?" the little girl said, breaking what felt like a spell that had come over me. An Adrien spell. One that needed no daily dosing of tea because it was naturally occurring.

Startled, I began to laugh as the woman scolded her daughter for pushing too hard for a sale, but Adrien wholeheartedly agreed with the little girl. Fifteen minutes later we walked away from the stall with a new skirt, dress, and another thicker shawl. Adrien insisted on buying it all for me and I wanted to protest, but I could also see how excited the woman and her daughter were to make the sales, so I kept my mouth shut. Between Adrien and Zane's generosity I'd never have to shop for clothes again.

We walked through the rest of the market before I thought to ask Adrien about the sailor. As soon as I did, his lighthearted attitude changed.

"A pirate sighting," he said, a sour note in his voice.

"Pirates?" I asked him.

He nodded as he led me over to where a small boat was tied to the side of the dock.

"Huge problem for me right now. They'll take your cargo and your ship, and then leave you for dead."

I cleared my throat, scanning the horizon for a pirate flag like in one of my novels. But of course, there was nothing there except the ships moored in the harbor.

He laughed. "They look like any old sailor, until you get close," he warned.

Yikes. I swallowed hard. I double- and then triple-checked that I had the Shadow Heart in the satchel attached to my waist, as Adrien helped me into the dinghy that would take us to his larger ship.

After untying the boat from the dock, he pushed us off and then settled onto the bench seat to start rowing. Holding a hand up to my forehead to block the sunlight, I asked which ship we were going to. There were a few bobbing in the harbor in front of us. He paused rowing to point to the largest one, a three-masted ship with square sails. The hull was painted white and there was a carving of a female attached to the bow. As we neared, I read the name along the stern. *Beatrice*.

"She's beautiful," I told him.

"My pride and joy," Adrien replied with a grin.

I fanned myself. I'd already taken off the shawl Adrien had wrapped around me and was grateful that one of Adrien's maids had provided me with a linen shirt that was tight around my torso, but loose in the sleeves, with matching pants that were more breathable than what I'd worn up in the Western and Northern Kingdoms. The sun was relentless here, something I wasn't used to.

"You must not get much warm weather in the Winter Court," he said, noticing that I scowled at the giant orange ball in the sky. I'm not surprised that was obvious. My skin was so pale it was practically glowing.

"I do not. And I like it that way," I told him.

He chuckled and kept rowing.

We reached the ship quickly after that and before I knew it, I was scaling a rope ladder and climbing over the railing. It was a flurry of activity up on the deck. Men rushing around, adjusting the sails, pulling ropes, moving around supplies. Honestly, I had no idea what they were doing, but it was obvious they were busy. So much so that hardly anyone took note of Adrien and me arriving.

I glanced over at Adrien next to me and he was beaming. He filled his lungs up with the briny sea air and then let it out slowly, closing his eyes as if he was savoring the moment. It would be clear to anyone with two eyes that Adrien loved being on this ship.

"Come on," he said, looking down at me. "I'll show you to your quarters for the duration of our trip."

I nodded and followed him past some men who gave me polite smiles and nods, and then through a doorway that led below deck.

The hallways in the ship were dim and narrow. We had to angle our bodies whenever someone passed so we could both fit.

Adrien led me to a surprisingly spacious cabin positioned at the back of the ship. There was a horizontal row of windows that afforded a beautiful view of the sea. There was also a desk bolted to the floor in front of the windows, and opposite the desk was a fairly large bed.

"This is the captain's quarters," Adrien said. "You can stay here."

I turned to him with a furrowed brow. I hated that I was taking someone's room. "Then where will the captain be staying?" I asked.

"I'll be staying in one of the smaller cabins," Adrien said with a grin.

"You're the captain?" That probably shouldn't have surprised me, but it did. I guess I just didn't expect an Ethereum lord to also captain his own ship. I was impressed.

Adrien laughed lightly at the look on my face. "Yes. *Beatrice* is my baby. I wouldn't trust anyone else to captain her."

I started to argue about the rooming. I didn't mind staying in one of the smaller cabins, but Adrien put a hand up. He wouldn't hear of it.

"So who is Beatrice? An old lover?" I questioned, surprised by the note of jealousy in my voice.

Adrien grinned. "I did love her. More than I've ever loved anyone in my life," he declared, and for some reason my heart squeezed painfully at that.

"She was my first dog. The most loyal and loving female I'd ever met," he finished, and I burst into laughter.

Beatrice was a dog!

A knock sounded at the door and when Adrien said, "Enter," an elderly fae hobbled into the room. He nodded kindly to me and then peered at Adrien.

"We're prepared to set sail in the next half hour, Cap'n," the fae said.

"Wonderful," Adrien replied. "I'll be up soon to take the helm."

The man nodded his head and then left.

"You're welcome to stay here, or come join the men on deck for the launch," Adrien told me.

"I'm definitely going back up," I said without even having to think about it. The room was nice, but I'd only ever been at sea one other time, so I wasn't about to waste the opportunity to be on deck when we left the harbor.

Adrien gestured for me to go ahead of him and we left the captain's quarters to head back up. Along the way, Adrien filled me in on some nautical terms and details about *Beatrice* specifically. Apparently the ship had six gunports on each side. It wasn't the largest ship in Adrien's fleet, but he said it was his favorite because she was both agile and fast.

Besides us, there were twenty-six crew members who were coming on the journey to the belly of the sea. The man who I'd met in the cabin a few minutes before was Brimsley, the chief officer and Adrien's first mate. Adrien said Brimsley had been sailing for longer than he had been alive, and that the aged sailor had an uncanny ability to detect when a storm was brewing.

When we reached the main deck, Adrien led me over to the ship's bow and told me it was the best place to be for the launch. With a grin, he left me there, striding across the vessel to the stern and up the short set of stairs to the quarterdeck, where the helm was. He nodded at one of his sailors who was manning the helm and then took over. I found myself smiling as I watched him shout orders to his crew. I'd never seen anyone so in their element.

Adrien's gaze drifted back to me, and he caught me staring and winked. I quickly turned, fixing my gaze on the brilliant turquoise waters, telling myself my cheeks were heating because of the sun beating down on me.

When we finally launched, Adrien kept to a slow speed until we exited the harbor. Once we cleared it, he shouted commands to his crew and they unfurled more sails as the ship lurched forward, cutting through the waves easily.

As the briny air blew through my hair, throwing the long strands every which way, I was in awe. The waters near the Winter Court were choppy and filled with peril. I'd only ever been out on it once because they were so dangerous. Only skilled fishermen braved the Ice Sea. Large shards of ice could puncture your hull in a moment and you'd be lost to the frigid waters. Nothing in the Winter Court was kind to life, which was what made us so resilient. No one would ever traverse the Ice Sea for leisure, but I could easily imagine spending time out here in these waves for the sheer pleasure of it. It's no wonder Adrien liked sailing so much.

I could have stayed on the bow all day, but around late afternoon I felt a presence and turned to see Adrien come up next to me.

"You're enjoying yourself," he said.

It wasn't a question, but I nodded anyway, taking in a full lungful of air. "Being out here feels . . ." I didn't know how exactly to put it into words.

"Like freedom," Adrien said, finishing my sentence when I trailed off.

I smiled and nodded, then glanced over at Adrien to find him watching me instead of the sea. And I liked that. More than I probably should have, considering it was still my plan to leave Ethereum as soon as I could. Mate or not.

That thought sobered me, and the smile slipped from my face.

"So you have a good idea where the belly of the sea is?" I asked.

Adrien tilted his head as he considered me. He seemed to have picked up on my mood change but didn't comment on it. He nodded and gestured toward the door that led below deck. "Let's go to my quarters. Or rather, *yours*. I have maps there and I'll show you where I think we should look first."

"Sounds good," I said without looking Adrien in the eye. He was right. It was time we got down to business.

Two hours later we had a plan. Adrien said that sailors reported not just strange compass activity, but also strange behavior in this southeast quadrant of the ocean. Sailors swore that at night they saw a bright blue glowing light coming from deep in the ocean in the center of this strange area. That's how it got dubbed: *the belly of the sea*. Because the light seemed to be emanating from the bottomless belly of the ocean itself. But when sailors tried to swim down to see what the glowing light was, they disappeared. Forever.

"Great, so that's confirmed. We are literally risking our lives for this," I said.

He gave me a handsome, half-cocked grin. "We are."

"And why does that make you smile?" I questioned.

He laughed. "What can I say? I like a little element of danger."

I don't know why I found that sexy, but it was.

Reaching out, I grasped his hand. "Seriously though, thank you. This will save so many people." I thought of my sisters, my parents, our people, the Summer and Spring Court refugees. The fate of the entire world of Faerie was quite literally resting on this one mission.

He laid his hand over mine and bore into my gaze. "You saved me from being married to a witch for the rest of my life. There is nothing you could ask that I would deny."

Kiss me, I thought wildly and then cleared my throat nervously, batting away the intrusive thought.

Giving him a small smile, I pulled my hand back. But I wasn't able to separate my gaze from him quite so easily.

As I peered into his eyes, my mind started to whirl. Adrien was handsome, and sweet, and very capable at things like sailing. Would kissing him really be a bad thing? I couldn't deny that I was curious to see if anything would happen. But there were some truths that perhaps I wasn't ready to face yet.

We were locked in a stare and as I watched him, he licked his lips to wet them. Oh, stars, was he thinking the same thing? My stomach flipped over, and the urge to close the distance between us became almost unbearable.

Maybe I should just do it, I thought to myself. *Just lean forward and kiss him.*

Assuming he wanted to be kissed. But he *was* staring at my lips.

I held my breath in anticipation as I leaned forward, and then came a loud bang on the door, causing us both to jump.

"Chow time, Cap'n," a sailor shouted, and I exhaled the breath I'd been holding.

Adrien looked annoyed at the interruption but nodded.

"Hungry?" he asked.

"Starved," I confirmed.

After a surprisingly good meal of charred corn, honey biscuits, and fresh grilled fish with lemon, Adrien returned above deck and I remained in the captain's quarters, feeling sleepy and sluggish even though it was still early evening. It had been a long few days and Adrien told me that if we sailed all night, we would reach the edge of the belly of the sea by morning.

I slipped into my nightdress that I'd packed and was asleep almost as soon as my head hit the pillow.

Chapter Fourteen

A hand pressed over my mouth, and my eyes flew open at the same time as I gave a muffled shout. The bedroom lamp had been lit, and I was staring into Adrien's terrified teal eyes.

My heart knocked in my chest as screams and a thump sounded from somewhere above. But it wasn't until my gaze fell to the green dampener rune on Adrien's bare chest that I felt a genuine terror of my own.

"Pirates have taken over the ship, and slit half my crew's throats. They got a rune on me before I could help. Can you use your magic to save the rest of my men? Are you powerful enough?"

Was I powerful enough? He had *no* idea.

He peeled his fingers away from my mouth, and I growled. "I'll kill every last pirate I lay eyes on."

"I was really hoping you would say that," he said, sounding relieved.

I reached over the edge of the bed and pulled out my faestone dagger. "And you can help," I told him. "Are you ready for it this time?" I asked, remembering how he'd reacted the last time my faestone dagger had come so close to his heart.

He nodded and brandished his chest.

Another scream and a thump above us. Were those bodies? Oh, stars, we had no time.

I swiped the blade over the rune and leaped out of bed, not caring that I was in only my nightgown. I needed to get up there before another man lost his life.

"Come on," I hissed at Adrien but when I reached the door, he was still sitting on the bed, staring in shock at his chest.

The rune. It hadn't come off. It was still glowing brightly. In frustration I rushed over and swiped my knife over it again. And again.

Nothing.

"No. *How?*" I asked.

Adrien frowned. "The fae you paid to rune me when I was coming off the tea. Did he see your dagger?"

My heart sank into my gut like a stone.

He . . . had. That bastard offered to buy it after telling me that's all I needed to dispel the rune he'd put on Adrien. Did he do this? I'd kill him.

Since he knew about my dagger it made sense that he'd somehow tweaked his rune to be impervious to it. Maybe he had nothing to do with this attack, but I couldn't think of another reason why my dagger wouldn't be working this time. And if it was him, that meant that this attack was my fault, at least partially, and that made me sick.

Adrien shook his head. "No matter. Let's go. It's up to you to save my men now, Isolde. *Please*," he begged.

He didn't have to say another word. I handed him my dagger

and my satchel with the Shadow Heart in it, and he took them. Then I held my hands about two inches from each other, pulling all of the moisture from the air to me, which was a lot when you were at sea. Frost began to appear at the edges of the windows, and my breath came out in a puff of white mist.

Adrien held my blade before him, and opened the door for me.

I was immediately met with a snarling unseelie fae wearing all black and brandishing a bloody sword before him. Forming a spear of ice, I sent it through his heart before he could even speak. His mouth opened like a gaping fish and then he hit the ground with a thud.

"Thank the stars," Adrien whispered behind me.

Had he assumed my powers were weak? He'd seen nothing yet.

I rushed down the hallway and up the stairs.

Stars have mercy.

Dead bodies littered the deck of Adrien's beautiful ship and alongside us—on our starboard side as Adrien had taught me—was another ship, bigger and more heavily gunned than ours.

Beatrice's deck was teeming with pirates who appeared to be stabbing anything that moved. But about a dozen of Adrien's men were still alive and fighting, so I'd have to be careful with my powers to avoid injuring them.

Across the ship I spotted a familiar fae in a bowler hat and three-piece suit, and anger exploded within me. It was, in fact, the man I'd paid to cast the rune. He would die first.

I flung a thick ice shard the size and sharpness of a large sword across the boat with perfect precision, and it sailed right through his chest. His shout of alarm was nothing over the screams on the boat, but my flying ice shard in the middle of the warm summer air had alerted more than a few pirates.

One by one, they turned toward me.

Yes. Come for me and leave Adrien's men alone.

Half a dozen of them ran in my direction, screaming and holding their stained swords aloft. I pulled the water from the sea and doused them with it, freezing them solid.

They stood like statues on the deck of the boat with swords still held in midair.

I moved deeper into the boat now, hoping to position myself in front of some of Adrien's men. Scrambling to the port side, I ducked quickly as a pirate came out of nowhere, dropping from some ropes above me. Before he could strike out at me, Adrien came up behind him and dragged my dagger across his neck before spinning and kicking out his foot into another pirate. His foot connected with the pirate's jaw and shattered it. The sound of broken bone filled the space before the man hit the ground, wailing. I appraised Adrien. Even without his powers he was useful.

Another half dozen men immediately descended on us. I froze who I could, and impaled the rest. I'd never had to move this quickly, or fight this many assailants at once. I was well trained, but this was madness.

I heard a deafening battle cry and when I looked up, over two dozen pirates rushed from the other ship onto ours. My stomach dropped. Too many.

Within moments the pirates were upon us.

I was madder than I'd ever been in my life. My hands shook

as I pulled up an ice wall between the two ships, cutting off any more pirates from crossing over.

The pirates in front of us shouted in alarm and drew their swords. Some even had magic. A small ball of fire caught my eye and nervousness ran through me. I'd never met anyone with fire magic: it was the antithesis of my very own power. Dawn came pretty close with her sunlight magic but fire . . . my magic was no match for it. It didn't matter. I'd fight to the death if that's what it took to keep Adrien and the remainder of his men safe.

Drawing on my power, I started to raise my hands, targeting one of the pirates closest to me.

"Look out!" Adrien shouted, and I spun around just as I felt a small prick in my back. Then it was like a heavy blanket had been placed over me, and all of a sudden, my powers were drained from my body.

A dampener rune.

No. I killed him.

I turned, and my gaze went to a tall female fae with burgundy hair and a feral snarl. She held a wand and was wearing a bowler hat of her own. The resemblance between her and the man I killed was uncanny. Perhaps his sister? And clearly the magic ran in the family because now I was in the exact same boat as Adrien. Powerless.

My mother had a dampener rune put on me once as a lesson, so I would know what it felt like. This was exactly how I remembered feeling. Helpless, empty, awful.

"Abandon ship!" Adrien cried out and was met with roars from his men.

One by one Adrien's men rushed to the edge of the boat and

jumped overboard. I gasped but had no time to dwell on the fact that they were all abandoning ship.

I looked up just in time to see a sword coming down right on top of my head. And then Adrien pushed me overboard.

With a scream, I tipped to the side, flailing, and cracked my head on one of the cannons as I fell toward the sea. Pain exploded behind my eyes and the second I hit the frigid water everything went black.

Chapter Fifteen

Sunlight hit my face and I awoke with a splitting headache.

"Mmm," I moaned.

"Isolde? Are you okay?" Adrien's panicked voice brought everything back. My eyes snapped open. We were floating. Everyone was treading water to stay afloat. I craned my neck to take in more of my surroundings and a spike of fear rushed through me.

We were in the middle of the ocean with no lifeboat, no land in sight, and treading water for . . .

"How long has it been?" I asked.

Adrien looked relieved that I was speaking, and I just now realized he was holding me afloat in his arms, in my white nightgown, soaking wet.

I scrambled out of his arms, but he kept his hands firmly on my biceps as I began to kick with my legs to keep from sinking. Since I wasn't the best swimmer, I let him assist me.

There were only eight men with us. Did that mean the rest were . . .?

A lump formed in my throat.

"We've been in the water for about four hours," Adrien said, and I noticed the men looked exhausted. Some were still bleeding from open gashes on their faces and necks.

"I'm so sorry I couldn't save everyone. There were too many. If I had my powers I could make a boat of ice," I told them. Even now I could feel the restrictive blanket over my power and a slight burn of the rune between my shoulders.

"Milady, ye saved our lives," one of the men said.

"We're grateful, even if we'll still drown," another said.

Drown?

My gaze flew to Adrien and the green rune on his chest, and he sighed. "We will eventually tire of treading water," he admitted.

No.

"Let's swim. Maybe there's land nearby," I offered.

Adrien shook his head. "There isn't and you'll tire faster swimming. We've been alternating between floating and treading water, but we will eventually need fresh water to drink. And when night comes . . ."

"No," I said stubbornly as I shook my head. This wasn't happening.

But it was true. We were stuck here in the middle of the ocean about to die. I craned my neck, searching for a boat in the water or land, but there was just a blue line as far as the eye could see.

"Try to cut through my rune. Do you still have my dagger?" I asked him.

He nodded. "And the crystal."

A trickle of relief ran through me. At least one thing was going in our favor.

I turned my back to Adrien so he could see where the rune clung to me and felt him deftly grasp my shoulder blades. Seconds ticked by, but that restricted feeling was still there.

"Did you try to cut through it?" I asked him, panic at the edge of my voice.

"Thrice," he confirmed.

No.

I peered at the men in the water with me. They were both seelie and unseelie. I was glad to see Adrien's first mate, Brimsley, was still with us. "What powers have you all got? We can figure this out."

"I can lift three times my weight," one said.

Okay, useless right now.

"I am powerless, milady," another mentioned.

"I sense where all the good fish are," another spoke up.

That could be useful when we were starving, but not if we had to swim miles to get there.

"Powerless," another said.

"I have bad taste in women," another said, causing the men to laugh.

Well, I appreciated that morale was still high. It seemed Adrien had hired a lot of fae without powers. They probably wouldn't have been able to find work without him.

"I can control the wind a bit," a shy teenage boy said, as he paddled to stay above water.

My head snapped in his direction at the same time as Adrien's. "Mathis, you didn't tell me that," Adrien said.

His cheeks went red. "Sorry Cap'n. It's not always easy to control, and I got fired at my last job for snapping the mast in half."

Whoa, that was some strong wind power.

Adrien nodded, swimming closer to him. "That's okay. Do you think you could call the wind now, to blow us southeast?"

Adrien had picked up on the same idea I had. If the wind carried us we wouldn't need to swim. We could cover more area that way and wouldn't tire as easily.

"How far is the nearest land?" I asked Adrien.

Adrien looked at me. "If we go straight through the belly of the sea, there is an island about two leagues from here. It's not inhabited, but reaching it would at least give us a chance."

The fae boy, Mathis, nodded. "I could try."

My legs were already fatigued from keeping afloat and the men had been at this hours longer than I had.

"Sir?" Brimsley called to his captain. "I've followed yer for many years and I knew the dangers of takin' *Beatrice* to the belly of the sea, but going there with no boat. We'll be eat'n alive by sirens."

"Sirens!" I shrieked.

Adrien gave Brimsley a stern look. "We have two choices. Either drown here or take our chances with sirens and possibly survive this. There's no land closer that we could reach."

With a resigned sigh, the man relented. "All right. If the sea takes me, then she takes me."

"The sea isn't taking anyone," I announced. "We're going to get through this."

But the tanned and weathered men just gave me polite smiles. Like they didn't agree.

I glanced at Adrien in panic and he slipped his hand into mine and squeezed. A calmness spread over me then. We were in this together.

"All right men, and lady," Adrien announced. "Prepare for some wind. Mathis, ready when you are."

The young fae swallowed hard and pulled his water-shriveled hands out of the ocean and held them up, palms to the sun.

He closed his eyes and took a deep breath.

I tensed, unsure of what to be prepared for. Choppy waters, wind, waves? Adrien hadn't let go of my hand and now his grip tightened as a breeze picked up around us.

"Try to concentrate the wind on lifting the water beneath us. Create a wave to carry us to shore," Adrien coached.

The boy gave a stressed frown, but nodded. The wind whipped harder, spraying saltwater in my face as the water began to churn.

Our bodies jolted left and right.

"Push the wind just against the water *beneath* us," Adrien tried to coach him. Mathis seemed unskilled but powerful: a highly dangerous combination.

Finally, a huge gust of wind slammed into the water next to us, and then we were lifted a few feet as the water rose up around us. Mathis had created a wave and we rose with it high above the rest of the water.

"Now push the wave southeast," Adrien called over the wind.

Mathis pursed his lips together as if concentrating deeply and then all of a sudden, we were moving.

Some of the men and I gave a shriek of surprise as we went from being stationary to blazing forward, our bodies cutting through the water as quickly as if we were on a boat. The force of speeding through the water so quickly pushed into my legs and stomach, yet Mathis miraculously kept our heads above the wave.

"You're doing great," Adrien encouraged, but I could hear the nerves in his voice.

This was *really* fast. And we were quite high. If anything went wrong we could be dragged under and drown.

We whipped through the sea with the wind batting against our skin and water spray dousing us. Though I couldn't complain because after about fifteen minutes, I saw land dotting the horizon.

"Land ahead!" Adrien cried just as the wind stopped and the water dropped out from under us, sending us plummeting down.

I wasn't able to take a deep breath in before I plunged under the water. The wave broke, which sent me into a spin and dragged me under deeper.

I kicked both feet and moved my arms to work my way back to the surface, but I quickly realized I'd been pushed too deep and I wasn't sure which way was up. Dizzy with panic, I twisted left and right trying to get my bearings.

Finally, I caught a glimpse of sunlight above me.

I kicked and clawed my way up toward the light, but my stupid nightgown tangled my legs.

I wanted so badly to inhale, but I knew my lungs would only fill with water if I did.

The surface still looked to be a good twenty feet above me when weakness overcame my limbs. I cursed the stupid rune stuck on my back. Without it, I'd simply use my power to propel myself to the surface. Now I was going to drown just feet from my goal.

I breathed involuntarily, my body unable to hold out any longer and took in a huge lungful of water. That's when Adrien swam into view and grabbed me by the waist, yanking me upward.

My throat burned as we reached the surface, and Adrien immediately began pounding me on the back. Hard. I hacked up a mouthful of water, struggling to get air into my lungs.

"I'm so sorry. There was some interference. My power just . . . stopped. Like I was overridden," Mathis said as he panted beside us.

Adrien rubbed my back, patting me as I struggled to breathe. My throat and lungs burned but I was able to get some oxygen in my lungs.

"Check him for a dampener rune," Adrien told one of his men but never took his eyes off me.

"Isolde. Are you okay?" he asked.

"You . . ." My voice was a croak. "Saved me twice."

He looked relieved I was conscious and speaking. "We aren't keeping score, beautiful Isolde."

Something about hearing him call me beautiful made my whole body warm.

I was exhausted from the struggle, and my arms and legs felt so weak. Adrien pulled me closer to him without question. I relaxed, letting him take my weight and feeling a little guilty about it as he trod water doubly hard to make up for it.

"No rune, Cap'n. Something else is afoot here."

"Probably sirens," one man said.

"Or the belly of the sea. Messes with powers too, my buddy said."

Belly of the sea. We were here?

I peered around, but saw no glowing water as Adrien had described earlier.

"You can only see it at night," he whispered to me.

We'd be long dead by then.

I looked over Adrien's shoulder at the speck of green in the distance. An island. I didn't think I'd be able to swim that far. It was difficult to gauge distance while bobbing in the sea, but if I had to guess, I'd say we were still at least three miles away, maybe more.

I already wasn't a good swimmer, but now I was exhausted and waterlogged from almost drowning. Getting to shore was our only hope though, so we had to at least try.

"All right," I said, steeling myself for what very well may be the last hour of my life. "Let's try to swim for it." I gestured toward the island in the distance and let go of Adrien so that we were both free to swim, but his grip on me tightened.

I glanced at his face to see him frowning. Unveiled concern shone from his eyes. "That's a long distance. It would be difficult for even the best swimmer," he said, pausing.

Tilting my head skyward, I guessed the time of day from the position of the sun. It was past midday, but blessedly still a few hours until nightfall. "Well, then we'd better start now."

I tried to disentangle myself from Adrien's grasp again, but he wouldn't let me.

I sighed. "Adrien, you're going to need to let me go so we can swim."

His gaze bounced over my face, seemingly memorizing each feature. "I don't know that you can make it," he confessed, his voice soft and gentle.

A rush of fear swept through me, but I forcefully shoved it away. Adrien's concern was valid, but now wasn't the time to panic.

"What choice do we have?" I asked, defeat in my tone.

Adrien's frown deepened, but he didn't refute me. He couldn't. He might not like it. I might not like it. But it was swim for the shore, or give up now and die.

When I scanned the faces of the other sailors bobbing in the water around us, I could tell that they knew the truth: not all of us were going to make it to land alive. But grim determination lined their features. No one was ready to give up yet.

With a reluctant nod, Adrien finally loosened his grip enough that I could slip from his grasp. I knew without him having to say it that he wanted to snatch me back, but he restrained himself.

I trod water clumsily, immediately feeling fatigue pull at my limbs, but I refused to let it show.

Adrien swiveled in the water so that he faced all of us. "Mathis, if your powers come back, let us know."

"Yes, Cap'n," Mathis said, but I was worried about the young sailor. He looked almost as tired as I felt.

"It's going to be a long swim," Adrien said to all of us. "Do what you can to conserve your energy. Take it slow and steady if you have to. This isn't a sprint. It's a marathon."

We all nodded and then his gaze landed on me. "If you start to weaken, say something and I'll carry you."

"You can't swim for the both of us," I argued.

"I can and I will. I won't let you perish in these waters," he told me, and the determination on his face almost had me believing that was true.

* * *

We'd been swimming for only ten minutes, but were making steady progress when a cramp seized my thigh. I gasped at the suddenness of the pain and pitched forward, dunking my head and only just avoiding sucking in seawater.

"What's wrong?" Adrien asked when I resurfaced half a second later.

The rest of his crew was at least twenty feet in front of us and even though I knew Adrien could easily outpace me, he'd refused to get more than a half-stroke ahead of me.

"Nothing," I lied. "Just needed a little break. I'm good now." I plastered a smile on my face that was probably more grimace than anything else.

Adrien peered at me skeptically, but I gritted my teeth and forced my legs to keep moving on willpower alone. A dagger felt like it was twisting in my leg with every kick, but I went on through the pain. Adrien's gaze weighed on me as silent tears leaked down my face that I hoped he mistook for seawater.

We went on for another couple of minutes like that when another cramp gripped my left arm. This time I couldn't stop the pain-filled cry that burst from my lips. Adrien was there in an instant, his arms going around me as I started to sink beneath the waves.

"You're cramping," he said, guessing correctly.

All I could do was nod as slices of pain shot through my arm and leg.

"Lay back," he commanded as he gently coaxed me onto my back. With his arms beneath me, he helped me float as he instructed how to stretch to work out the cramps and give my muscles a break.

I bit my lip against the agony as I massaged first my arm and then my leg. Eventually, the ache had subsided to a piercing discomfort, but there was no way I could keep swimming. My muscles just weren't obeying me anymore.

"I can't go on," I said, my voice catching. I had to swallow a sob that threatened to bubble up my throat.

"It's okay. I have you," Adrien said and then maneuvered so that he was at my head. He wrapped his arms around me, so that my back was on his chest, and started swimming us backward toward the island in the distance.

Adrien was strong and a fine swimmer, but he had his limits. I doubted he could reach the island if he was dragging me the rest of the way. His breath was coming out in huffs and puffs against my neck.

I had just worked up the courage to tell him to leave me behind when a scream rent the air. We both jolted, and then Adrien repositioned himself so we could turn toward the other sailors. They were even further ahead of us by now, but they'd all stopped swimming and were shouting to one another as they bobbed in the water, frantically turning in circles with their gazes cast on the water around them.

"Do you see Tanner?" one of them shouted.

"He was just here," another yelled.

I quickly counted heads to realize that one sailor was missing. *No.* My heart sank.

"What's going on?" I asked Adrien.

He shook his head, indicating that he didn't know just as a fin appeared.

"Shark," I gasped.

Fear knifed me in the gut. I hadn't thought extensively about how I'd prefer to die, but I knew that being eaten alive wasn't the way I wanted to go.

I watched in horror as another fin appeared in the water. Then another and another. They started circling Adrien's men, who shouted in alarm.

"Can you tread water?" Adrien asked suddenly, and I nodded. The cramps were only a dull pain now, and the adrenaline coursing through my body gave me a boost of energy.

Reaching down he pulled my faestone dagger and handed it to me. "Take this," he told me.

As soon as my fingers wrapped around the dagger, he took off, swimming with broad strokes.

"Adrien, no!" I screamed and started after him. What did he expect to be able to do against sharks with only his bare hands?

Unbidden, images of Adrien being shredded to pieces rose in my mind. The water turning red with his blood. His life, slipping from him as he was pulled to the depths in the jaws of a shark.

I thought I'd felt true fear a moment before, but the terror that ran through me now was nothing compared to anything that I'd ever felt before.

I struggled to follow him, my movements stilted and jerky. Adrien was already halfway to his men when a pair of gray scale-covered arms shot out of the water and grabbed Mathis from behind. The young sailor didn't even have time to scream before he was hauled under the waves.

What the stars was that?

A few of Adrien's men pulled the short swords that had been strapped at their hips and slashed out wildly at the water.

"Sirens!" one of the sailors screamed and then one by one, scaly arms and webbed fingers jutted from the choppy water and pulled Adrien's men under.

Sirens?

Shock ripped through me. I didn't know much about the fabled sea creatures except that they were bloodthirsty and cunning. They were said to use their voices to lure sailors into the waters where they dragged them under to feast on their flesh. But in this case, we were all already in the water, so they didn't need to use their deadly song to get us in the sea. We had swum right into their trap and were completely powerless.

Adrien stopped suddenly and turned toward me. "Swim, Isolde. Swim away!" he yelled, dread shining in his eyes.

He started to frantically paddle back toward me, his strokes fast and desperate.

I didn't know what to do. Swim toward Adrien and the swarm of sirens, or away? And if away, what was I swimming toward? This was their domain. There was nowhere for me to hide, so I stayed where I was, frozen by indecision.

Adrien was only two strokes away when his eyes suddenly went wide and from one blink to the next, he was yanked under the water.

Chapter Sixteen

"Adrien," I screamed, twisting in the water to try to see him, but clouds had rolled in, blotting out the sun, darkening the waves so I couldn't see more than a few feet down.

I was just about to dive to look for him when a hand wrapped around my ankle. I managed one final gulp of air before I was dragged down too.

Sharp claws dug into my flesh as I was yanked through the water. I couldn't make sense of up or down and my vision was a blurry mess of bubbles. On instinct I reached for my power, preparing to freeze whatever creature had hold of me, but of course nothing happened.

I wanted to scream in frustration, but held back. The air in my lungs was all I had left.

I kicked out, thrashing in the water like a madwoman, but my foot only connected with water and more water, and the grip on my ankle never loosened.

How much time did I have left before I passed out? A minute? Thirty seconds?

Already my lungs were starting to burn, and my energy was waning. The pressure on my ears was so intense that it felt like my head would explode at any moment.

Something flashed blue in my peripheral vision and I realized that by some miracle, I still held my faestone dagger in my fist. The chunk of kyanite embedded in the handle caught some errant ray of light that pierced the watery depths and flashed blue.

With what felt like my last bit of strength, I folded my body, tucking my knees to my chest, and blindly struck at the siren towing me through the sea. My first strike was fruitless, but the second one connected.

I had no idea where I'd stabbed the creature, but my blade sunk into it almost to the hilt. The clawed hand immediately released my ankle and then a shriek like I'd never heard before pierced my eardrums. I wanted to slap my hands over my ears to block out the noise, but I refused to give up my dagger to do so.

I pulled my dagger free and struck out again, feeling it scrape against something, and the scream intensified. The pain in my ears reached unfathomable levels, and then it felt like something popped in my head and the pain subsided. I knew I'd ruptured an eardrum, maybe both, but it was the least of my worries right now because I was well and truly out of air.

I could tell the surface was above me because of the hazy light overhead, but my limbs weren't obeying me. I tried to kick, but spasms made my muscles twitch.

How far down was I? Twenty feet? Thirty? More? Would the buoyancy in my body help me float to the surface?

My lungs screamed at me to breathe, but I kept my mouth shut, knowing that if I inhaled seawater, it would truly be over. But as the seconds ticked by, my vision started to wink in and out.

Suddenly, a face appeared in front of me and even in my weakened state, I jerked back. Even though my vision was blurry and distorted underwater, the creature was close enough that I could tell the face had some fish-like features. It had two large, all-black eyes and a flattened nose with two slits that looked more like gills than nose holes. Its flesh looked scaly and a mass of black hair grew from its head and floated in the water around us.

There was a jagged cut on the side of its face, that ran from its forehead, just narrowly missing its eye, down to its chin. It was clearly furious.

The creature opened its mouth to reveal three rows of serrated teeth and then the worse sound imaginable emerged. I quickly discovered I could only hear out of one ear—which I was thankful for in that moment—but even so, the noise scraped against the inside of my skull like someone was trying to scoop out my brain with a dull spoon.

The siren started to reach for my throat with its claws. I tried to swim away, but I couldn't, I didn't have any energy left, even to save my life.

Just as the creature was about to wrap its clawed hand around my neck, it froze. Its black eyes went wide as a blade punched through its chest.

My vision started to wink out as the siren's body was pushed aside and then strong hands grabbed the sides of my face. Before I knew what was happening, someone's mouth was pressed up against mine and then my lungs filled with sweet air.

The hands dropped from my face and I blinked once. Twice.

I could suddenly see perfectly under the water and floating in front of me was an unfamiliar man. His face was more seelie than the siren's, with familiar facial features: a nose, pointed ears, bright green eyes and a full mouth. But on either side of his neck were rows of gills and his skin was tinted green. He was barechested and when I glanced down his body, his lower half was a tail instead of legs.

Merman? Were those real?

Shock caused me to suck in a breath without thinking, but rather than my mouth and lungs filling with salty seawater, I breathed in sweet, life-giving air.

What magic was this?

The merman smiled at me when I pulled in more air, my eyes going wide in disbelief.

"I've used my magic to give you the ability to breathe and see underwater like we do until you resurface again. You're safe now," he said and even though we were underwater, I heard him just as clearly as I would out of it. At least with the ear that was still working. I appeared to be temporarily deaf in the other, but I hoped that my enhanced healing as a royal would repair the damage quickly.

"I'll take you to the others in your group," he told me.

The sailors. Adrien! Were they unharmed? Was Adrien alive?

My heart rate spiked again.

"Where are they?" I asked, discovering that I could also speak underwater.

I twisted in the water, but even though I could see through the depths now, the only things around us were regular sea life and coral. The clouds had clearly been chased away as the sun's bright rays pierced into the water, illuminating all for me to see. I didn't spot Adrien or anyone else.

"Is everyone all right?" *Was Adrien all right?* I wanted to ask, but the merman probably wouldn't know who I was talking about.

"Calm yourself," he said, reaching for me. "Let me take you to shore, where we brought the others."

I didn't want to waste time arguing, so I just nodded. I didn't put up a fight when he wrapped me in his arms, and then with a mighty swish of his tail we were propelled through the water.

Questions about what had just happened with the sirens and who my presumed savior was rose up in my mind, but I couldn't push anything past the knot in my throat.

Yes, I was traumatized by what had just happened, but fear for Adrien overshadowed it tenfold. I tried to tell myself it was concern for all the men that was choking me, but in truth, it was not knowing if Adrien was okay that left me paralyzed.

What if he was hurt? What if he was dead?

The merman cut through the water at a rapid pace and before long, we approached the shallows of the island we had been swimming toward. He slowed down his speed and brought us into a cove where I could see at least a dozen other unseelie similar in appearance to him under the water with us. They peered back at us with unveiled interest as we swam by.

When we were almost to the shore and it was shallow enough for me to stand, the merman surfaced. The instant my head broke through the water I heard shouting.

"Release me. I'm going after her." Adrien's furious voice echoed throughout the cove.

Relief poured through me, soothing my frayed nerves. He was alive.

"Cap'n, they said they'd bring her here. There's nothing you can do," I heard Mathis say.

Thank goodness the young sailor was alive as well.

The unseelie released me and I twisted to see Adrien struggling against his men atop a jagged bluff on the side of the cove. Many of them were bloodied and bruised, but all eight sailors and Adrien were accounted for.

Thank the stars.

Adrien continued to argue with his men, going as far as to threaten their lives if they didn't release him. It appeared he was trying to dive back into the sea.

I furrowed my brow. Was he trying to go back for me?

I called his name and he froze.

Jerking his head in my direction, his gaze connected with mine and it was like a spike of magic straight to my heart, making it pound harder than a Winter Court drum.

My breath caught as we stared at each other, and something intangible passed between us.

Since it was clear he wasn't going to try to swim back into the open ocean now, his men released him. Taking two purposeful strides forward, he dove off the cliff's edge and into the clear waters of the cove. As soon as he surfaced he started to swim toward me, his strokes long and quick.

When he reached me I expected him to stop, but instead he

brushed past the merman and scooped me up in his arms. He carried me from the water to the shore, his gaze never breaking from mine. It was only when he'd brought me clear of the surf to dry sand that he finally let me down.

My body slid against his as he gently let my legs drop, but he kept one arm wrapped around my back so that I couldn't go far.

"Are you all right?" he asked, his gaze now roaming over my face as if assuring himself I was really there.

I was breathless, even though I hadn't exerted myself. The merman had done all the work to get us to the cove. "I'm fine," I managed to get out.

Adrien heaved a relieved sigh. "Thank the stars." Reaching up, he cupped one of my cheeks. "I thought . . ." he started, but then let his words drift away. A shudder wracked Adrien's frame that I felt acutely because I was pressed closely against him.

"I'm fine. Unharmed," I said, choosing not to mention the ruptured eardrum and cuts on my ankle from the siren's claws.

Wrapping both arms around me, he crushed me to his chest and buried his face in the side of my neck as we stood on the sandy beach shore and held each other. Perhaps I shouldn't have let him pull me so close, but I felt a wild need deep inside to hold him tightly as well and wrapped my arms around his neck.

This feeling of needing someone was scary to me. But right now I needed to be closer to him.

We stood like that for a while, both of us trying to assure ourselves that the other was safe and well until someone cleared their throat.

"Excuse me, my lord," said a lyrical female voice. "But we must return to the open sea."

I could feel the reluctance in Adrien's arms as he released me, but he took my hand so I couldn't stray. I wasn't mad about that. For some wild reason, I wasn't ready to be separated from him either.

When I glanced back at the cove, a beautiful woman bobbed in the waves. She had long blonde hair with small seashells braided into it and bright blue eyes. Her face was round, and she had lush red lips that looked like they were in a permanent pucker. Her skin had a faint green tint to it like the male who'd saved me. I couldn't see her lower half, but I assumed she had a tail just like him as well.

"Lady Kira," Adrien said and then inclined his head in a sign of respect. "I thank you and your merfolk for saving us." His gaze flicked to me then, and something about the way he glanced at me brought a blush to my cheeks. "Especially the princess. I'm truly in your debt," he finished, looking back at Kira.

Merfolk. Just like I'd thought.

"You can repay us by stopping the curse headed our way," she said, her voice bold and clear.

Murmurs sounded, and I glanced around the waters of the cove to see the dozen other merfolk nodding as well.

"You know of the curse?" Adrien said, his hand tightening on my own.

She nodded solemnly. "If the black waters that plague the Northern Kingdom reach our seas, all life in the ocean will be in jeopardy. Already merfolk from the northern seas have started to migrate into our warmer waters."

Adrien exchanged a glance with me and then patted something

at his side. I looked down to see the pouch that held the Shadow Heart. It bulged, showing he still had the magical crystal.

"That's why we are here," Adrien confessed. "Princess Isolde of the Winter Court has been given a mission to destroy the curse, once and for all. But to do so, we need to get to the belly of the sea. Can you help us?"

A frown marred Kira's pretty features. "The belly of the sea is the sirens' domain. No land dweller has ever made it there and lived to tell about it."

My heart sank.

"The only hope we have of breaking the curse on our land is for Isolde and me to bring the Shadow Heart there to be unlocked. If we can't make it to the belly of the sea, all hope will be lost."

Kira chewed her bottom lip and glanced over at the male who'd saved me. He nodded once, and some concern seemed to clear from her face. When she turned back to us, determination lined the mermaid's features.

"I will gather our fiercest warriors and escort you and your princess to the belly of the sea."

My stomach flipped when she referred to me as his princess. Part of me felt like I needed to correct her, but I stayed silent for reasons that eluded me.

Kira glanced up at the sky and frowned. It was still daylight, but it appeared that night would fall shortly. I almost couldn't believe that we'd spent most of the day in the waters, battling the sea and sirens, although the exhaustion pulling at my mind and body told me it was true. I suppose multiple near-death experiences distorted my sense of time.

"It's not safe to approach the belly of the sea in the dead of night," Kira went on, her gaze dropping back to Adrien and me. "The sirens have the advantage in the dark waters. Their ability to see with little to no light is better than ours, so we'll have to wait until early morning when they no longer have the upper hand. We'll leave right after sunrise."

Twisting, she gestured toward a mermaid and merman behind her, who both came forward. I couldn't see until they were closer that they carried items in their hands. Freshly caught fish on a bed of seaweed, a large glass jar of water, and something that looked like folded clothes.

"Here," Kira said, and Adrien and I approached the water to gather their offerings. Adrien took the fish and water, and I accepted the folded clothes. Although the material was like nothing I'd ever seen before. It was stretchy and iridescent, like a fish scale, but soft to the touch.

"Food to regain your strength and clothes for the female," Kira explained, and I gave her a quizzical look, but when I glanced down at myself I immediately knew what she meant.

After everything that had happened today, I'd completely forgotten I was still in my wet nightgown that was most definitely see-through. With a gasp, I brought the clothing up to cover my chest, feeling the heat rise to my cheeks.

I supposed modesty wasn't the most important thing right now, but with my wet nightgown, I was practically naked.

"These clothes are special and will help you move more freely in the water tomorrow," Kira explained.

"Thank you," I said in a rush.

Kira and Adrien exchanged a couple more pleasantries and then decided on a time to leave the following day. It was agreed that we would sleep on the island tonight and then leave just before sunrise when the sirens were the most vulnerable.

Kira urged us to rest up and then she and the other merfolk disappeared into the sea.

The sun was beginning to set, and Adrien said that he and the men would create a makeshift camp for us for the night. I excused myself and walked a ways into the jungle, far enough that the men couldn't see me, but not so far that if I shouted, they wouldn't hear me.

I quickly shed my heavy, wet nightgown and pulled on the clothing the merfolk had given me. When I was dressed, I looked down at myself, not sure if I was more modestly dressed now or in the wet white nightgown.

The clothes they'd given me were a tight-fitted sleeveless top that swooped low in the front, and a pair of leggings that ended to my ankles. The parts of me that should have been covered were, but the material fit so snuggly to my body that every curve was exposed.

I looked at the nightgown I'd discarded on the ground by my feet and considered putting it on over the clothes, but I couldn't make myself put the torn and sandy garment back on. Adrien and his men would just have to deal with what I was wearing.

When I emerged from the jungle, the sailors had pulled large palm leaves from the surrounding trees and were making pallets to sleep on. They'd also collected a pile of coconuts.

No one noticed me for a few moments as I approached. Mathis, the first one to see me, stopped with his hand outstretched as he was about to add another coconut to the stack. His face went slack, and he blinked at me without uttering a word, and I suddenly wished I'd forced myself to don the wet gown.

"Mathis," I heard Adrien shout from somewhere in the jungle behind him. "What are you doing over there? The men could use your help pulling more palm leaves."

I was about to turn and flee when Adrien appeared, having just walked out of the trees behind the young sailor. He followed Mathis's gaze to me and then it looked like he caught his breath. His eyes flared as they ran over me, and I had the dueling urge to both cover myself and also turn so he could see even more.

Adrien began walking toward me slowly, and my throat went dry. "Go help the others," he said, dismissing Mathis, who finally shook himself free of whatever trance he was in.

He rushed away with a mumbled, "Yes, Cap'n."

Adrien kept walking until he was standing right in front of me. I licked my suddenly dry lips, and his gaze caught the motion as more heat infused his eyes.

I held my breath, at a loss for words, as Adrien continued to just stand there and stare at me.

I don't think anyone has ever looked at me the way he was looking at me then. Like he wasn't just seeing me, but that he was drinking me in.

"Umm. This is what the merfolk gave me. The nightgown was torn and dirty," I said, feeling like I needed to explain.

"I think I owe Kira an even bigger debt than I did before," he said, his meaning clear. He liked the outfit. And despite myself and my refusal to consider Adrien as my mate, I couldn't deny that I liked that he liked it.

"I'm sure it will be much better to swim in this," I said.

"Mmm," Adrien said and nodded, letting his gaze run down my front another time.

The look was so potent, it might as well have been a physical touch and heat rushed to my cheeks and elsewhere.

I cleared my throat and took a step away from Adrien, firmly reminding myself we were on a beach with eight other sailors. I was here to complete a mission, not to flirt. Adrien seemed to pull himself out of whatever reverie he was in as well, and taking my hand he pulled me along.

"We've made sleeping pallets for the night. We'll have the coconuts to eat and drink. I'm not sure if you've had them before, but I can assure you the milk is very refreshing."

He led me over to where the pallets were lined in a row, glaring at his men when they stopped to gawk at me. One look from their captain had them jumping back to whatever task they were working on before I'd distracted them.

We ate fire-grilled fish we'd caught, drank coconut water, and then chewed on refreshing mint leaves as we talked by the fire with his men for over an hour before sleep started to pull at my body. I noticed that Adrien had put my pallet next to his and backed them up to a few trees so that I was boxed in. Safe.

"Let's get some rest. Big day in the morning."

After wishing everyone good night, I lay down on my pallet and Adrien on his. We were mere inches from each other, maybe

LEIA STONE & JULIE HALL

a foot at most, and I couldn't help but stare into those blue-green eyes.

I remembered the way I'd washed his body when he'd had the fever and my cheeks heated. He was by far the most handsome man I'd ever laid eyes on. The way he was looking at me right now, with a burning intensity, made me yearn to know what was on his mind.

"What are you thinking about?" I whispered across the dark night.

He inhaled and then seemed to hold his breath for a moment. Leaning onto one elbow, he came closer to me and brought his lips to my ear. "I think you're my mate, Isolde." He exhaled, and the fresh smell of mint washed over me along with a whole-body tingle.

Mate. That word. So terrifying and yet, so right when it came to Adrien. I wanted to give in. I did, but also . . . I didn't. Because at this moment, as Adrien pulled back and hovered over my lips as if begging me to kiss him and prove him right, I couldn't help but think of my parents.

They had been madly in love, married for over twenty years and then everything just exploded. Now they barely tolerated each other. My father was broken by it. My mother too, but she hid it better.

I didn't want that. Mate. Love. It didn't matter. Nothing lasted forever.

When I didn't move to kiss him or to say anything to his sweet words, his face fell and he backed away, laying back down on his pallet and turning away from me.

My body buzzed with the urge to reach for him, spin him around and kiss him as proof of our mate bond rained around us, but I couldn't. I was frozen in fear, so I closed my eyes and pretended to sleep. Yet it was a long time before the darkness took me.

Adrien's words churned in my head for hours.

Chapter Seventeen

I awoke to a small nudge. My eyelids snapped open, and I came face to face with Adrien. It was barely light, so the early morning rays just kissed his features. Shadows still clung to parts of his face, but the lighting, or lack thereof, just made his eyes blaze that much more. The intensity in his eyes caused my stomach to flip over as I stared up at him.

"The merfolk are back. We need to leave," he said flatly, his voice void of the emotions his eyes betrayed. Then he turned his back and walked toward the shore.

I sat up rubbing my eyes, relieved to find that my ear had healed overnight like I hoped it would. When I looked down I spotted a small leaf plate before me. Some coconut meat was cut into cubes with mint leaves accompanied by a whole coconut full of water.

He made that for me? My heart pinched. It was so very sweet, especially after I rejected him last night.

It was just . . . the mate thing was so different to me and my culture. Here you kissed, found out you were mates, got married and popped out a kid? But a couple of weeks ago Adrien and I didn't even know each other and he was engaged to someone else.

It was too much, too fast. It terrified me. Mostly because I was starting to feel without a shadow of a doubt that if anyone in this realm was my mate, it was Adrien. But love only led to heartache, and I wasn't sure I could take any more of that.

I quickly shoved pieces of the coconut and mint into my mouth and chewed, then drank some of the coconut water. It put something in my stomach and the mint also freshened my breath. Afterward I met Adrien at the shore where he was talking to Kira and over two dozen merwarriors. They floated in the water with glowing spears and metal chest plates. We left Adrien's men sleeping. There was no sense in dragging them into this.

"Each one of these people are willing to die for the cause," Kira explained.

Adrien shook his head. "I couldn't ask you to force your people to—"

"I force my people to do nothing. They volunteered. Anything to stop the curse from killing our young and taking their future," she exclaimed.

It was a beautiful sentiment, but I really hoped no one was going to die today.

Adrien handed me the satchel that held the Shadow Heart, and I reached in and grabbed it. "I need to get this into the belly of the sea," I told them all and brandished it into the air.

A reverence fell over everyone. Gasps, open mouths and wide eyes.

"Then you shall," Kira stated. "Come into the water. We shouldn't delay any further."

I slipped the crystal back into my satchel and followed Adrien into the waves. I wanted to talk with him first and try to smooth things over from last night but there was no time now. He reached his hand out to steady me as I trod water and I gave him an apologetic look. He just returned it with a sad smile and a nod. Like it was okay. Okay that he'd told me he thought I was his mate, and I'd said nothing.

Dawn would kill me if she knew how much I screwed that up.

As we swam out to meet the merfolk I appreciated the clothes that Kira had given me the day before. They didn't impede any of my movements or tangle my legs like my nightgown had, and were so light and buoyant I didn't feel bogged down. But there was still something that was holding me back.

"If we are attacked, it would be easier to help fight if we didn't have these dampener runes concealing our powers," I complained to Adrien.

Kira swam up alongside me and gave me a radiant smile as I floated in the cove beside her. "I can help with that." She lifted her long blue nails above the water and clacked them together, indicating I turn around.

A shock of excitement ran through me.

"Really?" I asked.

She nodded, and then I gave her my back.

I expected her to cut through the dampener rune right away, but she didn't. I glanced over my shoulder at her and she had a frown on her face.

"I should warn you," she said. "Seelie magic is somewhat unpredictable around the belly of the sea. When we get close to it, you may not be able to use your powers, even after I cut this rune away."

"We saw that yesterday," I said, thinking of how Mathis's magic just gave out on him. "Hopefully my magic holds up. Either way, I need to be free of this rune."

Kira nodded, and I faced forward again.

"It only hurts for a moment," she said, and before I had time to even think about her words I felt a sharp slice between my shoulder blades. I hissed but then the pain was soon gone and I felt the floodgates open on my power.

The momentary pain was worth it. I'd go through worse pain than that to get my magic back. When the dampener rune was on, it was like I'd been missing a part of my physical body. I could still function, but I hadn't felt whole.

I thanked her and then she ducked underwater, saying she needed to talk to some of her warriors before we left. Glancing over, I watched a merman slice at Adrien's chest too. Once the green rune dissipated, he sucked in a big breath of air, closing his eyes to savor the moment. I could tell he was feeling the same thing I was. Relief. Joy. The rightness of having our magic returned.

He opened his eyes, and our gazes connected for a second and something indefinable but still powerful passed between us. I had the urge to swim closer to him, to reach out and touch him. I wanted to feel the warmth and smoothness of his skin beneath my fingers, but then a merman swam in between us, shattering the moment.

"Hello," the merman said and I blinked up at him. It took longer than it should for me to recognize him as the one who'd saved me the day before.

"It's you," I said, smiling back at him. "I never properly thanked you for saving my life."

The merman returned my smile, his eye crinkling in the corners. I didn't know if merfolk aged like seelie did, but if so, I'd say he was only a small handful of years older than me.

"My name is Marlin," he told me. "And it was truly my pleasure." He dipped his head and then peered back at me. "I'm glad to see that you are well." His tone was nothing but friendly, but I caught a glimpse of Adrien over Marlin's shoulder. The Ethereum lord was frowning at us as his gaze bounced between me and the merman. Unveiled envy shone in his eyes.

I almost laughed. Adrien had nothing to be jealous about. As much as I kept telling myself I didn't want him, he was truly the only man who filled my thoughts, but I still got a small thrill thinking he might be jealous.

"Well, if you hadn't breathed air into my mouth, I would have died," I told the merman seriously.

Marlin didn't get a chance to answer before Adrien's angry voice filled the air.

"What?" he swam over, shoving Marlin away from me. "You *kissed* her?" He ground the words out through clenched teeth, his body practically vibrating with barely controlled rage.

"Of course not," Marlin said, shaking his head as he glanced at Adrien's furious face and then he put another foot of space between them. "She was about to drown so I breathed air into her and then used my magic to allow her temporarily to breathe and communicate underwater."

His words didn't seem to assuage Adrien, who just glared at

Marlin. Taking my hand, Adrien pulled me closer to him and a swarm of butterflies took flight in my belly.

Stars help me, but I was in trouble because part of me enjoyed seeing him riled up like this.

"I assure you, it was only to save her life," Marlin explained, but then grimaced. "But I do need to use my magic on her again."

A noise rumbled in Adrien's chest that sounded a lot like a warning growl.

"I don't need to use my mouth to do that since we're not under the water," Marlin quickly added. "She was drowning before and I had to give her air quickly. I just have to put my hands beside her face, that's all. I promise."

Adrien's body stayed tense, and behind Marlin shadows started to gather.

Adrien's power.

The accumulating shadows meant it was time to put an end to this. I didn't think Adrien would truly attack Marlin, but I also wasn't sure.

"Adrien," I said gently, putting a hand on his shoulder. His muscles were tight and bunched under my touch. "Marlin saved my life yesterday. I'd prefer it if you didn't obliterate him with your magic. If we want to get to the belly of the sea, he needs to help me breathe underwater."

Adrien looked over at me, his eyes swirling with what looked to me like conflicting emotions. Several seconds ticked by before he finally pressed his lips together into a straight line and nodded. The action looked like it took effort for him.

Grudgingly, Adrien moved to the side and let Marlin get close enough to put his hands on either side of my face.

It only took a couple seconds for Marlin's magic to work on me, and then I convinced Adrien to let him do the same for him. After that, we dove under the waves and were able to breathe and speak like before.

When Kira returned, she told me to take hold of her and I hooked a hand onto her fin. She took off, swimming at twice the speed that I would have been able to, dragging me down and through the ocean.

Adrien held onto Marlin's fin and together we swam out of the cove and into the darkest water I'd ever been in. It was slightly terrifying. Not even the early morning light shone under here. Only the glow from the merfolk's spears lit our way.

"How much further?" I asked, still amazed that I could talk underwater.

"Up ahead. See that glowing cave?" Kira spoke back to me and the sound reached my ears perfectly.

I peered ahead and gasped when I saw the blue glow less than fifty feet ahead of us.

The belly of the sea. It was a cave.

"Attack formation," Kira suddenly snapped to her warriors and they aligned in a diamond shape all around Adrien and me. We were completely protected by them on all sides.

As we neared the cave I saw something slither in the dark waters.

"Three o'clock," Kira shouted, and then the glowing spear one of her mermen held was tossed in the direction that I'd seen movement.

A shrill rent the waters and I clasped my hands over my ears, but then it was cut off by a garbled wail as the glowing spear sank into the gut of a siren. With one flick of his wrists, the merwarrior called back his glowing staff, and it pulled itself from the dead siren and drew back to his palm.

Kira turned to face me. "You have maybe ten minutes. Then every siren in the area will be upon us."

My eyes bugged at the short timeline, but Adrien wasted not even a second.

"Thank you," he said and grabbed my hand, swimming with me toward the blue glowing underwater cave.

As we neared, I had to squint. There was a glowing wall that shimmered as we approached. I grew an ice spear in my left hand, prepared to stab whatever might be on the other side as we swam through. But the second we crossed the barrier . . . we fell.

A shriek flew from both Adrien and me as we tumbled downward and I landed on top of him. It took me a second to realize we were in some magical underwater cave that was filled with air. I peered behind me at the blue glowing wall of water in amazement. Then I looked down at the teal eyes boring into mine.

I was straddling his mid-section, and both of my palms were flat against his chest. I should have moved off him by now, but I hadn't. I was frozen, and the feel of his body beneath mine felt so right.

Adrien's eyes went half-lidded. "As much as I would love to lay under you all day long, we have nine minutes."

Embarrassment flushed my cheeks and I swallowed hard, letting out a nervous peal of laughter as I slid off him. "Right." We had a task to do.

There was a tunnel up ahead with crystals embedded into the walls that glowed and cast an azure hue over everything.

"Get behind me," Adrien commanded, and I did as he said. It was a narrow tunnel and we'd have to walk single file.

I kept my ice spear out and ready to stab anyone who came through as I followed Adrien. As the tunnel widened, Adrien stopped and I almost ran into him.

"Oh, no," he muttered.

Panic sliced through me. "What is it?"

I pushed my way beside him, hugging the wall, and my mouth opened in shock when I caught sight of what was before us. *Oh, no*, was right. How could we make it through a maze that size in time?

"Eight minutes. We should split up, but I can't bear the thought of you getting lost in there," he declared.

He grabbed my hand tightly, and I peered out at the labyrinth before us. We were standing atop a set of stairs that led down to a cave with high stone-walled passages that twisted and turned and went on and on into the distance. It reminded me of the one I used to run around in as a child, but bigger, and mine was made of ice. And in the very center of the labyrinth in front of us was a blue, glowing crystal of some sort that was hard to fully see from here.

The belly of the sea.

"Can we memorize the path?" I asked trying to spot the openings to the center. Left, left, right. No, dead end. Left, left, left, then right—

"No. We need to just go. Maybe you can use your magic to create an ice stair and we can climb up and see where we are at every few turns.

I grinned. He was a genius. "I can do better than that."

I moved past him and held up my hands, intending to make an ice shelf that I could push over to the center and then drop us down, but the second I stepped on the top stair, the shard I'd been using as a weapon fell from my palm, melted, the water forming a puddle at my feet.

Adrien frowned, stepping beside me. We both pulled for our magic, but nothing happened.

Adrien shook his head. "We can't use magic here."

"But we have to use magic to unlock the crystal."

Adrien glanced at the center of the labyrinth. "Let's hope once we get there we can. Come on. Seven minutes." He grabbed my hand, and we ran down the steps and into the unknown.

Chapter Eighteen

Adrien kept his hand clamped around mine as we raced through the labyrinth.

Left. Left. Right. Left. Right. Dead End.

Right. Left. Right. Dead End.

Right. Right. Right. Dead End.

Anxiety churned in my gut as the minutes ticked by, and we kept hitting dead ends.

Finally, I came up short, forcing Adrien to stop. "This isn't working," I told him. "We'll never find the right path like this. At least not in time."

"You're right," Adrien said, running a hand through his damp hair. Worry was etched into the dips and contours of his face. Neither one of us knew what to do, but we had to figure it out, and fast.

I don't know what made me think to do it, but I reached into my satchel and pulled out the Shadow Heart. My eyes grew when I saw a faint light in the middle of the black crystal. A spark of blue that pulsated like a weak heartbeat.

I took three steps forward, and the pulses quickened.

"Adrien!" I spun back to him, holding the Shadow Heart up between us.

"Keep going," he said. He'd been watching over my shoulder.

I nodded and turned back around, heading in that direction. The light within the Shadow Heart started to intensify as well as the speed of the beats. I jogged past a turn and the glow dimmed, and so I backtracked and it brightened, seeming to urge me in the right direction.

My own heart rate started to pick up as I dared to hope that the Shadow Heart was leading us where we needed to go. Adrien stayed on my heels as I followed the crystal's directions. We made two right turns, three left turns, and then another right and suddenly we were there, in the center of the maze and facing the large blue crystal I'd seen before we entered the labyrinth.

The Shadow Heart was now so bright that it cast a blue light over me. Its frantic beats matched my own. But now that we were here, what should we do?

The Wise Ones had been frustratingly vague in their instructions. They'd only told me to take the Shadow Heart to the belly of the sea and combine my magic with my mate's. But I didn't know any specifics. And all of this would only work if Adrien and I truly were mates.

Were we supposed to place the Shadow Heart somewhere? How did we combine our magic? Did we need to somehow push our magic into the Shadow Heart or just meld our magic together? I had more questions than answers, and that made me feel like even though we'd come this far, we were still going to fail.

As I stood steeped in indecision, Adrien was inspecting the

large blue crystal, running his hands over the smooth and angular surface. He seemed to have found something because he stopped and called me over. I was at his side in an instant.

"What is it?" I asked.

"Right here," Adrien said, pointing to a spot in the middle of the crystal I hadn't noticed before. It looked like there was a chunk of stone missing. "Try to put the Shadow Heart there," he explained. "It looks like it might fit."

Lifting my hand, I placed the Shadow Heart in the spot, and it fit perfectly. But then nothing happened.

"What now?" I asked, looking at Adrien for direction.

"Didn't you say we needed to combine our magic to unlock it?"

"Yes, that's what the Wise Ones said. But how do we even do that?" I'd never tried combining my magic with another fae before.

Adrien shrugged. "Maybe we just need to both blast it with our magic, your ice and my shadow, at the same time."

I nodded. "It's worth a try, but can we use our magic again?"

Adrien shrugged. "Only one way to find out."

Stepping back, we both lifted our hands, ready to unleash our powers, but when I pulled on my magic, it still wasn't there.

Terror ripped through me, and I glanced over at Adrien. The look on his face told me he was experiencing the same thing I was.

"My magic isn't back," I said.

"Mine neither."

I chewed on my bottom lip. How could we possibly combine our powers if we couldn't use them? It didn't make sense.

Frustration and anger hit me like a wave, stealing my breath. We'd come all this way and now nothing could be done?

I couldn't accept that. Wouldn't. We'd almost died. Some of Adrien's men *had* died, and Kira and the other merfolk were at this very moment risking their lives. Giving up now wasn't an option, but what else could be done?

"You need to kiss me," Adrien said, and when I jerked my gaze to him, I could see that his face was as serious as ever.

"What? I can't," I said, shaking my head even as my body screamed at me for denying it what it truly wanted. But my mind was stronger than my body, overriding my urges. The cold truth of it was that my fear of Adrien actually being my mate and what that would mean was fiercer than my desire.

Adrien took a step toward me, and I was so at odds with myself that I froze. Half of me yelled to move away and the other half demanded I close the remaining distance, but I couldn't force my body in either direction.

"I won't push you into this," he said, moving even closer. "I want you to know that I respect that you're hesitant about what might be growing between us. This isn't how I wanted this to play out, to pressure you. I'd planned to wait until you were ready. To wait forever if need be. You're worth that."

My heart stuttered at that. Was that true? Would he really wait forever for me?

Despite the internal battle I was waging, I couldn't help but soften.

"But if we are mates," Adrien went on. "Then there's a chance the magic of our mate bond could bring our power to the surface. That might be the key to unlocking this crystal."

"It could?" I asked and then licked my lips.

As Adrien nodded, his gaze dipped to my moistened mouth. His pupils flared, and my desire roared in response, demanding to match what I saw igniting in his eyes.

Adrien moved even closer until not much more than a sliver of space remained between us. "It's your call," he said, his voice soft as he gazed down at me. "It's just one kiss, and then we will know."

I shot him a look. "It's *not* just a kiss, and you know it."

He shrugged and moved even closer, dipping his head now. "Well, you did kiss my brother to find out if you were mates. It would just be like that."

"That . . . was different," I huffed instinctively, knowing that kissing Adrien would be vastly different than kissing Zane.

"Not so different," he said and a small swell of panic rose within me. What if we kissed and nothing happened?

I didn't know when it switched or how, but the thought of Adrien being my mate was no longer as terrifying as him not.

Adrien's lips were inches from mine, teasing me, waiting for me to make the move.

"I don't believe in mates," I whispered, but the words tasted like a lie.

"Prove it." The taunt barely left his lips when I lost all resolve.

My desires took over my common sense, and I crashed into him, our mouths seeking each other and opening the second they met. Warm tendrils of heat emanated from my chest and ran down my back.

Adrien's tongue slid against mine, and I moaned at the rightness of this kiss. This was what was lacking with Zane. *Passion.*

As we continued to kiss, our mouths coming back together

LEIA STONE & JULIE HALL

again and again like we were each other's air, the heat in my chest intensified, turning into an icy fire that somehow ramped up my craving for him even more.

I dove my hands into his hair as he wrapped his arms around me and hauled me closer. We were ravenous for each other. He nipped at my bottom lip and then swallowed my gasp on another kiss.

He tasted like mint and sunshine, and I knew I'd never get tired of this.

I kept my eyes shut as he pulled back and moved his mouth to my neck, sucking gently on the tender skin there until a low moan forced itself free. I felt him chuckle at my response as he traced a path with his lips up to my ear and then playfully bit my earlobe, causing a rush of desire to shoot through me.

I felt weak in his grasp as his mouth finally made its way back to mine, and he gave me the best kiss I think anyone had ever received in fae history.

He smiled against my mouth, and my eyelids popped open.

Oh, stars.

He was right. Adrien was my mate.

A fine, rose-gold dust hovered in the empty air around us, dancing on our skin. I stared at it in awe as it slowly faded away.

But Adrien hadn't just been right about being mates. I sucked in a surprised breath of air as power flared back to life in my chest.

"Adrien, my magic's back," I told him, breathless and reeling from our kiss and what it finally revealed.

"Mine too," he said.

I'd lost track of how much time had passed since we first

entered the cave, but it would be a miracle if ten minutes hadn't already come and gone. Either way, we needed to hurry.

Adrien picked up on my sudden urgency, and with an arm still anchored around my waist he lifted one hand toward the blue crystal and the Shadow Heart embedded in it.

I followed his lead and gathered my power as I lifted my hand as well.

"Together?" I asked.

Looking into my eyes rather than at the Shadow Heart, Adrien nodded. "Together," he said, and then we both unleashed our magic.

A wind funnel of black and white magic spun and swirled from our hands. Shadows from Adrien and snow from me. They collided and twisted together, creating a beacon above the Shadow Heart. I watched in anticipation as our magic was sucked inside the black crystal, and then it fissured, cracking in half.

I gasped as shock and sorrow rolled through me. "We broke it." This was awful. How would we ever stop the curse now?

Adrien leaned forward, picking up one half of the heart and a small vial containing glowing blue fluid dropped out with a tiny, rolled parchment tied with string to the silver stopper.

"No. We unlocked it," he corrected me.

"What is it?" I breathed.

The entire time the heart held a . . . potion?

Adrien held the parchment, no thicker than a green bean and no longer than an inch. He squinted his eyes and frowned.

"There's . . . a name on it."

"A name?" I plucked it from his grasp and held the impossibly small lettering up to the lightest part of the cave and gasped.

"Lorelei Maebry, Princess of Spring," I read out loud.

A vial. A note. For Lorelei? How? It didn't make sense. But neither did the Wise Ones and all of their knowledge. Had they known about this? I wanted to rip open the small seal and read it right now but it wasn't addressed to me.

"We have to get this to Zane," I told him, in a daze, but when I looked over at Adrien, he was still staring down at the piece of the Shadow Heart in his hand, a confused look on his face.

"What's wrong?" I asked.

"Nothing, probably, but . . ." He shook his head and then glanced up at me. "It's just that we always believed that the Shadow Heart is what powered our world. At least that's what the old stories say. But now half of it is sitting in my hand, so how could that be true?"

"Maybe it's what was inside that was the true source of power?" I offered, thinking about the mysterious vial. "Or perhaps the stories are wrong."

I knew from experience how stories could be false. Look at all we've been told about the Ethereum lords. Most of that wasn't true, yet we'd always accepted it as fact back in Faerie.

Adrien slipped his hand into mine. "I guess it doesn't matter now. Let's get out of here while we still can and we'll see that my brother gets that." He nodded down to the vial still held tightly in my hand.

Nodding, I handed the vial to Adrien who took it and the two halves of the Shadow Heart, and placed them into the satchel. Then we ran for the exit, my mind spinning the entire time.

Chapter Nineteen

After exiting the underwater cave, Marlin used his magic so we could breathe underwater again and we rode to the surface. There were a few dead sirens in the water but Kira and her people had handled it and all lived to tell the tale. Once we got to shore they had a small, weathered sailboat with Adrien's surviving crew members already aboard waiting for us. We thanked them for their kindness and help before pointing the boat toward Soleum and leaving. Adrien assured me that since he had not checked in back home, there would be an entire second crew and ship coming to look for us as pirate encounters were so common. Sure enough, after just three hours one of his ships found us and took us on board.

"We found *Beatrice* twenty leagues north and flying a pirate flag. Got her back for you, but she'll need some work," the captain of the new ship told Adrien as soon as we'd boarded.

Adrien nodded. "Glad to hear you got her back, Haron. Any other news I need to be aware of?"

The man glanced at me and then back to Adrien. "A rumor that might interest you perhaps . . . in private."

Adrien frowned. "Then let's step onto the captain's deck and speak."

The man started toward the back of the ship, and I prepared to wait for Adrien while he talked with his man when his hand slipped into mine, and he tugged me along with him. We were led onto the captain's deck where the helmsman was steering the ship. The fae, Haron, dismissed him and then took hold of the wheel himself.

Once the helmsman left, we were alone.

Haron peered at me and swallowed hard. "My lord, are you sure you don't want this conversation to be private?"

Adrien nodded. "I'm sure. You can say anything in front of her. What is it?"

Haron sighed. "One of your spies got word to me via raven that someone with ice magic, who looks very similar to Lady Isolde, was seen at the southern tip of the kingdom."

It felt like lightning struck the top of my head as shock rushed through my body. Someone with ice magic that looked like me? That . . . that wasn't possible. Right?

Adrien peered at me with confusion. "How many sisters did you say you had?"

My stomach sank. No. She wouldn't. She couldn't. Right?

"Seraphina," I breathed. But how could she be here? I guess it might be possible. She was a Winter princess, and the portal was technically still open. I just hadn't expected Seraphina to do something so rash and dangerous. Nor for my mother to allow her.

Queen Liliana. Of course. When I didn't return right away she would have sent Seraphina, probably against my mother's wishes.

I prayed that she wasn't brainwashed by Queen Liliana's lies and didn't actually try to kill an Ethereum lord while she was here. She might only be seventeen years old, but she was very capable and well-trained in the art of fighting.

"I need to speak to this spy right away," I said, my heart hammering in my chest.

Haron dipped his head to me. "Of course, my lady."

"Thank you, Haron." Adrien took my hand and squeezed it before leading me below deck.

We entered the level where the cabins were and Adrien led me into one of them. I was in a state of shock, just following Adrien through the halls as I thought of my poor terrified sister walking through that mirror portal with zero training on the Ethereum realm.

"I'm sorry to hear about your sister," he said when we were alone in the room.

My mind was frantic with worry for her.

I reached up and rubbed my temples and Adrien stroked my upper arms. "What do you need? How can I help?"

I was on the verge of a panic attack. My little sister was here. All alone.

"Your men wouldn't kill her, right?" I dropped my hands and looked up at him.

He shook his head. "Not if she looks like you. Not even if she tries to kill them. They will detain her. How powerful is she?"

I swallowed hard. "Not as much as me, but . . . enough."

He was being so supportive and yet this was overwhelming. The kiss we shared, the mate confirmation. It was real. He was my mate and even though that felt so right, it terrified me. Now that my sister was here, I had to focus on that. But I couldn't until we'd talked over what happened back in that labyrinth.

"Adrien, about that kiss," I hedged.

He just peered at me adoringly. "Yes, Isolde?"

I swallowed the lump in my throat. "The truth is, I went to a dark place after my parents' divorce and I'm terrified of the idea of marriage."

His gaze softened and he took my hand in his. "I can be a patient man if I have to. But please know that there is nothing more I want in this world than to call you my wife."

It was the sweetest thing he could have ever said, but when he uttered the word "wife" a small spike of fear raced through me that I tried to hide, but Adrien was perceptive enough to see it.

He cupped my face in his hands. "I would never pressure you to do anything you weren't ready for. Just being by your side is more than enough for me. But there are more important things we have to focus on. We will find your sister. Together."

I knew then that I'd never have to be alone in anything and that was comforting. Love, marriage, it all terrified me, but I also couldn't ignore this bond between us and having him at my side, going at my pace, brought me comfort.

After a rough night's sleep we reached the shores of the Southern Kingdom and docked back in the same wharf we'd left from. One of Adrien's spies was waiting for us because we'd sent a raven from the ship to alert the castle that we were on our way back. The spy was wearing a black hooded cloak that was coated in dust, from the desert area, I presumed.

I ran over to him, charging ahead of Adrien. "Do you have her? My sister?"

Please say yes.

He pulled back his head covering and a puff of sand fell to his shoulders. His face was scabbed and bruised.

"I do not, my lady." Then he met Adrien's gaze. "She was taken by Elisana, who is *very* much a blood witch. They went north. Robbick is dead."

Dizziness washed over me, and Adrien caught me as I fell against his side.

"What are we going to do?" I asked Adrien.

He glanced at his spy. "The north is nearly completely taken over by the curse. Why would she go there?"

The spy spoke softly as some passersby walked near us. "Her village sits away from the curse for now. On the Midlands border. We think Elisana went to check on her mother who still lives there and once she gets her to safety, she will . . . do whatever she has planned with the girl."

"No," I whimpered.

We did our part. We unlocked the crystal and got the vial inside, and now we needed to bring it to Zane, not go on a hunt for my little sister. Yet, there was nothing that would stand in my way of rescuing Seraphina. Not even trying to save two worlds.

"My lord, there is one more thing." The spy looked like he didn't want to deliver the next blow. "The curse has begun to creep over the border. The date trees are dying."

"The curse has struck the Southern Kingdom?" Adrien asked,

LEIA STONE & JULIE HALL

his voice laced with confusion. But then he looked down at me and his gaze cleared.

"What?" I asked, seeing that he'd figured something out.

"We assumed the curse would hit the Western Kingdom next because we thought you were Zane's mate, and the curse seems to be following the lord who finds his Faerie mate. But—"

"I'm your mate, not Zane's," I finished for him, filling in the blanks myself.

Adrien nodded. "But even so, it's weeks earlier than was expected. The curse must be speeding up."

A look of determination settled over Adrien's features, and he turned back to his spy. "And the people?"

"Okay for now," the spy reported.

"Prepare a contingent of two dozen men to ride north with us and get Isolde's sister back," Adrien said. "And send a letter to my brother Zane that we need to see him."

The man nodded. "And the curse on our lands?"

Adrien sucked in a deep breath. "I will not sit by as things get worse and risk lives. Evacuate the northern refugees first. Send them to Windreum. Once they are safe, begin sending waves of our people west as well. It might take a week but I want everyone out before the real damage starts."

My heart bled for him. As a leader, to make such a decision was so hard. But it was the right thing to do.

"Hopefully just a precaution," I told him, indicating my bag and the vial inside for Zane.

He nodded but didn't seem fully convinced.

Adrien then reached out and grasped my shoulders, determination

208

etched into every feature. "Zane's trains don't run to the border where Elisana's village is. If we skip taking a carriage and ride on horseback as fast as possible straight through the Midlands, we can reach Elisana in just under two days. We can leave right away."

He was choosing to help my sister first over his own people.

I nodded, feeling relieved. "Thank you." I was tired from all that had happened on the sea, but of course I wanted to leave as quickly as possible.

Adrien jumped into action, sending a messenger before us to the castle to ready the horses and prepare travel packs for us. By the time we returned to Soleum, two horses were already saddled and ready, loaded with supplies. We mounted immediately and rode through Soleum as quickly as possible. We rendezvoused with the spymaster and the two dozen he gathered outside of the city.

Adrien didn't bother dismounting his horse as he spoke to the group, quickly telling them where we were headed and why. I was such a ball of nerves I barely heard what he said, really only catching the part about how we were only going to stop when we had to in order to rest the horses and ourselves for a few hours at a time. We were trying to cut a four-day trip in half in order to reach Seraphina as quickly as possible.

My heart softened to him a little more in that moment, seeing him work so hard to help me find and save my sister. He was a good man. And so were the other Ethereum lords I'd met. Queen Liliana was so wrong about them. We all had been.

A swell of thankfulness that I'd found him rose inside me, threatening to destroy the mountain of fear I had built up about the future of our relationship. But I'd carried the trauma of my parents' divorce for too long to let it go easily.

After that, the whole group of us took off, galloping through Adrien's kingdom at a breakneck pace for as long as the horses could. Eventually we had to slow, and then long after the sun had set we stopped to rest, although only for a small handful of hours. We were up again before dawn, racing through the sandy terrain.

There was a stark beauty about Adrien's kingdom that I could appreciate. The sand, the palm trees, the small blooms that managed to spring up despite the lack of water. I found myself comparing his land to my own court. Most fae would consider the Winter Court a harsh environment as well. But the one big difference here was the heat.

The sun was unrelenting, and seeing me struggle around noon on the second day, Adrien insisted I drink part of his ration of water as well as my own. I would have refused, but there was a serious chance that I might pass out, and I didn't want anything to slow us.

"We've made good time," he said as he watched me drink and our horses walked next to each other on one of our rare breaks from traveling at top speed. "The temperatures will drop soon since we are leaving the Southern Kingdom. We should be well into the Midlands by late afternoon and then with luck, the border of the Northern Kingdom by nightfall. Elisana's mother lives in a small town just beyond the border."

I didn't miss how Adrien's eyes hardened when he mentioned his ex-fiancée.

I handed him back his canteen and our fingers brushed. Even

that small touch sent a thrill through me, and the hardness was wiped from Adrien's gaze and replaced with heat. Heat that we could do nothing about because we were riding to save my sister with an audience of over twenty of his men.

"How did you even meet Elisana?" I asked because I was both curious and needed a distraction from the desire growing inside of me and knew that nothing would douse the fire in both of us as quickly as talking about Adrien's ex.

I could see that it worked on him as well as it did on me. His mouth pinched, and I suddenly felt bad that I'd brought it up. Of course he didn't want to talk about the blood witch that had kept him under a love spell.

"I'm sorry," I started. "I shouldn't have asked. Just, never mi—"

"No, it's okay," Adrien said. "It actually has to do with where we are going, her home village. I met Elisana when I was traveling through the Midlands to get to the Northern Kingdom. The Midlands can be a hostile territory, especially for Ethereum lords."

My eyebrows raised at that.

"Don't get me wrong," he was quick to add. "Most of the Midlanders are peaceful, but there are those who live in the land between our kingdoms because they are fleeing crimes, and it's a hotbed for fae who would like nothing more than to overthrow one of the lords and take the kingdom for their own."

"Then why were you traveling through the lands if they are so dangerous?"

And why are we? I thought.

"Well, not much is truly dangerous for an Ethereum lord. Our power is unparalleled in this realm." The way he said it didn't make it sound like he was boasting, but rather just stating a fact. "And I was also traveling incognito, so I didn't think I'd be recognized."

"But you were?" I guessed.

"What I was," he said, "was distracted." Some color suddenly appeared on Adrien's cheeks that made me think he was blushing. "A group of bandits snuck up and managed to unhorse me by slapping a nasty dampener rune on me. I fought hard, but there were a dozen of them and eventually they knocked me out.

"When I woke, I was in Elisana's home just over the Midlands' border and looking into her eyes, already under her love spell, I guess. She told me she'd come across the group in the middle of the night and saved me. I hadn't thought to question how she got me away from so many men and transported me to her village because I was already besotted with her."

He shook his head, a sour look on his face. "In hindsight, Elisana most likely arranged the whole thing."

Sympathy for what Adrien had been through pricked my heart. Elisana had used him in an awful way. I didn't even know how you would trust someone after something like that happened to you, but Adrien, as amazing as he was, didn't appear to be letting that stop him from opening his heart to me. Maybe I needed to follow his lead?

"I stayed with Elisana for three days while I recovered from my injuries. Drinking a *painkilling* tea each morning." He emphasized the word painkilling because we both now knew what that tea was. "At the end of the three days, we were engaged and she traveled back to the Southern Kingdom with me. She kept me drinking her potion after I'd complained about how poorly I was resting. I don't know how I've been such a fool."

I wanted to lay a hand on him to offer him comfort, but we were too far away so I used my words instead. "It wasn't your fault, Adrien. You were enchanted. Even a mighty Ethereum lord isn't immune to magic like that."

"Thank you," he said, giving me a small smile, and clearing his throat. "But there are a couple of things you need to know about the village we are traveling to. First, it's very remote, and second, it's populated by only women." He gave me a pointed look.

"Only women? Is that normal?"

Adrien shook his head. "It's not. Elisana told me that the men had been killed in a mining accident two seasons before I met her, but now that I know what she is, I have to assume that's a lie as well."

"Why would she lie about that?" I asked, not understanding.

"Because it is a convincing cover story for a coven."

I gasped. "Of blood witches?"

He shrugged. "I don't know for sure, but I think we should be prepared that they might be."

Sudden fear for Seraphina quickened my heartbeats. A whole town of blood witches. If they were all as powerful as Elisana, they'd be almost unstoppable. "Is that why she's taking my sister there? For backup."

"I don't know that either. It could be just as my spymaster thought, that she's gone to check on her mother and bring her to safety, but I think we'd be foolish not to prepare for anything to happen once we get there. I'd like to move into the village covertly.

If it is teeming with blood witches, our best chance at saving your sister will be to get her out as quietly as possible."

I nodded and even under the blasting sun, a foreboding chill swept through me. But I would do anything, *anything*, for my sister. And that included facing a village full of blood witches if I had to.

I hardened my resolve. We would find Seraphina and get her to safety, or die trying.

Chapter Twenty

We reached Elisana's hometown by nightfall and Adrien sent his spies out into the village to learn what they could about my sister. Because this was a village of strictly women, they had to stay cloaked in shadows and only listen at the open windows of houses or taverns. Adrien and I began to stack ourselves with weapons as we awaited word from them. It was late and I was exhausted, but there was no way I was waiting even one more moment to learn the fate of my beloved sister.

"Adrien, I want you to know something," I told him as I strapped a sword to my waist. He peered at me quizzically.

"I'm not sure of the laws of this land, but if Elisana has harmed a single hair on my sister's head, I will kill her. Consequences be damned."

He gave me a half-cocked grin that made my stomach flip. "Oh, Isolde, I'll give you a full pardon to murder the blood witch, but you'll have to get her before I do."

I grinned. Okay, I guess that wasn't going to be an issue. Now I just had to find the woman.

The sound of crunching rocks pulled our attention to the right and I formed an icicle in my palm but dropped it to the ground when I recognized one of Adrien's men dressed in all black.

He bowed, pulling back the black hood that kept him hidden in the dark night. I recognized him as Eldon, one of Adrien's most loyal. He was a master of his craft and seemed to take this mission very seriously, which I appreciated.

"My lord, lady." He rose from his bow. "I've found your sister. She's alive but is being kept from using her power."

My heart flipped over at the way he said she was being kept from using her power.

"How is she being kept from using her power?"

Eldon sighed. "She's got a dampener rune on, my lady."

Damn those stupid runes. I hated them.

I began to pace as my mind ran wild with thoughts.

"How many guard my sister's room?" I asked him, rolling out my neck and readying my magic. I'd freeze the witch solid within seconds.

He chewed on his bottom lip. "Just Elisana."

I cocked my head to the side to make sure I'd heard him correctly. "Inside, but at the door? The back gate? The end of the street? How many total?"

He shook his head. "It's just her and . . . the windows and doors are wide open. It's like she wants you to find her."

Adrien let a curse word fly and I frowned. "Why is that bad? It's just her and she wants me to come, so good. Let's go." I started forward and Adrien's hand snaked out and grasped my upper arm.

"Isolde, she knows how powerful both you and I are. If she's alone it's because she has something over your sister that is bad. This is a trap."

It felt like he'd poured ice water down my veins. I wanted to argue, but Adrien was right. This probably was a trap. Elisana, despite all of her many faults, was not a stupid woman. She wasn't going to just leave herself open to harm.

"Elisana is cunning. She took your sister for a reason. She has to know we're coming for her and my guess is she's going to use your sister against us."

Dread crept into my heart. What could she have over my sister? She'd already rendered her powerless.

Adrien laid a hand on my shoulder and when I glanced up into his eyes, they were alight with compassion. "Let's go and find out what she wants."

I chewed my lip. "You just want to walk in there and *ask her*?"

He nodded, slipping his hand into mine. "I fear that if we go in hot, Seraphina will die."

Those three words, *Seraphina will die*, were the most terrifying words I'd ever heard in my life.

"Let me lead, okay?" he asked.

I'd been shocked into submission; so scared of losing my sister, I simply nodded.

How did this happen? How did we get here? At that moment my little sister was a hostage in Ethereum at the hands of a blood witch. I had enough on my plate, like stopping the curse that was ravaging both of our worlds. I didn't want to deal with this as well.

But I would. I had to. For Seraphina.

"That's not all," Eldon said, and from the sound of his voice I knew it was more bad news. "There wasn't a male in sight and from looking through the windows, most of the spies reported seeing cauldrons, herbs, wands, crystals and other dark magic items."

"So it's as I feared," Adrien said with a frown. "We are in a coven of witches."

"It looks to be that way," the spy said with a grim look on his face.

Panic clawed at my chest. Adrien squeezed my hand, his gaze conveying to me that we were in this together. It didn't take away my fear, but it did give me hope.

Eldon led us down the cobblestone road and through the quaint northern village. I wondered if the black waters would soon swallow this place too but tried to just focus on my sister.

"Adrien, I can freeze the woman solid in a moment. Just distract her for ten seconds. That's all I need."

Adrien shook his head. "I have a bad feeling that she's expecting that. She's very cunning."

Anger roared to life inside of me. I just wanted to kill this woman. Adrien said by his own admission that he wanted her dead too, but now he was telling me to wait?

Reading the anger on my face, Adrien squeezed my hand again. "Trust me, please," he quietly begged.

He was asking a lot, but the look on his face told me he knew that. I had to take several slow breaths to regain control over my emotions, but I finally gave him a small curt nod. I wouldn't kill her right away. I would trust him.

The corners of his mouth turned up in a sad smile of acknowledgement and he swiped his thumb gently over the back of my hand.

When we reached the small brick house with the porch light on and the door cracked open, Eldon slithered into the shadows, seemingly to watch from elsewhere.

Adrien gave me one final glance and then walked up to the open door and knocked on the frame. "Elisana," he called. His voice was calm, but I heard the hatred in her name.

"My darling," came an excited reply as the door was yanked open.

Elisana looked better than ever. She was wearing a pastel pink dress with her hair curled in waves over one shoulder and a full face of make-up.

And I immediately wanted to murder her.

Forget Adrien's weird feeling and stupid plan. Instead of freezing her solid, I decided I wanted to see her suffer. With a flick of my wrist I shot a serrated icicle into her left shoulder. She cried out in pain, falling back against the open door, but then another scream rose up deeper in the house. One I recognized.

Seraphina!

Elisana ripped the icicle out with a grunt, and it clattered to the floor just as I rushed past her and to the sound of my wailing sister. I passed through a sitting room and into a larger living area where my Seraphina was sitting on the couch, holding her shoulder, blood pouring from a wound.

No.

"Sera!" I ran to her, frantically trying to assess what had happened, but there was no weapon, just an open puckered hole in her left shoulder, right where I'd struck Elisana.

How?

Elisana clicked her tongue behind me, and I looked over my shoulder to see her enter the room with Adrien behind her. "Naughty, Isolde. You hurt your dear sissy."

I felt absolutely feral as I glared at the blood witch. There were dried herbs and crystals and small bowls littering the coffee table and I knew at that moment that she'd done something, forced my sister to drink one of her vile potions.

"What did you do?" I growled.

Elisana grinned. "My best spell yet. Little Seraphina and I are soultied. Now any harm that comes to me will be transferred straight to her." She peeled her torn sleeve down to show me that her shoulder was unharmed.

No. That wasn't possible.

I looked back at my sister who was whimpering in pain, and at the bloody hole in her shoulder. Knowing I caused that made me sick.

Adrien was right. Elisana was cunning and she knew what she was doing. Had I frozen her solid as I'd planned to, my sister would be dead.

"What do you want?" Adrien asked, his voice held a false kindness, one you used on an animal you were scared of that you didn't want to spook.

Elisana looked at him and I could see the envy in her gaze. "I want my fiancé back. I want *you*. Isolde kidnapped you from our wedding, and she's not even behind bars." She growled the last part, shooting me a scathing look that bounced right off me.

Seraphina leaned into me and I reached out and held her hand, squeezing it, knowing we couldn't speak freely here.

Elisana walked over to the table where there was a small cup of brown tea and my stomach clenched. "Adrien, darling, you've been without your tea for too long." She picked it up and I stood.

"No!" I shouted but Adrien caught my gaze, and I paused. There was something in that gaze that told me to trust him.

"Yes, I've been sleeping horribly," he told her. "If I drink this tea you'll let them both go? Seraphina and Isolde?"

Elisana glared at us. "Of course. I don't want them to stay here a moment longer than they have to. Look what she's driven me to do to protect myself," she said as she handed him the cup, giving me her back.

"Adrien, no," I whimpered.

We couldn't do this again: not the tea. I wanted to knock that cursed cup to the floor and watch it shatter.

Adrien took the cup and looked past Elisana right at me. His gaze was filled with sorrow and longing.

"Now drink up and let's get these unwanted houseguests out of here. Mother is on her way back to town and she's so excited to meet you."

I bit my lip, as silent tears fell from my eyes and down my cheeks. I shook my head, silently begging him not to do this, but also knowing he had no choice. If I hurt Elisana, I hurt my sister. If Elisana flew into a rage and tried to hurt Adrien, myself or Seraphina, then I couldn't protect us because I wouldn't be able to retaliate. I was stuck.

With slightly shaky hands, Adrien upended the cup and chugged the whole thing down in one go. I had to suppress the sob in my chest.

I tugged my sister's arm, forcing her to stand with me. I had to get her out of here soon or she might bleed to death, but I couldn't leave Adrien. How could I leave him with her?

A slightly glassy look came over Adrien, and he leaned forward and pulled Elisana into his arms. Seeing her in his embrace made my stomach roil and I almost rushed forward and ripped them apart, but then Adrien looked over Elisana's shoulder and stared directly at me, clarity shining from his eyes.

"I love you," he said, and my heart hammered in my chest. It felt like the world around us stopped as we stared at each other.

He was looking right at *me* when he said it.

The words hung in the air between us like the beautiful rose-gold shimmers that appeared when we kissed, but then Elisana's grating laughter pierced the moment, shattering it.

"I love you, too," she told him. "I've missed you."

But he was holding *my* gaze. I knew then without a shadow of a doubt that he was talking to me, not her.

Did the tea not work this time? Was he fighting it?

"*Go*," he mouthed.

I was torn, but then my sister sagged next to me and I glanced over to see her face was a deathly shade of white. I had to get her to safety and get help. The only person I could think of was Dawn.

Elisana pulled away from Adrien and turned to face me with venom in her gaze. "Get out. You've overstayed your welcome."

Reaching into the folds of her skirt she pulled out a small wand. A glowing rune danced at the tip, ready to be cast.

Throwing my sister's arm over my neck, I yanked her forward, holding her shoulder as we ran out of that house so fast I almost tripped and fell on my face.

Chapter Twenty-One

Adrien

I had to lock down my emotions as I watched Isolde flee with her sister. Everything inside me screamed to cut Elisana down, end her here and now, and leave with my mate. But I couldn't. A strike against my ex-fiancée was a strike against Isolde's beloved sister, and I would never cause Isolde that kind of pain. So I fought my desire for revenge and stood rooted in place, watching the love of my life run in the other direction, taking half of my heart with her.

I'd taken a gamble drinking Elisana's potion, but it had been a good one. I'd consumed the liquid over a minute ago, and though I felt pulling at my thoughts to shift to Elisana, I was easily able to fight it. Now that Isolde and I had bonded, the magic that connected us was stronger than Elisana's potion. I had hoped that would be true before I drank. But even if I'd been wrong, it would have been worth it to give Isolde the opportunity to escape with Seraphina. And I reasoned that Isolde had already broken the spell once, so I had confidence she would be able to detox me of this poison again if she had to.

She was amazing, my mate. Fierce, loyal, kind, and brave. I truly believed there was nothing she couldn't do, but even so, I was relieved to find I was still in my right mind.

I only had to convince Elisana I was under her spell for a few more moments. My plan was to immobilize her as soon as Isolde and Seraphina were safely gone. I might not be able to strike Elisana down, but I could render her useless with my magic, and then I would search this house from top to bottom for some way to break the soul-tie she'd created with Seraphina.

The front door slammed, marking Isolde's and Seraphina's exit, and relief shot through me.

Thank the stars, they'd made it out of the house. But right on the heels of that relief was a longing and sadness so acute it felt like my heart was being squeezed in a vise. I wasn't meant to be separated from my mate like this.

Turning back to me, Elisana leaned against me with her head on my shoulder, seemingly content. I gathered my shadows, pulling them closer as I readied my snare. In a moment I would shove her away and then spring my trap, boxing her in shadows.

Elisana didn't seem to notice the shadows slithering toward us. Her fingernails ran over the back of my neck as she draped her arm across my chest, and a wave of revulsion rolled through me that I played off like a shiver of desire. I glanced down at her, forcing my gaze to remain a mask of loving devotion.

"I'm so glad to have you back, darling," she said, using her favorite term of endearment for me as she snuggled closer.

It took everything inside me not to rip myself away from her, but instead I concentrated on playing my part.

"I've missed you," I said.

The words tasted vile in my mouth, but I managed to deliver them with a smile. I wasn't sure I was convincing enough though because Elisana's eyes narrowed ever so slightly and she pulled back a little.

A spike of apprehension ran through me, telling me it was time to act. I was just about to unleash my shadows, trapping Elisana within them, when there was a prick at the center of my chest and a familiar and unwanted heaviness settled over me. Every shadow I'd conjured in the room behind her dissolved into nothing.

I reeled back, but it was too late.

Looking down, I spotted a dark purple glow and realized with growing horror that she'd put a rune on me, but this one felt different from a dampener and wasn't the normal sickening green color. The rune on my chest wasn't just smothering my powers, it had also started to trickle into my mind, making me foggy and seemingly allowing Elisana's potion to do its work—not enough that I fell completely under her control like I had before, but I knew I was impaired.

Fear clawed its way through my chest for the first time since I'd consumed her tea tonight.

When I glanced back up at Elisana, she stood a few feet away from me, holding her wand. There was a haze in the air around her, and my feelings of anger started to soften even as I tried to hold on to them.

"Ah, that's better," she said with a smile on her face.

I blinked a couple of times, shaking my head against the fog of confusion that dulled my senses. "Why did you do that?" I asked.

Stepping forward, she patted my cheek affectionately. I didn't lean into it, but I didn't swat her away like I wanted to either. "Just as a precaution, darling."

I tried to rouse my fury again, but it doused itself almost the moment it was ignited.

Setting down her wand, Elisana took my hand, holding it between both of hers. Part of me wanted to yank it away from her, but another part of me welcomed the contact. I stood still as the two opposing forces warred within me. The potion was strong, but my love for Isolde was stronger. I had to fight this.

"I know I was pushing for a big wedding, but all this has made me realize that I don't need that. I just want you," Elisana said, and I looked into her brown eyes. They were quite beautiful, with gold flecks interspersed throughout the bronze. Had I ever noticed that before? I wasn't sure.

"Now that you're back to yourself," she continued, "we'll finally be married like we should have been. I've already started preparing for a ceremony right here in my hometown."

I found myself nodding without meaning to, and a huge smile broke over Elisana's face, even though inside I was screaming, thrashing in a cage of my own mind.

Married? No. I would never marry *her*. There was . . . someone else. There was . . .

As I stared at Elisana, another woman's image appeared in my mind's eye. A raven-haired beauty with ice-blue eyes and full lips. Curves that were made for my hands and a husky laugh that made my blood sing.

Isolde. My mate. My love.

Fight it. Think of Isolde, of her stunning blue eyes and the way she laughed, I told myself.

I fought to hold on to her image, knowing my feelings and connection to my mate would be my only saving grace. The longer I held Isolde's image in my mind, as Elisana prattled on about our wedding, the more I returned to myself. The disgust and wrath I felt toward the blood witch helped burn away some of the effects of her magic still trying to get a stronghold on my mind.

It was going to be a battle, but I knew that I somehow had to keep control of myself while still convincing Elisana I was under her spell. Because if I couldn't use my magic on the witch or physically hurt her, I was stuck with only one option: to play along until I could figure out a way to break her soul-tie to Seraphina and kill her. Or wait for Isolde to return and do it for me.

Chapter Twenty-Two

Isolde

I burst from Elisana's house and nearly ran right into a group of Adrien's spies. "He's . . . I . . ." I couldn't speak, I was so distraught.

"We heard. Eldon is staying back to make sure the lord is safe. We will flee with you and help your sister," the man in the black face wrap told me.

I simply nodded, on the verge of a breakdown as I clung to my sister and fought the urge to run back to Elisana and freeze her solid.

Adrien drank the tea and then looked right at me and said he loved me. That was for me, not her, right? I had to hope he could fight the powers of the potion while I sought help.

"Isolde," my sister whimpered, nearly tripping over her feet. She'd lost a lot of blood and I felt so guilty that I'd been the one to cause it. If only I had listened to Adrien, and not lashed out at Elisana, my sister would be okay.

"We need a healer," I said frantically to one of Adrien's men as we ran full speed to where we'd stashed the horses. My hand was applying pressure on Seraphina's wound but that wouldn't last.

When we reached the horses, one of the men ripped off his black wrap and began to tear it to shreds. "I'm not a healer, but I'm trained in these situations," he said.

He worked quickly draping the six or seven long strips of cloth over his arm. He then balled up some cloth so that it was about the size of the open hole in her shoulder. He was going to plug the wound with dirty cloth?

"Seraphina?" He approached her with a kind smile, but I could see the concern in his gaze as he looked at her left shoulder. I followed his line of sight and had to swallow a whimper. Her clothing was soaked in blood. No wonder she was so quiet. She was on the verge of losing consciousness.

My sister nodded at her name.

"I need you to lay down for a second while I dress your wound, and even though this is going to hurt, I need you *not* to scream. Can you do that for me?" He peered over his shoulder at the village, and I knew he feared retaliation from Elisana or the other witches that lived here.

My sister bit her lip and nodded.

I helped her lie down on the grass and then held her hand. "I'm so sorry, Seraphina," I whispered, and my sister just looked up at me with wide terrified eyes. Adrien's spy, whose name I had yet to learn, peeled her fingers away from the wound.

"Be strong for me, okay?" he told her.

She whimpered, and then he reached out, and he pushed the little ball of cloth into her wound.

Seraphina sucked in a breath and opened her mouth to scream but I clamped my hand over it. She moaned into my palm and my heart broke for her. The man then made quick work of wrapping the black strips of linen around her shoulder to hold the cloth plug in.

"Does she have any self-healing abilities?" he asked me.

I nodded.

"Okay, then we'll keep an eye on it and pull out the plug so it doesn't become embedded. It should keep her from bleeding out, though."

"Thank you. What's your name?" I asked him.

"Leif," he said, and both Seraphina and I startled.

That was my father's name. A pang of sadness entered my heart. I missed my family terribly, but it seemed that this was a sign that even from another world, my father was looking out for us.

I helped my sister up, and she swayed on her feet as we got her onto a horse with me.

"I need to get to Windreum as fast as possible and speak to Zane," I told the men. And also Dawn and Zander who I was hoping would be with him.

He nodded. "Let's ride west. We can pick up the train to Windreum in a small town I know of and maybe even find a healer there."

Relief rushed through me. The train would shorten our travel and be easier on Seraphina.

Without any further discussion, we kicked our horses and galloped off into the night. It was hard because the farther we rode from Adrien, the heavier my heart got.

Would Elisana still want to marry him? Would she kiss him? Would he fall subject to her love spell again and I'd lose him for good?

The last thought horrified me and made me realize I wanted Adrien for myself. Forever. Yes, my parents' divorce had left its mark on me, but that didn't mean my marriage would end the same way. I had to change my thoughts about that and not let my fear stop me from having the life I wanted. And right now I wanted nothing more than to grow old with Adrien.

* * *

We rode through the night. My sister slept with her back against my chest and I kept her secure with my arms around her and on the reins of my mare. Her wound was closing and Leif said that we would need to pull the cloth plug out soon or risk it embedding in her skin and causing long-term issues or infection. But to pull the cloth out meant she would again be in danger of bleeding out.

We needed a healer, but we were in the middle of nowhere.

I looked up at the night sky and prayed to every star in it that my sister be spared. By the time we reached the town of Tarrin, where the train station was, it was almost first morning light. I breathed a sigh of relief when I saw there was a large gathering of people on the platform waiting for the train to take them to Windreum. I had no idea when the train would arrive. It could be anywhere along the line between capital cities right now, but if there were people waiting, it meant it might come along sooner rather than later. Hopefully sometime today, but in the meantime, my sister's wound needed to be dealt with.

Leif helped me get her off the horse and then he peeled back the cloth, wincing slightly.

"What is it?" I asked, looking at the wound.

I could see my sister looked better. She had color to her cheeks, but I noticed a thin layer of skin had started to form over the packed cloth.

"Just leave it in," my sister said, her voice stronger. "I don't mind it."

I met Leif's gaze before glancing back at Seraphina. "If we do, you will lose all range of motion and this arm might become unusable. Not to mention infection will form. We need to cut it out before it goes too deep."

"Cut it out?" I yelled so loud that a few passersby turned to look at me.

Leif scanned the crowd at the train platform and then glanced back at me. "I'll be right back," he said, and walked away.

Seraphina peered up at me with slight fear in her eyes and I realized this was the first time we'd been truly alone since I'd found her.

"Sera, what are you doing here in Ethereum?" I tried but failed to keep the scolding tone from my voice.

She looked ashamed. "Trust me, sister, I don't want to be here. But when you didn't return, Queen Liliana panicked. She threw me into the portal against my will."

That wench! How dare she?

Anger toward the Summer queen rose up inside of me, but

I forcefully tapped it down, softening my voice so Sera didn't think it was her I was upset with. "It's okay." I reached out and took her hand. "I've got you now."

She squeezed my hand. "Things are bad back home, Izzy. Our people had to flee to the Spring Court and some got trapped in the ice mountains and . . . succumbed."

No.

"Mother, Father, our sisters?" I asked in a panic.

"All okay. But the Winter Court is . . ." Tears lined her eyes and she blinked them back. ". . . pretty much gone."

Gone? What did she mean *gone*?

Leif ran over with an elderly woman who carried a black leather bag in her hands. Her silver hair was tied into a bun at the nape of her neck and her pointed ears stuck straight up.

"I found someone who can help," Leif said.

The woman looked at Seraphina with concern. "Can I have a look, dear?" she asked and reached for her shoulder.

"I packed it with cloth, but I'm worried if it's removed . . ." Leif said, not finishing. We all knew what he meant. That my sister might bleed out.

"Are you a healer?" I asked desperately.

The woman smiled kindly at me. "No, honey, I'm not. But I have delivered over three hundred healthy babies and sewn their mothers back up after tearing."

My stomach dropped. "You're a midwife?"

No. My sister was going to die.

She ignored my shock and probed the wound gently with her wrinkled fingers.

"I'm the best thing you got, hun. Let's go to my office." With that she ushered all of us across the street to a small brick shop that said *Healthy Child Midwifery by Hannah* in gold paint over the top of the black door.

She unlocked the shop and we stepped inside. It was clean with dust-free wood floors and white walls. It smelled of antiseptic and lavender. She rushed us back to one of the treatment rooms where there was a wooden table next to a desk filled with sterile instruments and bottles.

Seraphina went to lay down on the bed and winced.

"Are you in a lot of pain, dear?" the woman, who I assumed was Hannah, asked.

Sera nodded.

The woman soaked a rag with a yellowish liquid and peered at me. "Sisters?"

"Yes." I grabbed Seraphina's hand.

"The resemblance is uncanny," she told me.

We've always been told we looked alike. "What is that?" I gestured to the yellow fluid.

Hannah smiled. "Something to make her rest comfortably while I operate."

Operate? My heart picked up speed.

The woman walked over to my sister and looked down at her with a bright smile. "My name is Hannah, and I'm going to put this over your mouth and nose. Then you're going to take a little nap while I fix your shoulder, okay?"

Sera nodded but whimpered, "I'm scared."

"Don't worry. I haven't lost a patient yet and I don't intend to start now." Those were the last words my sister heard before

Hannah put the rag to her mouth and nose. Seraphina inhaled deeply and then her eyes drooped and eventually closed, When her hand went slack in mine I had to swallow a sob.

"Please help her," I begged the woman.

Hannah pulled a small blade from her desk and I took one look at it and swayed on my feet. Thinking of her cutting my sister open made me sick. "Do you think you'd be more comfortable in the waiting room?" she asked.

I would but . . . I didn't want to leave her.

"I'll stay and assist," Leif told me and I sagged in relief.

"Okay . . . thank you."

With that I walked numbly out of the office and went to wait in the room with my head held in my hands.

Please let her be okay. I just need her to be okay.

* * *

Thirty agonizing minutes later Hannah stepped out of the treatment room wearing an apron with blood on it. I bolted into a standing position. "Is she okay?"

Hannah smiled. "She did great. I was able to remove the cloth and stop the bleeding. It will probably leave a nasty puckered scar, but with her self-healing ability her range of motion should be fine within a few weeks."

Oh, thank the stars!

"Thank you." I rushed over and hugged her.

She patted my back. "You're welcome. You can go in and see her now. She's just waking up."

I didn't want to be insensitive to my sister's healing but I couldn't help but think of Adrien being stuck with Elisana. I really needed to get to Windreum. "Can she travel? We are needed urgently in Windreum."

Hannah nodded. "Your friend told me. I've given him a pain tincture for her with instructions, and another one for infection, just in case."

Appreciation for this fae rose within me. "I don't know what we would have done if you weren't here." Emotion was tightening my throat and making the words hard to get out.

She smiled kindly at me. "It was my honor, my lady."

Just as I turned to head in and see my sister, the train whistle blew somewhere in the distance. It was here, and not a moment too soon.

I glanced over my shoulder toward the platform and could see the northern refugees starting to collect their belongings through the window. A few of Adrien's men jogged across the street to Hannah's shop, and I gave them instructions to help me get Seraphina on the train. I also made sure to pay Hannah some coins for her service.

Less than ten minutes later we were settled into the packed train. A kind fae saw the condition my sister was in and offered her their sleeping compartment. I was overcome with gratitude. Seraphina had been through an ordeal and needed as much rest as possible to heal over the next week or so.

I sat on the floor beside Sera's bed, holding her hand as the train moved along the track, taking me closer to Windreum and farther from Adrien every minute that passed. And with each moment that ticked by, worry for him grew until he was all I could think about.

By the time the train rolled into Windreum later in the day, I knew one thing for sure. I never wanted to be parted from Adrien again.

Chapter Twenty-Three

"I solde?"

Dawn's voice pulled me from my thoughts, and I spun to see her coming down the stairs in Zane's foyer, as quickly as she could in her pregnant state.

Dawn practically waddled as she descended the last couple of steps. Was she even bigger than the last time I saw her? It had been almost two weeks since we met at the station in Noreum, but her stomach protruded even more. There surely couldn't be just one baby in there.

When she reached me, Dawn threw her arms around my shoulders and pulled me toward her in an awkward hug because her belly was in the way. I squeezed her back the best I could. Just seeing her gave me a boost of strength that I happily soaked up.

Stepping back, she looked at me with a concerned expression and asked, "Was that Sera I saw being brought into the castle?"

I nodded. When we arrived at the station in Windreum, not more than an hour ago, we immediately headed for Zane's castle. I traveled with Seraphina in a hired carriage, but one of Adrien's men secured a horse and went ahead of us to alert Zane.

The moment we arrived, Zane had been there waiting for us with a healer. Although Sera was doing much better, I was still so thankful for Zane's thoughtfulness. He had some of his staff whisk my sister to a private room where she would be cleaned up and cared for before resting.

I'd given him a very brief version of what had happened with Elisana and how she was holding Adrien. Then he'd left to gather Dawn and Zander, who he hadn't had time to notify before we had arrived.

I'd been relieved when he told me Dawn and Zander were here. I was glad they weren't in the Southern Kingdom with the other northern refugees. After boarding the train when I saw them last, they'd only traveled as far as Windreum. They wanted to stay as close as possible to their kingdom to make sure their people were evacuated, which ended up being a good decision since the Western Kingdom was the only remaining place in Ethereum that the curse had yet to cross. And it was good for me because I was going to need everyone's help to break the soul-tie between Elisana and Seraphina, and save Adrien.

"What is she doing here?" Dawn asked, clearly shocked.

"When I didn't return with a heart, your mother pushed Seraphina through the portal," I told her, and immediately Dawn's features darkened.

"She did *what*?" Anger began to radiate from her.

I didn't answer because the question was clearly rhetorical.

"I can't believe it," she said, shaking her head. "I know my mother is driven and single-minded at times, but how could she have forced an untrained child into this mess?"

There was no love lost between me and Queen Liliana. What she did had almost cost Seraphina her life, but I believed the situation in Faerie was indeed dire and it drove Queen Liliana to do desperate things. Dawn left Faerie when the curse started in her kingdom. She didn't fully understand how bad things had gotten throughout the realm.

In the carriage ride over, Seraphina had given me even more details about what was happening back at home. The land was uninhabitable. Fae were dying. And those that survived had lost everything. It was as if the world was truly coming to an end. So it wasn't as if I agreed with what the Summer queen did, but perhaps I understood what drove her to that point.

"We need to talk," I told her. "Zane said he was going to get you and Zander."

Dawn nodded. "Yes, we're to meet in the drawing room. He found me first and told me you were down here. He'll get Zander and bring him there. Come on."

Taking my hand, Dawn led me back up the stairs and then down a long hallway, stopping in front of large wooden double doors. She didn't pause before pushing it open to reveal a sizable room. There was a giant stone fireplace along the back wall and three green velvet couches positioned in front of it. On the opposite side of the room there was a card table with bucket chairs where Zane must entertain guests in the evenings to play cards.

Zane and Zander were already there. Zander came over to give me a quick hug in greeting, telling me that he was glad I was safe, and then we all settled into seats around the circular card table off to the side.

243

I quickly updated them on all that had happened recently. I started with how Adrien and I had located the belly of the sea and unlocked the crystal. Both Zane and Zander looked surprised and a little confused, as Adrien had when I explained how the Shadow Heart had cracked in two, but they didn't interrupt. I told them how we discovered that Seraphina was in Ethereum but that she'd been captured by Elisana before I even had a chance to find her. Zander and Dawn seemed to already know that Elisana was a blood witch who was drugging Adrien to love her, so I assumed that Zane had told them.

I explained that we'd tracked Elisana down in a small village in the Northern Kingdom only to find out that she had soul-tied herself to my sister and we couldn't hurt her. And finally that Adrien had drunk her potion that had kept him captive to her before, but that I didn't believe it had worked this time.

"In order to defeat Elisana and save Adrien, we have to find a way to break the soul-tie," I finished, looking each one of them in the eye. "Do any of you know how we can do that?"

The looks on their faces gave me their answers before anyone uttered a word.

"I don't think any of us know enough about blood magic to be able to break a soul-tie," Zane finally confessed. "But we do know a blood witch, Rowena, who might be able to help us," he went on, and Zander's gaze immediately darkened.

"No," Zander said forcefully and Dawn laid a hand on his arm, seemingly to soothe him.

Zane looked at his brother. "She helped us before, for a price. Maybe she would again?"

Zander grumbled something under his breath and Zane sighed. "Our brother's life is on the line, along with the fate of not one, but *two* worlds. I don't like it any more than you do, but I don't think we really have an option at this point. Do you have a better idea?"

Zander pressed his lips together in a hard line, but after a few tense seconds he gave a sharp shake of his head.

"Then I'll send my men to go get her," Zane said, sounding resigned rather than happy to have won the argument. "She's actually in my kingdom. They can retrieve her and be back hopefully by tomorrow."

Zander raised one eyebrow at his brother.

"I've been keeping tabs on her since we last met her in Stryker's kingdom," Zane said by way of an explanation.

"That was smart," Zander replied.

Zane gave his brother a glare. "I'm not an idiot. She has my blood."

I cocked my head at Zane. There was a story there, but I wasn't sure I wanted to know it.

Glancing over at me he asked, "Do you have the Shadow Heart with you? Or at least what's left of it?"

I nodded, and then reaching into the satchel hanging from my waist, I pulled out what had been hiding in the Shadow Heart plus the two halves.

"Is there something written on that?" Zane asked, pointing to the small vial and even smaller scroll attached to it.

I nodded and then held the vial out, so they could see the sealed rolled note with Lorelei's name on it for themselves.

I glanced at Dawn and she leaned in at the same time as Zane did. They both gasped at the same time.

"Lorelei?" Dawn said in awe.

I nodded. "I think we need to get this to her." Then I glanced at Zane. "Have you found a way to get to Faerie?"

He nodded, but his expression remained grim. "I think I have. But it's going to take all four of us brothers to do so. I've already sent a raven to Stryker letting him know that I need him. I haven't heard back from him yet, but I'm hoping he and Aribella will be able to make the journey here soon. Once we defeat this blood witch and get Adrien back, I don't want to waste a single moment getting to Lorelei."

Interesting. He said getting to Lorelei rather than getting to Faerie or ending the curse. Despite the direness of this whole situation, I had to smile a little internally. Zane deserved happiness, and I was sure he was going to find it in the sweet Spring princess. Zane was truly an amazing man. Lorelei didn't know how lucky she was.

After that, Zane left to arrange for his men to locate the blood witch who he thought might aid us, leaving Zander, Dawn and I to start planning for Adrien's rescue after we broke the soul-tie.

"And you're sure Elisana's potion didn't work this time?" Zander asked, a crease forming between his brows. "We all witnessed the power this blood witch had over my brother before. He would have done anything for her. I think we need to know, going in, what we should be prepared for. If he's under her thrall again, it's not just Elisana we'll be battling, but Adrien as well. If he's not in his right mind, he'll defend her, even against us."

The thought of Adrien fighting against his brother to protect Elisana made me sick to my stomach.

"I'm sure," I said, holding my tongue against any doubts I might have.

"I wonder why it didn't work this time," Zander mused, running two fingers over his lower lip as he tried to work it out.

"Well, I have a theory," I said, clearing my throat.

I was suddenly shy. I hadn't told them Adrien and I had confirmed we were mates yet, but there was really no reason to hold the information back. I'd seen the power of our bond work when we couldn't access our magic in the belly of the sea. If I had to guess, I'd say that's what was keeping Adrien clear-headed right now. I only hoped that Elisana didn't realize because I didn't know what she would do to Adrien if she thought he would never love her again. She was clearly unhinged.

Dawn and Zander patiently waited for me to explain. "We found out we're mates and solidified our bond, so I think the magic of the bond between us is more powerful than Elisana's potion."

"You're mates?" Dawn's eyes started to well as a huge grin appeared on her face. "I knew there was something between the two of you. It was all over your face when you called Elisana a wench. I guess ending up in front of Adrien instead of Zane meant something after all." Reaching across the table she grabbed my hands and squeezed them quickly.

Zander glanced over at his wife with a look of such deep affection that it made my heart ache. I'd seen that look before when Adrien gazed at me. Would I ever see it again?

"I know I speak for Dawn when I say that we couldn't be happier for you and my brother," Zander told me. "We're extremely excited for your future together."

"We'll only have a future if we can defeat Elisana and I can get him back," I said.

"You will," Dawn replied with such conviction that I couldn't do anything but believe her.

* * *

Later that night, Zane found me alone on a balcony overlooking the lights shining throughout the city of Windreum below. He cleared his throat to announce his presence and came up next to me, resting his forearms on the railing.

Zane may not have turned out to be my mate, but there was still a connection that had formed between the two of us during the time we spent together. It was similar to the connection I had with my sisters. It was comforting to have him here, even if he wasn't saying anything.

After a few more moments of comfortable silence, Zane said, "I came out to check on you. How are you holding up?"

Truthfully, I was a wreck, but I knew I needed to stay strong for my sister and Adrien. Now wasn't the time to fall apart, even though I felt a hair's breadth away from shattering into a million pieces.

"I'm fine," I lied, and a small frown turned down the corners of Zane's mouth.

Even though I knew he saw right through me, he had the decency not to call me out on my lie.

"Dawn told me some interesting news," he said, not able to keep the corners of his mouth from lifting in a smile.

"Oh, yeah?"

I had a feeling that I knew what he was going to say, which was confirmed when he asked, "So, do you believe in mates now?"

"It's not that I didn't necessarily *believe* in mates," I started, but then Zane gave me a look that I couldn't help but laugh at. But my levity quickly faded as Adrien entered my thoughts.

"He said he loved me," I confessed, my eyes suddenly starting to sting.

A gentle look softened Zane's features. "Of course he did. And how could he not? You're fierce, determined, beautiful, and a million other things that make you the perfect counterpart for my brother. He never stood a chance," he finished with a smile.

I sighed. "But we haven't known each other for very long. Hardly any time at all when you think about it. And there's still so much we don't know about each other."

Zane shrugged. "So, why does that matter?"

I shot him a look that said that it should matter.

Zane tilted his head as he regarded me. "Let me ask you something. Do you feel the same way he does?"

Yes, I felt the same way. But those feelings scared me, so rather than admit them, I deflected. "Feeling so strong about each other so soon . . . it's just, not logical," I argued with a shake of my head.

Zane turned to me fully, looking me right in the eyes. "Love isn't logical, it just is."

"That simple, huh?"

He nodded. "Yes, that simple."

Something inside me started to crumble. I'd held it together the best I could over the last day as I got my sister to safety, but here, standing on this balcony thinking about how I left Adrien, and what I'd given up in order to save her, suddenly became too much, and I broke.

"If I love him, how could I have just left him there?" I asked as unwanted tears started to stream down my face. I could no more hold my sobs in than I could stop loving Adrien as much as I did.

"You didn't leave him there. He told you to go," Zane reminded me as he wrapped his arms around me. He let me cry without judgment for a little while, making me wish I'd had an older brother.

"What if I never see him again? What if I never get to tell him I love him too?" My words were barely above a whisper, but somehow, Zane still heard.

"You *will* see him and you *will* get to tell him how you feel," he said, his voice firm and sure. "But I know my brother, so I'm pretty sure he already knows."

Zane's words washed over me like a healing balm and my tears eventually subsided. I took in a cleansing breath and stepped back to wipe my face with my sleeve.

"Feel better?" Zane asked.

"Yes," I said with a nod, feeling something inside me click into place.

I finally knew that it was time. Time to let go of my fears and embrace my future. And that future included the seafaring Ethereum lord I'd fallen in love with, and I wasn't about to let something like a blood witch or an evil curse stand in my way.

Chapter Twenty-Four

Adrien

Laying wide awake on the lumpy couch, I strained to hear Elisana across the room, waiting for her breaths to lengthen and even out to confirm she was asleep. The couch in her bedroom was the only concession she'd allowed me. She wouldn't let me sleep alone last night or tonight, claiming that our separation had caused her trauma, and now she wanted me close all the time. I hadn't been able to come up with a way to convince her that we should sleep in separate rooms without tipping her off that I wasn't fully under her love spell.

Thank the stars we hadn't shared a room before, because I was at least able to stay out of her bed without raising suspicion, claiming that I still wanted to wait until we were wed to share that intimacy. She'd pouted but relented.

The last day and a half had been torture, pretending to be infatuated with her as she paraded me in front of her friends and fellow blood witches in the village. Her touch made me shudder, yet I had to act like I was utterly besotted.

There were times when her magic had swelled, threatening to pull me under thanks to the rune she'd put on my chest, but I always fought against it. Time and time again I brought up Isolde's face in my mind's eye and focused on my mate, and the effects of Elisana's magic had dimmed. But it was a tricky line to walk, keeping Elisana believing I was in love with her while searching for a way to break her soul-tie with Seraphina so that I could kill her.

Especially since the witch barely let me out of her sight.

I was running out of time. The only thing keeping Elisana from insisting we take our vows immediately was the return of her mother, who'd been blessedly absent since I arrived.

I'd never met the woman but apparently, as the leader of Elisana's coven, she was the one who would preside over our nuptials. Elisana was anxious about the delay, but determined to have her mother marry us. She didn't say anything directly, but I got the impression from little things she said here and there that her mother would be able to bind us in ways that were more permanent and deeper than simple marriage vows.

A fact that horrified me.

According to Elisana, her mother was expected to return any day now.

There was no way that I would ever betray Isolde and utter vows to another woman, much less the blood witch who had enthralled me, so once her mother appeared, it was only a matter of time before Elisana discovered I was faking my affections for her.

As restricted as I was right now with the rune on my chest, I would no doubt be in chains or worse when my deception was discovered. I had to find a way to break this soul-tie before that happened, so I was waiting for Elisana to drift off so that I could search her home for something useful.

It was well into the night when I was finally confident Elisana was deep in sleep. Her breaths were slow and even as she snored softly.

I held my own breath as I carefully sat up and slid off the couch. I padded to the door in my stockinged feet, my gaze fastened on the lump underneath her covers the whole time. The door squeaked as I pulled it open and I froze, waiting for Elisana to jump out of bed. But she didn't wake and only turned in her sleep.

Opening it just wide enough to fit me, I squeezed through the doorway as soundlessly as possible and crept down the stairs.

There was one place in Elisana's house that she'd been careful to keep me out of. It was a small room off the kitchen that I'd only gotten a glimpse of once when she ducked in to return her wand. From the brief look I'd gotten, I'd seen jars, vials, ingredients for her potions, and stacks of books. If there was information somewhere in this home about how to break a soul-tie, I was willing to bet it would be there, but when I reached the room, the door was locked.

I let out a quiet groan of frustration. If I had my powers, I could easily send shadows into the lock to pick it. Without them, I could break the door down with force, but that would undoubtedly wake Elisana.

I cast my gaze around the kitchen, looking for something I could use to pick the lock or unscrew the hinges, when I caught a set of eyes peering at me through the kitchen window. I almost shouted in surprise before recognition settled in.

"Eldon?" I mouthed, and my most loyal spy pulled back his hood to reveal the rest of his face to me.

So not all of my men had fled with Isolde. That was both comforting and terrifying. I hoped she and her sister had made it out okay.

I gestured for him to go around to the door that was off the kitchen, and he nodded again and disappeared briefly. It was late, so there was a good chance no one was walking around to see him, but I didn't want to take any chances of being seen speaking with him.

"My lord," Eldon said quietly as he entered the kitchen, his voice barely a whisper. "I've had to stay concealed during the day, but I've caught several glimpses of you from afar, and you've seemed . . . not quite yourself." Concern was written all over the spy's face and his gaze darted around as if he expected Elisana to appear at any moment.

I knew what he was trying to say. He wanted to know if I was under Elisana's thrall again or not.

"I am in control," I told him. "Now that Isolde and I have solidified our mate bond, Elisana's magic isn't strong enough to sway me. I can feel it trying to work, but I've been able to push it aside. I've been acting around her this whole time."

"Mate bond? Congratulations, my lord. I'm so glad to hear you've only been acting," he said, his voice infused with relief.

"Where is Isolde?" I asked, conflicted on whether I wanted her to be far away and safe, or close by.

"She fled with Leif and the rest of the men. They headed for the Western Kingdom to seek help from your brother, Zane. I stayed behind to keep an eye on you."

Relief that Isolde was most likely safely tucked away in Windreum right now outweighed any disappointment that she wasn't near. "Good, I'm glad she's safe. My brother will take care of her, and thank you for staying behind to look after me." Good men were hard to find. I'd have to promote him when I eventually made it out of this mess.

"We should leave, my lord, before the witch awakens," Eldon said, casting a frantic look in the direction of the stairs that led up to Elisana's bedroom.

"We can't just yet," I said and explained to him quickly that we needed to try to find something to help break the soul-tie between Seraphina and Elisana. Then we could flee.

After telling him that the door to Elisana's secret room was locked, Eldon reached into a pouch at his waist and pulled out a small case that held long, thin pieces of metal. Some were straight and others had slightly hooked ends.

Lock picking tools.

Stepping aside, I let him attend to the lock and after only a few moments there was a click and the door popped open.

"Quick. Help me look for anything that might be useful to break a soul-tie." I pointed to the rows of small bottles positioned on shelves across from me. "Check all the labels and I'll check these books."

We got to work right away. When Eldon had checked all the bottles, he turned to me and shook his head, telling me he hadn't found anything. I pointed to another part of the room and he started examining the herbs and potion ingredients without having to be told, while I continued to thumb through the books as quickly as possible.

I was halfway through the stack when I came across a black leather-bound book. I could tell the tome was old because the leather casing was cracked and worn, and the pages within were yellowed with age. I knew exactly what I was holding the minute I opened it.

A grimoire. Either Elisana's or perhaps her family's.

A bolt of excitement shot through me. I didn't know much about blood witches, but it was common knowledge that their spells were passed down to each generation through grimoires. There was a very good chance that the spell Elisana had used to bind her to Seraphina was in this book. And if it was in this book, the instructions on how to break it were most likely in there as well.

"Did you find something, my lord?" Eldon whispered, appearing next to me.

"Perhaps," I answered quietly, without taking my eyes off the pages as I thumbed through it, looking for the soul-tie spell.

I was halfway through the book when I finally came across it, the spell for the soul-tie. And it was at that precise moment that a floorboard creaked above our heads.

Both Eldon and I froze, hoping it was just the groans of an old house. But then another creak sounded, making it obvious that Elisana was awake.

Without taking time to think it through or even check to see if there was something that explained how to reverse the spell, I ripped the page from the grimoire and shoved it at Eldon. After quickly replacing the book where I found it, I hurried him out of the room, closed the door which locked automatically behind us, and rushed him out the back door.

"Go," I whispered frantically. "Take this page to Isolde in my brother's kingdom. And tell her I love her."

"My lord, come with me," Eldon said. "You can escape as well. We can go to her together."

I shook my head. I wanted to, desperately, but if Elisana realized I was missing, she'd go looking for me immediately, probably rousing half the village to help her. There was no guarantee I'd be able to escape a whole coven, but a good chance Eldon could because no one knew he was here. Getting that page to Isolde was now the priority. Not to mention the fact that I wouldn't put it past Elisana to cause her own self harm just to hurt Seraphina. She was completely deranged. I had to wait until the soul-tie was broken.

"I can't," I simply said, and then shoved Eldon out the door. I'd only just closed it behind him when Elisana appeared in the kitchen doorway.

Her shrewd gaze swept the room. I didn't miss how her eyes went first to the door to her potion's room before anywhere else and was glad I'd thought to shut it.

"What are you doing?" she asked sharply, when she didn't see anything amiss.

If I was going to keep my ruse with her going, I needed to think fast.

"What? Where am I?" I turned in a wobbly circle as if taking in my surroundings for the first time. "How did I get here?" I asked and then grabbed my head, pretending to be foggy-headed, like I'd sleepwalked my way down here and was confused.

"You don't remember walking down here?" she asked.

I shook my head. "I was sleeping on the couch. I kind of

remember feeling thirsty. I must have come down here half awake, looking for water."

Elisana's eyes narrowed, and I didn't miss the suspicion simmering in them. Her gaze flicked to the back door behind me and I knew with a sinking feeling that I was going to have to do something drastic to convince her.

Up until now I'd gotten away with keeping Elisana at arm's length. Some hugs and a few chaste kisses to her cheek and forehead had been enough to mollify her, but I hoped I wasn't going to have to step it up now to convince her I was still under her magic.

Elisana walked toward me, her gaze fastened to the back door, but I couldn't let her go out there to give Eldon time to escape. I sprung forward and gathered her in my arms. She stiffened a little, telling me that I was right and she wasn't, in fact, fully convinced that I'd stumbled down here by accident.

"My love," I said, the words tasting like ash in my mouth as I forced myself to lift a hand and softly stroke my fingers against the column of her throat. To me it felt like snake scales, and I had to ward off the shudder that threatened to run through me, but Elisana's eyes fluttered and a flush pinked her cheeks. "Why don't we return to your room?"

"We will. I just want to check the back door—" She started to pull away from me, but I tugged her back and ran the tips of two fingers over her bottom lip, back and forth, and Elisana started to look as dazed as I'd pretended to be a few minutes beforehand, the back door all but forgotten.

I smiled internally, even as my stomach roiled at having to continue to touch her and hold her near.

"Come sleep in my bed," she said, her voice thick with seduction, but the sound didn't rouse even a speck of desire within me.

I shook my head. "I can't," I made my words sound pained. "Being so close to you would be too great a temptation," I lied. "You said yourself your mother would return shortly. We've already waited this long. A day or two more won't kill us."

Elisana groaned in frustration. "It's one of the reasons why I love you so much, that misplaced honor of yours. But fine, we'll keep our separate sleeping arrangements . . . for now."

Taking my hand she turned and then tugged me after her, leading me back upstairs. Each step felt like a monumental task because all I wanted to do was rip my hand from hers and use it to squeeze the life from her instead, but I couldn't because that would kill Seraphina.

Hurry, Isolde, I thought.

There's no way I was going to be able to play along for very much longer. Because I knew next time Elisana would expect me to take her in my arms and kiss her passionately, and I wouldn't be able to, even to save myself.

Chapter Twenty-Five

Isolde

I slept fitfully that night, tossing and turning beside my little sister as she snoozed peacefully. Whatever tincture they had given her for the pain had worked very well and I was grateful. But my mind was a jumbled mess.

Would this Rowena woman come? Would she agree to help us? Was my mate sleeping next to Elisana right now?

By the time the morning light bled through the cracked open curtains I'd barely gotten a few hours' rest. After checking on Sera and leaving her in the capable hands of her nurse, I went down to have breakfast.

Dawn was already there with a full plate of sausages, boiled eggs, and some delicious, glazed pastry with fruit filling.

"Someone's hungry," I teased.

Dawn grinned. "This is my second plate."

I shook my head. "Do we know how many you are carrying? Because no offense, but that belly is too big for one."

She laughed. "The midwife used a stethoscope last night to hear the heartbeats . . ."

She let that word linger in the air. Heartbeats. Plural.

"And?" I sat before her in rapt attention.

She lowered her voice. "At least three."

My jaw unhinged. "You poor woman."

Dawn's bright chuckle filled the room and she just beamed at me. "Oh, Isolde, I've missed you and that dark sense of humor." She leaned forward and hugged me, holding me for longer than normal.

Best friends know when something is wrong, and without words she was telling me she knew how much leaving Adrien must have distressed me.

"It will be okay," she whispered before releasing me.

I nodded, thankful for her comfort. "You have to name one of them after me, their future favorite aunt," I teased.

She smiled softly. "A royal having all girls is common in Faerie, but here they have all boys, so . . ."

Oh. That was interesting. A direct opposite. I knew we sometimes referred to Ethereum as the mirror world, but I didn't think the differences between realms would extend to something like this. "Well—"

There was a knock at the open door to the dining hall. I turned to see Zander standing there. "Rowena is here."

My eyebrows lifted. That was faster than I'd thought. Zane sent his men for her just last night. At best, I didn't expect them to be back until later in the day, but I was glad to be wrong.

Dawn went to stand, and Zander moved across the room to stop her. "My love, please, if you care about the health of my heart, stay in here while the blood witch is present."

Dawn frowned, looking annoyed, but I thought it was really sweet.

"Are you going to stay with me?" She put a hand on her hip in defiance.

He nodded. "Sure. If you want me to."

She looked surprised at that, but then Zane stepped up behind his brother and Zander turned to him. "Can you handle the witch with Isolde alone?" he asked.

Zane nodded confidently.

Zander pointed a firm finger at his brother. "No blood," he chastised.

Zane clapped his brother on the shoulder. "I got this."

Even though I was hungry, I left the table and followed Zane to the drawing room we'd met in yesterday.

The only blood witch I'd ever met was Elisana, and she was a nightmare, so I wasn't sure how I felt about meeting another and asking them for help.

"You trust this woman?" I asked Zane as we walked down the hallway.

"No," he said simply, and chills rose up on my arms.

"But she might be the only one who can help us?" I asked, and he nodded once.

Steeling myself, I let Zane lead, entering the drawing room after him.

One of Zane's men was standing next to a tall woman with light-purple-hued hair. She had her arms crossed and looked like she didn't want to be here.

"Luckily for us, she was one town over from Windreum, here in the Western Kingdom," the spy said and bowed to Zane before leaving to post himself at the door.

"This is the only kingdom currently not affected by the curse, so yes, I am staying here." Her voice held an air of superiority.

The tic in Zane's jaw showed how much he liked her dwelling in his kingdom, but he didn't comment on it. Instead, he cut to the chase. "We need your help again."

She stood a little taller then, running her fingers over her smooth face. "And I would love to help you again, darling. Your blood was absolutely divine. What can I do for you?"

Zane looked at me, and I saw apprehension slip over his gaze. "I need you to project us to the Faerie world like you did last time. This time in front of Lorelei, the Spring Court princess."

My head jerked back like I had whiplash. "What?" I said.

"There must be payment. Like last time." The witch held out one hand and pulled a dagger from her belt with the other.

Zane turned to me frantically. "I'm sorry but I have to see her, to tell her I'm coming. Then we can ask for help with Adrien."

I swallowed hard. Was this what they'd done when they'd projected their ghostly apparitions into my room that day?

"Zander said no blood," I told him as I stared at the witch's outstretched palm and the dagger.

Zane pursed his lips. "What my brother doesn't know won't hurt him," he said and then held out his hand out to Rowena.

With that, the witch sliced the tip of his finger and let the crimson fluid leak out onto her dagger, filling the tip. She then pressed the tip of the cold metal to her tongue and licked it off. I began to shiver.

Right before my eyes, the woman seemingly looked younger. It was incredible and horrifying to see someone lose five years of their face and skin.

"Ahhh," she sighed in contentment. "I *am* enjoying these little meetings we have, Lord Zane."

"Get on with it," he growled.

She rolled her eyes. "Since there are only two of you, it will be much easier this time."

Pulling a small box from her cloak she opened it, revealing a long, sharp needle. She gestured for my hand and I gave Zane a look, but he just nodded solemnly, telling me she'd only take a drop. After pricking my finger she blotted it with a small square of red cloth and then did the same to Zane.

"Thank you for doing this," Zane said beside me.

I understood his desire to check in on Lorelei, even I wanted to see her, to speak to her and ask how things were going. She was his mate and he was protective. I admired that. I just hoped it was quick since my own mate was in trouble.

The witch then began to chant and wave the cloth into the air. "Once you have the place I need to take you in mind. Grasp my hand," she told me.

Right. Lorelei.

I closed my eyes, remembering my last visit to Spring. It had been a diplomatic one. My mother was in need of food as our rations had run out early and so we'd begged Queen Gloriana for some. She had graciously given us more than needed as the Spring Court was always bursting with plenty. Lorelei and I had spoken in the gardens of their palace. A peaceful place where Lorelei often tended to her crops and flowers. She had been sweet and soft-spoken and generous.

I focused on that memory now as I reached out and grabbed the witch's cold fingers. As soon as our hands connected, the cloth caught fire and started to burn with green flames. Rowena's eyes then went completely black as she continued to chant, and then suddenly she threw back her arms and her magic slammed into me. The moment it did, I was sucked from my body and then floated before being hurled into a different realm.

When I opened my eyes I blinked rapidly at the plumeria bushes. I was there, in the palace garden inside of the Spring Court.

I did a full three-sixty, seeing Zane beside me but no Lorelei.

"It's beautiful here," Zane breathed. He was a ghostly apparition on my right, and I was starting to wonder if we'd have to search the castle for her when I heard her delicate singsong voice.

Lorelei loved to sing and she did it often. I turned in the direction of the sound to see her coming through the vegetable garden with a large basket in her arms. The sun shone on her long brown hair and the butter-yellow dress she wore swayed in the breeze.

I flicked my gaze to Zane to see the look of wonder in his eyes, and I couldn't help but grin. The way he watched her, as if he was in awe of her beauty, warmed my heart.

Now I had to try to speak to her without completely freaking her out.

"Lorelei," I called softly.

Her gaze shot upward, zeroing in on Zane and me, and she dropped her basket of veggies with a terrified yelp.

Well, I guess there was no way to do that gently.

"It's me, Isolde. I'm in Ethereum and we've used a witch to help us talk to you." I rushed the words out by way of explanation.

She grasped her chest, eyes wide as she went from me to Zane, and back to me, before resting on Zane again and sticking there. Something shifted in her gaze then, and her face relaxed as she looked at him.

Zane bowed to her. "I'm Lord Zane, the Ethereum Western lord and . . . I'm your ma—"

"Man helper," I shot back, cutting Zane off. Was he seriously going in with the mate thing right away? No way. She'd freak out.

"Man helper?" Lorelei cocked her head to the side. She still had her hand on her chest and hadn't moved an inch. Processing the shock no doubt.

"Yes, a man who wants to help you with your task to end the curse," I fumbled and widened my eyes at Zane.

He nodded, getting my point. "Yes. I'm here to help you. I have important information and something I need to get to you."

Lorelei looked left and right across the garden as if searching for other people. Then she stepped forward a few feet and got closer. "Isolde, I got your letter. About Dawn, Aribella and the Ethereum lords visiting you as ghosts. It sounded . . . nonsensical. But Queen Liliana is already here, and she's . . . acting off."

"Off?" I asked, a chill racing up my spine.

She swallowed hard. "Disturbed. When I questioned where you or Seraphina were, she . . . struck me." She brushed her fingers over a small bruise on her cheek that I hadn't noticed before.

A low and menacing sound came from next to me and I looked over at Zane, who was practically vibrating with fury. "I'll kill her."

Lorelei looked up at him in surprise, and I laughed nervously. "He's very protective of all of us. Dawn, too," I lied.

He needed to tone it down or she would be totally freaked. Or maybe that was just me? Maybe I was the only one who would have a hard time accepting this mate concept right away.

"You have to be careful around her," I warned Lorelei. "Lord Zane has found a way to come to you. In order to bring an end to this curse on both of these lands, you have to do something together."

Lorelei softened her posture. "Together?"

She was so innocent and naïve. I wanted to wrap her up and protect her from the world. She'd always been that way and a secret part of me worried she might be too soft to face what lay ahead.

"If that's okay? Just wait for me. Stay safe until I can reach you and we will end this," Zane told her.

She chewed at her bottom lip and nodded once.

A frigid chill ran over my body, and I stood there for a moment wondering how it could be so cold in the Spring Court when a hand passed through my chest, and then Queen Liliana was there. She had stepped through my ghostly apparition and spun around, facing me with a menacing snarl.

"You are a traitor to all seelie," Queen Liliana growled, and then lashed out with a blinding light.

There was a flash of light and a crushing weight on my chest, and we were back in the drawing room at Zane's castle and the lavender-haired witch was grinning. "Ohh, I like that woman."

"Would she hurt Lorelei again?" Zane asked me immediately.

"No," I lied because I could see the terror in his face. Queen

Liliana had already hit her, so I wasn't convinced she wouldn't do it again, or worse. But I could tell that Zane was spiraling, so I didn't point that out to him. Before he could do anything to help Lorelei, we had to get Adrien back. Something I needed him for right now.

"Zane, I need you to focus on Adrien and help me," I told him. I'd done what he asked. We'd checked on Lorelei and told her he was coming, and now I wanted my mate back.

He took in a cleansing breath and nodded. "We need one more thing," he told Rowena and then looked at me in anticipation.

I knew more about the situation so it was probably best I explain. "A blood witch is holding someone I care about captive. She's created a soul-tie with my sister so we cannot harm her."

Rowena's eyebrows bunched together. "A soul-tie? That's powerful stuff. Who is this witch?"

"Elisana, she—"

"Elisana?" Rowena stumbled backward shaking her head as she eyed the door and the window, seemingly looking for an escape. She began to pack her things, strapping her dagger back on her belt and moving for the door.

"Wait a second, you have to help us." I stepped in front of her.

She shook her head, looking frightened. "There are few blood witches I would refuse to go up against, but Elisana is one of them. You may imprison me, torture me, do as you please, but I will not help you."

What in the world?

Zane looked confused. "Is she more powerful than you?"

Rowena's lips flattened and her nostrils flared as if she wouldn't dare admit such a thing. But finally, she relented and gave a short nod of her head. "Not just that . . . she has power over me, over *all* blood witches. Her mother is the coven leader," she explained.

"And that means?" I asked her.

"It means when I was born my blood was taken and is currently being held in her house. One drop and she could end me. I cannot help you with this, and that is final." Her tone was pleading, and I looked at Zane in defeat.

He sighed and called to his man who hadn't left his post at the door. "Take her back to where you found her but keep an eye on her. We may need to revisit this."

* * *

The rest of the day passed in agony. We scoured Zane's extensive library but found nothing about a soul-tie. Dinner was pretty silent that night as I tried to come to terms with the fact that I had nothing to help Adrien.

"We can start planning our attack on Elisana's village. Ready the troops and even get them in place one town over," Zane offered.

I swallowed hard. "But we can't move until the soul-tie is broken, and right now we have nothing on that."

Dawn reached over and slipped her hand into mine. "Stryker and Aribella have sent word: they are having some troubles in their kingdom with the curse, but they can be here in two days' time. Maybe they will have some knowledge—"

"Two days?" I whimpered, suddenly losing my appetite. "Adrien doesn't have two days."

Dawn frowned and said nothing more.

After dinner I checked on my sister and was pleased to see she was up and laughing with her nurse.

"You're feeling better?" I asked.

She smiled at me. "I am, thank you."

The nurse was only a few years older than Seraphina and she was showing her a book. We'd grown up around sisters and we were never alone, so I was glad she'd made a friend.

Stepping out onto the balcony, I looked out over Zane's beautiful land. Orange leaves fell from the trees in a soft swirling motion as they made their way to the ground. I sighed, looking up at the moon and praying Adrien was okay. As I glanced at the fountain in the middle of Zane's garden, I froze.

A figure dressed in all black snuck through the moonlight, toward the castle. At first I thought it might be a thief or an attacker, but I noticed the telltale outfit he wore and recognized this as one of Adrien's spies.

I rushed through my sister's room, out the door and flew down the stairs. By the time I reached the back door, it was just in time to see the man slip inside.

He saw me and pulled his head covering off.

It was Eldon, the one we'd left back to make sure Adrien was safe.

"Please tell me he's okay," I begged. My heart couldn't take it if he was about to tell me Elisana had killed him or forced him to marry her.

He broke into a handsome grin and then pulled a piece of worn paper from his pocket.

"He's okay. He says he loves you, and he wanted me to give you this." He handed me the paper and I scanned it.

Soul-ties—how to make them, how to break them was printed in neat scrolling handwriting at the top.

I stared down at the spell on how to tie a soul to another and my stomach roiled. She'd taken my sister's hair, blood and fingernails for this.

I fast-forwarded to the breaking part and relief rushed through me.

"*If you find yourself wanting to break the soul-tie, place the vial containing the blood, hair and nails into the fire until they fully burn.*"

That's all? I just had to find the vial of my sister's stolen elements, and destroy it by fire.

My heart felt so light in that moment I could have sworn it grew wings. I burst forward and pulled Eldon into a hug, laughing as tears leaked from my eyes. "Thank you."

He hugged me back but then pulled away and met my gaze with a more serious one of his own.

"He fights the pull of the love potion, but Elisana plans for them to marry soon. We have to leave tonight."

My heart hammered in my chest at that. Leave tonight? We didn't have an army or a blood witch to help us against Elisana or if it came to it, her whole coven as well.

But if Elisana was planning on marrying him . . . Anger flashed through my body like boiling water. No. I couldn't let that happen.

I ran into the house and Eldon followed me as I roused Zane, Zander, and Dawn from their beds. Looking tired, they shuffled downstairs in their sleepwear.

I quickly brought them up to speed, and Zane flew into action. "We have two Ethereum lords: we don't need an army," he growled as Zander nodded, rolling out his neck.

"My lords, with all due respect, the entire village is teeming with blood witches," Eldon said.

Dawn chuckled. "I can cut their heads off with a sunlight beam, and Isolde can freeze them to death. Let's do this. Ready the horses. Call the train," she ordered.

Zane and Zander shared a look.

"My love," Zander started and Dawn stood so fast her chair fell over.

"No, you will *not*. Not this time. I'm not staying behind. If we don't get Adrien back so that he can help make a portal to send Zane to Faerie, all hope of any safe world to leave to our children is lost."

He sighed. "I know you are strong, but Elisana has dampener runes. What if she throws one at you? Then your power is useless."

Dawn crossed her arms. "Then don't let her get close enough to me to do that."

Zander sat a little taller as if taking her words to heart.

"You both protect Isolde and me from any witchy stuff and we will cleanse this town and save Adrien, I promise." That was the Dawn I knew. A fearless leader.

Zane and Zander shared another look, and then both nodded.

"You get weak when you use up too much power," Zander reminded her. "The babies—"

"Babies?" Zane asked, surprised.

Dawn smiled. "At least three."

Zane grinned, clapping Zander on the back. "Just like Mother."

Zander nodded, but didn't return the smile. "I don't want to treat you like you're fragile, Dawn, I know that you're more than capable, the fiercest warrior I've ever met. But you're carrying our family inside of you. I couldn't bear it if anything happened to you or the babes."

She reached out and stroked his cheek. "I won't use enough magic to weaken me. Just enough to cut down half of the witches."

I had to keep the smile from my face. It was such a Dawn thing to say. She was born and bred to be an assassin.

"Okay," Zander sighed, still looking hesitant but resigned.

* * *

We rode fast and hard from the castle to the train that awaited us. Zane had held it in the station since the day we arrived, anticipating we'd need to get back to Adrien quickly at some point. Before leaving I'd told my sister I would be back soon. Once we were settled on the train I pulled out the ripped sheet of paper Eldon had brought and looked at it more closely, to make sure I didn't miss anything.

Dawn saw me inspecting the spell and reaching over she squeezed my hand. "We've totally got this."

Her confidence was admirable but I was a ball of nerves. What if I couldn't find the vial? What if there were more blood witches in this town than I thought?

I glanced at Zander to see him watching his wife with worry, his hand going to her swollen belly in protection.

Was it right to bring Dawn? She was a total badass, but she was a mother now, carrying life. Shouldn't she avoid all risks to them and her?

Was it selfish of me to allow her to come?

As the train rocked, I felt sleep pulling at my limbs. We wouldn't be at our stop for several hours, and sleep would do me good.

All I could think about was Adrien.

Hang on, I'm coming.

Chapter Twenty-Six

Adrien

I'd done what I could, I'd bought as much time as possible, but today was the day I married Elisana.

Or so she thought.

I would never be able to go through with it. I'd try to run, but she'd either catch up with me and kill me out of anger, or harm Isolde to get back at me.

Where are you, Isolde? Had Eldon gotten her the page from the grimoire? Did it have useful information on how to break the spell?

"Your tea, my darling," Elisana said in a singsong voice.

I plastered a smile on my face as she approached. Her hair was all done up in curls and she wore a full face of make-up that made it hard to even recognize her.

I took the tea, as I had the last few days, and chugged it in one full go. She looked pleased with that and stroked my arm as she took the cup from me.

"My mother has just reached the edge of town. She will be here any moment," Elisana squealed.

"Wonderful. I'm so excited," I lied.

Elisana peered at me with concern. "Now, I wanted to talk to you about my mother."

I sat up straighter. "Okay . . ."

"Don't be frightened by her looks . . . she's, well, she's very healthy," Elisana offered.

I frowned. Healthy? What did that mean? I didn't ask because I figured the tea would make me compliant and non-questioning.

A few minutes later there was a knock at the door, and Elisana got up to get it as I moved with her. I'd have to really put on the charm with her mother as well, to buy as much time as I could until hopefully Zane and Isolde, and whoever else, came back to help get me out of here.

When the door opened, Elisana squealed, "Mommy!"

She rushed forward and hugged the woman, and then stepped out of the way so that I could see her.

When I did, my face fell.

"Rowena?" I gasped.

The purple-haired witch, who'd appeared to be in her twenties was Elisana's *mother*? Perhaps I shouldn't have been so shocked. I'd seen the woman take ten years off her face with one slurp of my brother's blood, but even so, to think that this whole time she'd been Elisana's mother. It took me by surprise and for a few moments my carefully placed mask slipped.

Elisana looked surprised. "You know each other? I know we look more like sisters but Mother, this is Adrien. The love of my life."

Elisana reached for me, and it took every ounce of my acting ability to give her a small smile and grasp her fingers.

Elisana pulled me closer to Rowena who was scowling at me with an impenetrable gaze. After looking me up and down she peered back at her daughter.

"Darling child, you have a problem. The love potion is not working on him. I can see it."

At that moment, Elisana clamped her fingers around mine like a vise and growled. "I knew it. Help me hold him down, Mother."

One second I was turning to flee, and the next something sharp cracked me in the back of the head.

Chapter Twenty-Seven

Isolde

The train stopped, and we disembarked and rode to Elisana's village in the morning sunlight. It was a little slower going than I wanted because Dawn had to ride in a carriage instead of on horseback, but we still made it to the woods surrounding the village by midday. As we neared, it became apparent that something was going on there. There were carts of flowers and food being brought in from all the surrounding places.

When we got to the very edges of the village and tied up our horses to a tree, my stomach sank as I realized what all the fuss was about.

A wedding was happening. From our hiding place within the trees, we could see that the road was covered in rose petals and a garland of flowers adorned every head.

We backed a safe distance away from the village, my mind screaming at me to charge forward and find my mate before it was too late, but I forced myself to hold back. I'm sure my restlessness was evident to everyone because I couldn't stop pacing.

"You ready to break up another wedding?" Zane asked me, and I was grateful for the confidence in his voice.

I nodded. "Find the vial of Seraphina's blood, destroy it, kill Elisana. Until then she's off limits," I told everyone. They knew what she looked like, so we were good there.

"But everyone else is fair game." Dawn cracked her knuckles, and Zander raised one eyebrow.

"Okay, little bird, get behind me and remember your promise. Take it easy." He coaxed her behind him, and she groaned.

Going under the cover of night would be ideal, but this would have to do. We agreed to split into two teams. Zane and I would go on foot to Elisana's house and try to find the vial while Dawn and Zander scoped out where the wedding was going to take place and prepare to attack.

After agreeing on a safe location to meet again, Zane and I took off, sticking to the tree line as long as possible until Elisana's house could be seen through the brush and foliage. This time we didn't walk down the cobblestone streets and enter her home through the front door. Instead, we crept toward the back entrance. We weren't sure if Elisana or her powerful mother were there, but if so, it didn't benefit us to announce our presence.

There were no shadows to hide in so we sprinted from the trees to the home, only breathing a small sigh of relief when we were pressed up against the side of the house. Zane put his finger to his mouth, indicating I should stay silent, and then carefully peeked into a couple of the windows.

"I don't think anyone is home," he said when he returned to me.

"Good. Let's find that vial."

With a nod, we moved to the back door that led into the kitchen, finding it unlocked. I hoped it wasn't that way because of a trap, but I suppose if you lived in a village with only other members of your coven, you weren't worried about someone breaking into your home.

Even though we didn't think there was anyone home, we were still careful as we entered the house. We kept a sharp ear out for any noise, but it was quickly clear we were the only ones there. That was good for searching the house, but bad for Adrien. It meant he was probably already at the wedding site, which caused my anxiety to spike. We needed to find that vial now.

I glanced at Zane and he saw the fear in my eyes. "Let's make this quick. You take upstairs, and I'll search down here," he said.

I nodded and then took off. The upstairs consisted of three bedrooms and a small bathroom. I flew through each room like a tornado, looking in every drawer, under each of the beds and mattresses, behind the curtains, and even checked for loose floorboards, but I didn't find what we were looking for.

My only hope was that Zane hadn't come up empty-handed as well, but my heart sank when I returned to the kitchen to find him standing in the middle with his hands on his hips, looking grim.

"Anything?" I asked, but he shook his head.

"I found her potions room." He pointed to the end of the kitchen where an open door led to a narrow room filled with what looked like ingredients for her potions and spells, books, and even a wall of vials. Before I could get excited about the vials, Zane said, "All the bottles and vessels in there are labeled. None of them are what we are looking for. And I checked every drawer and hiding spot in the kitchen and the rest of the floor. I don't think the vial is here," he said, his voice filled with regret.

A ball of frustration and anger swirled in my chest, growing bigger and bigger until it detonated. Throwing my hands out toward Elisana's potion room, I released my magic, freezing everything in the room. With a scream of frustration the ice then exploded, destroying everything in there. Her potions room wasn't the target I wanted, but it did make me feel a measure better knowing I'd destroyed all her things.

"Wow," Zane said, blinking at me after my show of power. "That was impressive."

"Thanks, but that was nothing compared to what I'm going to do when I get my hands on Elisana," I told him.

"I believe you," he said.

"Come on." I waved Zane over to the back door. "She must have the vial on her. Let's go check in with Dawn and Zander."

Zane nodded and followed me out of the house. This wasn't how I wanted it to happen, but I wouldn't let myself lose hope. We could still attack and stop the wedding. I just couldn't hurt Elisana until I'd burned that vial.

As quickly as possible, we hurried to where we'd agreed to meet up with Dawn and Zander. They'd beaten us back to the designated meeting spot, and Dawn was pacing when we arrived.

"Did you get it?" she asked immediately.

I shook my head. "It's not in her house. She must have it on her."

Dawn and Zander exchanged a look.

"What?" I asked.

"We think it's around her neck," Zander answered. "We caught a glimpse of her going to the ceremony location, which is an outdoor amphitheater on the other side of the village. She's wearing a gold chain with a small vial hanging on it."

"That has to be it," I said. "It's not ideal, but at least we know where it is now."

Dawn stepped forward. "That's not all." The look on her face and the tone of her voice said that I wasn't going to like what she said next.

"Is Adrien all right?" I asked, because that's all I really wanted to know at this point.

She bit her lip, but nodded. "He seems unharmed, but they have him tied up. It's obvious he's not a willing participant, but it appears they are going to go on with the ceremony anyway."

"Can they do that?" I asked. "To get married, both parties have to say, 'I do', right?"

"Perhaps not," Zane said, speaking up. "This is a blood witch ceremonial wedding. They might be able to bind Adrien to Elisana without his consent. We just don't know."

Fear wanted to pull me under, but instead I strengthened my resolve. No. I wouldn't let that happen. Adrien was my mate, and I wasn't going to let Elisana keep us apart for even one more day.

"It's time," I said. "Take me to the ceremony site. We have a wedding to stop and a groom to save."

* * *

We made it to a hill overlooking the open-air amphitheater just before the ceremony appeared to be starting. Seats were filled with women dressed in their finery on both sides of an aisle that led to the lowest part of the structure, which served as a stage. It was eerie to see no men, and it made me wonder how the women had children. And where were their husbands or lovers?

I assumed this was a site they used for rituals as well as wedding ceremonies, but I couldn't know for sure. I tried not to think too hard about what a group of blood witches would need a place like this for, or the flat stone structure that looked an awful lot like an altar on the stage below.

I spotted Adrien right away, standing at the end of an aisle, a little ways from the stone altar. He was tangled in vines that came up from the ground and wrapped around him from below his knees all the way up around his arms to his shoulders, completely incapacitating him. There was a gag in his mouth, keeping him from crying out as he thrashed against his bindings.

Everything about this sham of a ceremony was sick. From the unhinged bride to the unwilling groom.

Suddenly, all the women stood, and I glanced down the aisle to see Elisana dressed in a gossamer ballgown as she started to walk toward my mate.

Fury like I'd never felt before rose inside me, and I was about to start down the embankment toward the amphitheater when Zane caught my shoulder, only just stopping me.

I swung my gaze to him, annoyed that he was trying to hold me back when he said, "Look," and pointed toward the end of the aisle where Adrien was still fighting to free himself.

"I know, Adrien is there," I all but snapped at him.

"No, behind him," Zane said, and I followed where he was

pointing to see a woman with purple hair standing not far behind him.

"No, it can't be," Zander said, coming up next to me.

But it was. Rowena stood proud, watching Elisana move down the aisle toward her and Adrien. I could only assume she was the one presiding over the ceremony.

A traitor and a liar.

I shook my head. It didn't matter. Elisana was already halfway to Adrien, so pulling from Zane's grasp I took off, stoking my magic as I rushed forward. I heard Zane and the others following behind me, but I didn't stop to wait for them.

I was almost to the amphitheater when I finally released my magic with a roar, freezing the aisle from back to front in a sheet of ice and making Elisana tumble to the ground. I winced a little, knowing those bruises would show up on Seraphina, but I'd had to do something to stop her.

Shouts of alarm and rage sounded from the blood witches in attendance, but we'd already agreed that the others would focus on containing the witches so I could go after Elisana. Out of the corner of my eye I caught Zane, Zander, and Dawn beginning to battle with them so I paid them no mind as I rushed forward with one goal in mind. Reach Elisana.

Elisana was trying to rise to her feet when I got to her. I so badly wanted to punch her in the face, but I held back and instead I thrust my hand out and grabbed the vial strung around her neck. Elisana gasped in surprised as I ripped it free, and before she had a chance to retaliate I did the only thing I could think of. I pulled the moisture from the air and encased Elisana in an ice bubble.

My sister was a Winter princess and therefore not as susceptible to the cold, so it wouldn't hurt her if Elisana was there for a little while. I needed to keep the witch someplace safe and out of the way until I could burn this vial.

From within the ice bubble, I heard Elisana's rage-filled scream as she beat against the ice, but I knew it was too thick for her to get through. At least quickly.

With the vial grasped in my hand, I lifted my head and glanced down the aisle to where Adrien was still held captive. Rowena was gone from sight, which made me nervous, but I focused on my mate.

I was close enough to read the fear in his teal eyes and knew in my heart he wasn't worried about himself, but rather that fear was for me. But he needn't worry. I was too close to having what I wanted to let it go now.

Zane suddenly appeared next to me. He had a cut on his forehead that was dripping blood down the side of his face, but other than that, he appeared unharmed.

"Do you have the vial?" he asked, and I nodded, holding it up between us so that he could see.

"Good. Let's free my brother and then destroy that."

"I couldn't agree more."

Pulling some of my magic back, I unfroze the ice covering the aisle to make it easier for Zane and me to run across it, and then we took off. A mix of Zander's shadows and Dawn's light magic zipped around the amphitheater as they fought the coven of witches while Zane and I ran toward Adrien.

The witches pulled out wands and threw spells, but I noticed some ran away screaming, "*Ethereum lords!*" in fear. I could only imagine what a formidable pair Dawn and Zander were right now, but I couldn't waste any time to check on them. I told myself that Zander would protect Dawn, and Dawn was strong enough to keep these witches occupied a little while longer.

Zane and I had almost reached Adrien when a figure stepped in front of him, blocking us.

Rowena.

Chapter Twenty-Eight

R owena stood in front of us, holding a wand in one hand and a feral look in her eyes.

"How dare you interfere with my daughter's wedding," she growled, the wand clenched in her hand.

Daughter? Elisana was her *daughter*?

But Rowena looked young enough to be Elisana's sister, so how could that be?

An image of Rowena reverse aging in an instant after she'd drunk Zane's blood rose in my mind.

Ah.

"I've got this," Zane said and then lifted his hands toward her. I assumed he was trying to use his magic against her, but nothing happened.

Zane's eyes widened in shock and disbelief as Rowena chuckled huskily. "I've tasted your blood, my lord. Your magic is useless against me now."

Without missing a beat Zane pulled the dagger that had been sheathed at his waist. "Free Adrien," he said to me quickly, and then he rushed Rowena, who seemed caught off guard that he would attack her without magic.

She recovered from the surprise attack fast, pivoting to the side so that Zane wasn't able to embed his blade in her gut. But on his next strike, he slashed her hand and she dropped her wand. He came at her again, and she spun out of the way, leaving an opening for me to reach Adrien, which I wasn't about to waste.

Jolting forward, I reached my mate. Pulling my faestone dagger, I started to hack at the vines holding him in place. He uttered a muffled shout that I took as a warning and I turned just in time to punch an ice spear through the chest of some random witch who had been about to drive a dagger through my back.

She stared at me with surprised wide eyes before crumpling to the ground at my feet. I didn't even spare her a glance before spinning back around. I cut more of the vines away, using my magic to freeze some of them and snap them off. I almost had all the vines entwined around his upper body removed when suddenly more of them started to grow at his feet, twisting up his legs and snacking toward his torso. I grunted in frustration as sounds of battle between Dawn and Zander and the witches rang out behind me.

I doubled my efforts, snapping off frozen vines as quickly as possible until Adrien was finally able to get an arm free.

He ripped the gag out of his mouth. "The rune. Cut it off."

Of course!

I glanced down at the shining purple rune on his chest and quickly swiped my faestone dagger across it. It disappeared, and with a roar, shadows around us raced toward Adrien and shredded the vines still holding him in place.

Impressive.

Rushing forward, he took me into his arms, kissing my lips briefly before pulling back to see the carnage behind us.

"Tell me the page in the grimoire helped you figure out how to break the soul-tie." Even as he spoke, shadows raced out of him and slammed into the witches nearest us, sending them flying across the amphitheater.

I nodded and held up the vial. "I need to burn this to break the connection between Elisana and my sister. Then we can finish her."

Adrien grabbed my hand, and we sprinted to the back of the ceremonial stage where a small fire burned. A black pot of bubbling potion sat above the flames. I didn't want to know what this potion would have done if they'd made him drink it.

Zane's roar cut through the air at the same time Rowena shrieked and then I heard breaking ice.

No.

Rowena was setting her daughter free from my ice cage.

"Do it now," Adrien shouted and I threw the vial into the fire, watching it crack in half and be consumed by flames.

"You bastard!" Elisana screamed at Adrien, and when I spun in her direction she was free of her ice cage and running at us.

I paused before acting. Afraid she would kill my mate, but equally afraid that maybe the soul-tie wasn't fully broken yet and I would kill Seraphina.

Shoving Adrien behind me, I shot an ice shard from my hand, aiming for Elisana's right shoulder as a test to see whether or not the soul-tie was actually broken. The ice blade slammed into her and she staggered back. Blood immediately bloomed over her shoulder and started to drip down her arm.

"A little help!" Zane yelled, grabbing my attention.

I snapped my gaze across the amphitheater to see Rowena holding her wand up in front of her, aimed right at Zane's face.

I didn't think. I just acted and flicked my wrist toward Rowena, unleashing a huge amount of my power and freezing her solid from head to toe. Without pause, Zane smashed the hilt of his dagger into her chest and she shattered into a hundred pieces.

"No!" Elisana roared.

My gaze flicked back to her to see that she was still bleeding from her right shoulder; the wound had not transferred to my sister.

Relief flooded me. The soul-tie was broken, and her attention was consumed with her mother.

Now I could end her.

I raised my hand, a breath away from freezing her like I did her mother when Adrien grasped my fingers, staying me.

"Let me?" he asked.

Anger and fury swirled in the depths of his teal eyes. She had done the worst to him after all.

I nodded.

Elisana sensed her impending doom and took off running, heading for the back of the aisle while holding her bleeding shoulder, but Adrien's shadows were faster.

She hit the shadow wall and tried to change course, but he blocked her in on all sides, giving her nowhere to run. She spun to face us, her chest moving up and down with rapid breaths.

Her eyes filled with fear as she watched Adrien walk down the aisle toward her. As she watched death coming for her.

When Adrien reached her and glared down at her, I didn't feel even a flicker of remorse. She had brought this upon herself. This was the reckoning that she deserved.

"There is nothing I can think of that is more evil than forcing your will on another," Adrien said, his voice as cold and sharp as one of my ice spears. "You deserve to be ripped apart limb by limb."

Elisana whimpered, cowering before him.

"But I'm a decent man, and so I'll offer you a quick death."

Elisana's head snapped up and in an instant the fear melted off her and her face sharpened into a hate-filled mask. Screaming, she lunged for Adrien with her fingers bent like claws, but she didn't reach him before his shadows consumed her.

One second she was there, the next she was eaten by darkness. There were screams and the sound of a struggle, but then the shadows disappeared.

Elisana was dead, collapsed on the floor, face blue like the oxygen had been taken from her lungs.

I sighed in relief as Adrien turned to me and we took stock of what threats were left.

Some witches at the back of the theater were being chased out by Dawn and Zander. There were a few lying dead in the surrounding area, but everyone else seemed to have fled.

"I will never give a witch my blood again," Zane declared, which caused Adrien to smile slightly.

I stepped closer to him, needing Adrien to see me fully and hear what I was about to say.

"I thought I was going to lose you," I told him as he pulled me into his arms. "I thought you would die, or be forcefully married off to another without knowing how I truly felt."

He stepped back and peered down at me with an adoring gaze as he stroked my cheek. "And how do you feel, Isolde?"

I took a deep breath. "I love you. I can't imagine being without you, and I think love is enough. Our love is enough."

A huge grin graced his face and he pulled me in for a toe-curling kiss.

Dawn whooped and clapped as I smiled against Adrien's mouth.

When Adrien drew back, he peered down at me. "Does this mean you're not afraid of marriage anymore?" He sounded hopeful.

"Not with you. In fact, I can't imagine spending one more moment not married to you," I declared. "Marry me? Right now?" I begged.

He looked around at the flower-decorated altar and then to the dead bodies on the ground. "Hmm, this place wasn't quite what I envisioned for us."

I laughed.

"Hey, there is a waterfall down here," Dawn called out. She was at the top of the amphitheater steps, looking down on the canyon.

A short ten-minute hike later we all stood at the base of a small pool at the bottom of a twenty-foot waterfall. The water that cascaded down from the ledge above was crystal clear and sparkling in the last rays of the dying day's sunlight. It was breathtaking, and free of the carnage from our battle.

Dawn stood on my right holding a handful of wild flowers and thistles she'd picked on her way down here. Zane stood on Adrien's right.

Zander stood in front of Adrien and me to officiate the wedding. Since he was the Ethereum lord of this Northern Kingdom, he had the power and authority to legally marry us.

"My father once told me that our mate is the one whom our soul chooses," Zander said, beaming at the both of us. "Adrien, do you choose to love, care for, and be loyal to Isolde for as long as you still have breath in your lungs?"

"A million times," Adrien breathed while staring into my eyes.

My throat tightened with emotion when Zander asked me the same question. "I do. Forever."

Zander smiled. "Then you are now—"

Adrien leaned in and stole a kiss, which made Dawn cheer in excitement and Zane laugh.

"Husband and wife," Zander finished after we broke apart and I laughed.

We were dirty, covered in blood and the signs of battle, but I knew in my heart that Adrien was a partner that I could go through all of life's ups and downs with.

With a shout of excitement, Dawn leaped into the pool and created a big splash.

"Dawn, be careful," Zander scolded and jumped in after her, swimming to check on her.

Dawn rolled her eyes at her husband when he reached her. "Oh, relax, I'm just swimming."

Zane shrugged and pulled off his shirt and dove in as well.

Adrien looked at me, holding my hand, and walked us to the edge of the water.

Our job wasn't over yet. We still had to help Zane get to Faerie and end the curse. We still had to protect Adrien's people from the curse, but for now . . . we could have this one small reprieve.

With a shout of joy we both leaped into the crisp, cold water, and I plugged my nose as I submerged. The cold bite of the water was refreshing and cleansing, and I felt renewed when my head broke the surface.

Adrien popped up next to me and took me into his arms, gazing into my eyes. "I'm the luckiest man in all the realms."

"I beg to differ," Zander piped in, and we all laughed.

This day ended as perfectly as possible, and for that, I was grateful.

Chapter Twenty-Nine

I never expected my wedding night to be spent on a train with not one, but *three* Ethereum lords and my best friend who'd been raised to kill them, but here I was.

In all fairness though, I'd never really imagined my wedding night before because I hadn't thought I'd get married, so it was not as if it wasn't living up to expectations.

Married. I was married to Adrien. I was Adrien's wife, and he was my husband.

I thought there'd be a wave of panic and regret to accompany those thoughts, but there wasn't. Not even a little. Instead, I felt at peace. Maybe even for the first time in my life as I snuggled into Adrien's side.

After our spur-of-the-moment wedding, all of us had taken a quick swim in the pond at the base of the waterfall to wash the battle off. We then returned to the station where Zane's train was waiting and departed for Windreum right away. We were hopeful that Aribella and Stryker would be there when we arrived so Zane could leave for Faerie soon. And we knew that the train was needed to bring refugees from the south to the west, where all of Ethereum was now traveling to safety. We didn't want to take it up any more than we had to when so many others had need of it.

The original plan was for Adrien and me to retreat to one of the sleeper cars to spend our wedding night alone once we all briefly discussed our next steps, but I'd been so exhausted I'd fallen asleep against him almost immediately.

I'd been embarrassed when I'd woken hours later and realized I'd slept almost the entire way back to Windreum, essentially ruining our opportunity to have time alone together. But Adrien had just looked at me lovingly as he ran his fingers over my cheek and told me we had a lifetime together, so there was no rush. It was the perfect response and made me fall even deeper in love with him.

According to Zane we were now less than a half hour from Windreum. Dawn and Zander sat in the passenger car a couple of rows in front of us, cuddled together. I glanced across the aisle at Zane who sat alone. His gaze was trained out the window even though it was still too dark to see anything. I could see his face in the glass's reflection, and there was a faraway look in his eyes. I knew his mind wasn't with us right now, but instead fixed on Lorelei.

If Stryker and Aribella were already in Windreum, Zane wanted to try to leave for Faerie immediately. His plan involved creating a portal using the brothers' combined powers, and none of us knew if it would work or what it would do to the lords. Zander and Adrien had both insisted Zane spend the day preparing and get one good night's sleep before attempting his half-cocked plan. Zane hadn't agreed, so they were in somewhat of a stalemate currently.

As much as I knew it pained him to wait even one more night,

I agreed that Zane needed the rest, and waiting just one more day would also give Dawn, Aribella and me some time to teach him all we knew about Faerie. He didn't know what he was going to face when he arrived there, so journeying exhausted and ill-prepared wouldn't do him any favors. Even now, I could see the dark smudges under his eyes in his reflection, telling me he hadn't slept at all.

Seeing the forlorn look on his face made my heart ache for him, but what he didn't understand was that Queen Liliana was as ruthless as she was cunning. Zane had come to mean something to me, and if he was going to have to face off against the Summer Court queen—which I feared might end up being the case—he needed to be rested and at full power. So if I got a vote on the matter, it would be to wait the extra day as well.

The train whistle rang, letting us know we were getting close to the Western Kingdom's capital. I sat up fully, but Adrien wouldn't let me get far. Putting an arm around me, he tugged me so that we were still pressed up against each other with my head resting on his shoulder. I couldn't look into his eyes from my position, but I felt his steady heartbeat beneath my hand where it rested against his chest, and the distracting movement of his thumb as it brushed back and forth over my hip.

Adrien shifted, and I felt the press of his lips as they whispered over my forehead in a gentle kiss. "Having regrets?" he asked, his voice light and laced with humor, but he tensed when I didn't immediately respond.

I pressed against his chest, forcing some space between us so I could look into his eyes. I saw concern and doubt there, and my heart squeezed.

Of course I had no regrets. I hadn't meant to make him insecure about my feelings for him, but I wanted to be looking in his eyes when I told him that so he could see the truth as well as hear it.

Reaching up, I placed a hand against his cheek and ran my thumb over his full bottom lip, enjoying the smooth contrast to the rough stubble against my palm. His eyes became heavy and dark with desire, which sent a sudden bolt of awareness through me that I tried my best to ignore.

"Adrien," I said, speaking deliberately. "I know I was scared before, but hear me when I say there's nothing in this realm or any other that can make me regret the decision to be your wife."

He released a heavy sigh, his relief clear as a soft smile turned up the corners of his mouth. But I wasn't done.

"We don't know what the future brings," I admitted. "But whether we have a lifetime together or just a few more days, marrying you will always be the best thing I ever did."

Adrien growled low in his throat and tugged me closer. "We *will* have a lifetime together," he vowed, his voice deep and dripping with conviction. "I won't allow anything less."

"And I look forward to every single day of it," I said as I smiled up at him.

I loved seeing the fire stoke in his gaze as I ran my fingers slowly down the column of his neck until my hand rested over his heart once again. This time, it beat a furious pace under my palm.

He let out another low noise that was half growl, half moan. "Do you think we have time to find that sleeper car?"

I grinned, liking where his mind was going. I opened my

mouth to tell him it was worth a try when the train whistle blasted, interrupting me.

"We're fifteen minutes from the station," Zane called from somewhere behind me, and Adrien heaved a frustrated sigh, looking up at the roof of the train car before tipping his head back down to me.

Reaching out, he traced my upper lip and then lower lip with the tip of his finger, his gaze following the path. His attention made my mouth feel extra sensitive, and I wanted nothing more than for him to kiss me, and kiss me hard.

"As anxious as I am to get you alone," he said, his voice dropping an octave and making a delicious thrill run through me, "what I have planned for you will undoubtedly take longer than a quarter of an hour."

His words caused a fire to stoke low in my gut, and it was my turn to smother a groan.

A smile broke out on Adrien's face at my reaction. Leaning down, he placed a feather-light kiss on my lips that in no way satiated the desire now running through me before pulling back again. "The wait will be worth it."

"Do you promise?" I asked breathlessly, even though I'd done no physical activity.

"Always."

* * *

It was a flurry of activity when we reached the station in Windreum. Stryker and Aribella had arrived only a few hours before us in the middle of the night. The sun was just starting to crest the horizon as we traveled through the city to Zane's castle. Once we arrived, even though it was early, we all went to meet Stryker and Aribella in Zane's drawing room.

I wasn't as close to the Fall Court princess as I was to Dawn, but our reunion was still a warm one. We hugged and her face beamed when she heard that Adrien and I were married. She introduced me to her husband, Stryker, who was as handsome and fearsome in person as I remember him being when he'd appeared in my room with the rest of them.

Stryker didn't come off as a particularly warm fae. I could tell it would take more than one interaction to feel at ease with the brooding lord, but what sold me on him was how he looked at Aribella. The way his eyes lit up with unveiled love and his face softened told me everything I needed to know. There was no doubt in my mind that he loved her deeply, and that was enough for me.

After strategizing the whole morning and listening to Zane argue with his brothers again about trying to make a portal immediately, we all finally convinced Zane to wait another day. Yet the compromise was that he would leave at first light and not a moment later.

Assuming this portal he and his brothers intended to make even worked. He hadn't explained much in detail, just that with their combined magic they should be able to do it and it would leave them all weak for a day afterward. I just trusted that they knew what they were doing.

We disbanded after that, Zane going to gather what he needed for his journey. Since we'd all been traveling and were tired, Dawn,

Zander, Aribella and Stryker retired to their rooms to rest. Before resting myself, I wanted to check in on my sister and explain to her about my marriage to Adrien. It was going to be a shock to her to find out that I'd married the Ethereum lord, and I didn't want her to hear about it from anyone else.

I told Adrien I also wanted to clean up. I wasn't a particularly fussy princess with regards to fashion and appearance, but my hair felt like a litter of squirrels had made their home in it and my clothes were stiff and uncomfortable. And if I were being honest, less than fresh smelling.

Adrien was gracious about my wanting to visit my sister, and gave me a toe-curling kiss before letting me go that almost had me abandoning my plans.

I went as far as to turn to follow him when my name was called, snapping me out of it.

When I glanced over my shoulder I saw my sister running up the stairs to meet me, her dark hair streaming behind her. Zane's healer must have been one of the best because the color had returned to her face, and since she was running, she didn't appear to have any lasting physical effects from her ordeal.

Thank the stars.

Sera and I collided in a giant hug. I wasn't sure who squeezed who the hardest, but my ribs were sore when we finally broke apart. Sera wanted to know everything that happened with Elisana, down to the last detail, and so it took more time than I would have liked to relay the entire story.

Finally, I got to the part where I'd basically proposed to Adrien and then our hasty wedding.

Her brows shot straight up her forehead. "You're married?" she asked with something akin to awe.

I nodded.

"I'm . . ." she said.

I bit my lip, bracing myself for her reaction.

". . . glad," she finished with a soft smile, and then it was my turn to be surprised.

"You are?" I asked. I'd expected her to be at least a little upset that I'd married an Ethereum lord, our supposed enemy, but the look on her face only conveyed sincerity. She truly seemed happy for me.

Reaching forward, she took my hand in between both of hers, her face turning serious. "Yes, I am. I know that what happened between Mother and Father hit us all hard, but I think in some ways as the eldest, you the most. I've been concerned that you would never open yourself up. That you would only ever push love out of your life, but I can clearly see that you've let it in. When you talk about Lord Adrien, joy shines from your eyes. It's apparent to me that what you have with him is special."

I blinked back at my sister, wondering when she'd gotten so wise. "Thank you for understanding," I said with unexpected tears prickling the back of my eyes.

"Of course," she told me. "It makes me happy to see you happy." She grinned. "Now go on. You've already wasted enough time with me. I appreciate you humoring your sister, but you have a handsome lord waiting for you. If our situations were reversed, I certainly wouldn't still be here with you."

* * *

Much to my disappointment, I couldn't find Adrien right away. I searched a whole floor of Zane's castle for him, but he was nowhere to be found. When I finally questioned one of Zane's staff about where the Southern lord was, she directed me to what was supposed to be our shared bed chambers, but he wasn't there either. There was, however, a steaming bath already waiting for me. The woman who showed me to the room said it was filled for me at Lord Adrien's request and then with a wink, she left me.

The bath felt amazing, but I couldn't fully enjoy it because I missed my new husband. At some point, Zane had had all the clothes he purchased for me in Soleum moved to this room, and so after I'd thoroughly washed my body and hair, I changed into a pretty deep purple dress that hugged my ribs and flared at the hips. It was a little lower cut than I was used to, but I felt beautiful in it.

I chuckled to myself when I realized that Adrien had never even seen me dressed as a princess before. The dress wasn't as extravagant as what I might have worn in the Winter Court, but it was a far cry from the torn and dirty pant and shirt combinations I'd mostly been in around him.

I was sitting in front of the mirror vanity, combing out my mostly dry hair when the door to the chamber opened behind me. Adrien appeared in the mirror's reflection, his gaze connecting with mine immediately. The look on his face was one I knew I'd never tire of seeing. It was part awe, part desire. He gazed at me like he was a starving man, and I was his meal. And I loved it.

Warmth gathered inside me, growing in heat and intensity the longer we stayed locked in our stare. He looked like he had bathed as well, hair wet and slicked back with fresh clothes on.

Finally, Adrien moved toward me, practically prowling, his intent clear. I stayed perfectly still, keeping my gaze connected with his in the mirror's reflection as my heart pounded furiously in my chest.

He took his time reaching me, drawing out the moment. It was an exquisite kind of torture to wait for him to make a move.

When he stood right behind me he finally broke our stare. Glancing down at me he reached forward and pulled the length of my long raven hair over one shoulder, exposing my neck to him. My breath caught in my throat when he ran his fingers gently over the base of my neck, and I tilted to give him more access.

"You are the most beautiful creature I've ever laid eyes on," Adrien said.

His reflection was no longer enough for me, and I twisted in my seat so I could look up into his true face. His eyes shone with love, overwhelming me.

"I don't deserve you or your love," he said, his voice barely above a whisper.

A touch of sadness infiltrated my haze of desire. Adrien was the most amazing man I'd ever met. Brave. Honorable. Kind. Not to mention irresistible. He was more than deserving of me and my love.

"Don't say that," I said, reaching up to place my fingertips on his lips. "I love you."

He softly kissed my fingertips and then took my hand. "I love you too, and I will spend a lifetime making sure you never regret the decision to marry me, starting now."

With speed I wasn't aware he was capable of, Adrien reached down and gently ringed my waist with his free arm, pulling me to my feet. I blinked and then was standing with my back to the thick bedpost and my front crushed against Adrien's chest.

My heartbeat started to race like the flapping of a humming-bird's wings as anticipation bubbled inside me.

"I can't wait to give you the wedding night you deserve," he said, his mouth mere inches from mine.

Yes, I wanted that too.

I glanced over his shoulder to where the windows were letting in the early afternoon sun. "Wedding night?" I asked with a coy smile. "But it appears to still be day, my lord. Does that mean you intend to make us wait until the sun sets?" I joked.

Bending his head, he ran the tip of his nose from the base of my neck up the column of my throat. The light touch felt criminally good, and when he reached the sensitive spot behind my ear a soft growl rumbled in his chest. "The length of a single night isn't long enough for what I plan to do with you, so we need to start early."

"Is that so?"

He made a purring sound at the back of his throat that sent a wave of warmth straight to my belly.

Adrien pulled back slightly, and I already missed the full press of his body against mine. "This is a lovely dress," he said, running his fingers over the edge of the low-cut bodice, making a shiver of pure desire run through me. When he looked up, his teal eyes were blazing. "Do you mind if I rip it off you?"

With those words, my mouth went dry and my mind went blank, so all I managed to do was nod.

A wolfish smile appeared on his face, and I knew then that Adrien was right. The length of a single night was certainly not long enough.

Chapter Thirty

After spending the afternoon and night with my new husband, I had to force myself out of my love bubble to support Zane. The curse was only getting worse across Ethereum and I knew it would be the same in Faerie. Aribella, Dawn and I spent the early morning hours telling Zane all we could about our world and Queen Liliana.

When everyone had eaten breakfast, Zane stood, rubbing his hands together in a nervous fashion. "Let's do this."

Dawn stood and set a folded bundle of something on the table. "I'm not sure if you will need these to cross through the portal, but it can't hurt."

She indicated Zane take whatever it was. He opened the cloth package and I noticed two beautiful stones. Sunstone and Carnelian. Stones that used to be embedded in the hilt of her and Aribella's daggers. I'm sure there was a story there.

"Oh, take mine too. Dawn is right. We cross into the portal with these and can't go back without them." It wasn't like I would need mine anymore.

I laid my blue kyanite dagger on top of the two other stones.

Zane bundled them carefully and slipped them into his pouch. With that, we headed outside to the woods behind Zane's palace. He warned us that the magic he and his brothers used was powerful when directed through the earth but would make them very weak, possibly even causing them to pass out.

I was anxious for Adrien but knew he had to do whatever it took to help Zane.

When we reached a clearing in the woods, I faced off with Zane. "You have the Shadow Heart potion and the two halves?"

He tapped his satchel.

"And you also have the maps we drew?" I asked.

He reached out and grasped my shoulders. "I'm going to be fine. Thank you for being such a good friend."

With that, he pulled me into a hug, and my heart pinched. Zane and I shared a special bond and always would. I cared about him like a brother. And now he *was* my brother.

"Be safe," I told him and pulled away as everyone else stepped in to give hugs and say their goodbyes.

Once we had, Zane stood in the middle of his brothers and glanced at Zander. "You've always been the strongest with this type of magic. I need you to give it all you got."

Zander nodded once and then reached down and pulled off his shirt, rolling out his neck as if he were getting ready to fight.

"Showing off those muscles, brother?" Stryker teased.

Zander smirked. "I'm from the north: if there isn't snow, I'm hot."

I grinned at that. "Same."

"I'm not complaining." Dawn fanned herself as she looked at her mate and I couldn't help but peer around at our little crew and allow the love to overflow my heart. Not only did I find my mate and marry him, but I'd also gained three brothers. Something I never thought I'd have.

The Ethereum lords got into place, fanning out around Zane who stood in the middle of the triangle they formed as Aribella, Dawn and I stayed back and out of the way.

Zane looked at his brothers. "Remember when we visited Isolde in our spirit form in the blood witch's spell?"

They nodded. "This will be like that. You will envision going to that place, Faerie, and then hit the earth with all the power you can, connecting with each other. I'll then pull the magic up and hopefully create a portal."

"Hopefully?" Stryker asked.

Zane swallowed hard. "This has been done once before, hundreds of years ago, and the notes left behind are in the worst ink-stained handwriting I've ever seen."

"It will be okay. You've got this." Aribella cheered everyone on.

I wondered who created a portal to our world hundreds of years ago. Probably something that had been covered up.

"I'm ready," Zander said with a deadly calm, sinking his fingers into the earth and holding on.

"Me too," Stryker offered, following suit and falling down onto his knees.

"Same." Adrien bent to one knee and began to dig his fingertips into the ground as well.

This was it. Dawn slipped her hand into mine and then I reached out and grasped Aribella's. We all stood off to the side and watched in anxiety as the men breathed in and out slowly.

"Ready," Zane finally said and sat on his heels, digging his hands into the soil like all his brothers had.

What happened next was one of the most beautiful things I'd ever seen.

It started with Zander. A golden glow rose up from where he crouched and moved to Stryker, washing over him like a wave and then going to Adrien. It covered my husband and then disappeared into the earth before popping up around Zane and cocooning him.

"Wow," Dawn breathed beside me.

I inched forward, still clinging to Aribella and Dawn. The golden magic seemed to solidify over Zane as he grunted, no doubt trying to make his portal.

"The image of Faerie in my mind's eye isn't enough," Zane growled.

I had an idea then of what might help. Letting go of Dawn and Aribella's hands, I rushed into the center of the circle, feeling a buzz come over my skin as I crossed the threshold.

Zane peered up at me pleadingly as I reached into the satchel around his hip. I grasped the two stones from Dawn and Aribella's dagger and then my own and pulled them out, placing them under his palms between his skin and the earth. The second I did this I was nearly blown off my feet with a force of power.

"What was that?" Zander shouted.

I stumbled out of the circle and looked back to see a small window had opened in front of Zane. A window to our world. But it wasn't large enough for Zane to go through, and it was flickering.

"Those are the Harvest Mountains," Aribella exclaimed.

They were indeed the Harvest Mountains of Fall Court, and they were as black as night, covered in what looked like oil. The image flickered in and out.

"I can't hold on much longer," Adrien cried.

Zane grunted in defiance. "I just need it to get a little bigger so I can jump through."

Should he be going through on the other side of the Harvest Mountains? It wasn't Spring Court, it wasn't healthy. But it was his only shot, so I knew he would no matter what.

"Maybe we can help them," Dawn said, rushing forward to kneel beside Zander.

"No, stay back," Zander grunted, sweat beading down his face.

She dug her hands into the earth next to him and I could see sunlight beams pour out of her fingertips and into the soil.

The portal suddenly stopped flickering and blew open wider.

It worked!

Aribella and I rushed to kneel next to our husbands without another word and added our magic as well. I fed my icy tendrils into the earth and then felt as it took what I offered. It was like a drain had been pulled from a tub and magic started sucking out of me.

I peered up to see the portal open to the size of a door, and black sludgy water poured inside of our world as Zane met my gaze.

"No, it's too dangerous. We'll try again another day," I yelled to him. This wasn't the Spring Court.

"I'll stop the curse, or die trying, and I won't let a hair on Lorelei's head be harmed." He declared it like an oath and then

leaped into the portal, ripping his hands from the earth and bar-
reling through just as it snapped shut behind him.

The rest of us fell backward, panting as exhaustion pulled at
our limbs. Laying on the forest floor, I peered over at Adrien and
my heart broke for Zane. We all had each other, and he'd just gone
on a one-man mission to save both of our worlds.

May the stars be with you.

Epilogue

Lorelei

O ne second, Isolde and the handsome Lord Zane were standing in front of me in the garden, and the next, Queen Liliana showed up and they disappeared.

"I knew I couldn't trust you," the Winter queen seethed, her face contorting into a reflection of rage as she stalked toward me.

I backed up a few paces, holding my hands up in surrender. "I didn't know they would be here."

She shook her head. "You can't save us." Her words hit me in the chest like arrows, piercing me deep.

"I want to," I said more timidly than I'd intended to.

I wasn't a warrior. It literally went against my magic. I gave life, I didn't take it. But even so, I hadn't lied. I did want to save our world.

As the queen advanced I backpedaled until my shoulders hit the tree behind me. I held my breath as Queen Liliana walked right up to me. "You fancied him, didn't you? That lord who said he was coming for you?"

She'd heard?

My heart pounded in my chest. The letter Isolde sent to me had sounded unbelievable, but now I wondered if it were true.

"Are they our mates?" I dared to ask, my voice no louder than a whisper. "Is it true?"

We didn't have mates in Faerie, but I still understood the concept. I'd only ever heard the term in fairy tales: myths and fables our parents read to us as children. It was said there was no connection stronger than mates. That it wasn't just love that bonded the pair, but magic as well.

The queen's upper lip curled so that she was sneering at me. "Yes. A small price to pay to bring peace for a hundred years."

I whimpered at the confession, despair filling my heart. All these years, the Summer princess champions had been sent to Ethereum to kill their mates. And Queen Liliana expected the same of me now.

I shook my head, a tear falling down my face. "I can't. I won't hurt him."

If the handsome man who'd come in the vision with Isolde was my mate, I wouldn't harm him.

Queen Liliana nodded, a slow smile streaking her lips and causing a foreboding shiver to slither down my spine. "I know you won't, delicate Lorelei. That's why I'm going to use you as bait to bring him to me so *I* can carve his heart from his chest myself and end this once and for all."

"What?"

No! I can't let her use me like that.

I burst forward, intending to run, when she reached out with something shiny and cracked the side of my head.

I had about two seconds to process the fact that the Summer queen had just struck me, and then everything went black.

Acknowledgments

A big thank you to my amazing co-author and best friend Julie for being so fun to write with. Also a huge thank you to our publishers HQ, and editors Cat and Seema, for loving and believing in this series as much as we do. To my agents Flavia and Meire at Bookcase Literary for all they do, and a special thanks to our readers for supporting us all these years. I can't believe I get to call this a job!

~ Leia

My first thanks go to Leia for putting up with all my quirks and keeping our co-writing ship moving forward. It's an unbelievable pleasure to work with such a talented co-author and amazing friend. To Flavia and Meire at Bookcase Literary Agency, thank you for championing this series for us. We're so fortunate to have you in our corner! Thanks to Seema, Cat, and the whole HQ team. We're thrilled that *Cursed Fae* has found a home with you. And finally, thanks to all our amazing readers. You're the reason we get to do what we love!

~ Julie

Captivated by *Broken Hearted*? The story continues in the Cursed Fae series . . .

To save my kingdom, someone must die . . .

Book 1: Cold Hearted

Every hundred years, a curse descends on Faerie, ravaging its lands and killing its people. For the last two millennia, the Summer Court princess has always been the one to stop it.

Book 2: Faint Hearted

With the curse that's plagued their lands for the last two millennia running out of control, the task now falls to the Fall Court princess, Aribella, to stop it from spreading further.

Book 3: Broken Hearted

The Winter Court princess must find the next piece of the puzzle to end the curse ravaging her lands.

Book 4: Black Hearted

With the curse threatening to destroy not only Faerie, but Ethereum as well, the last princess of Faerie must work with one of the dark Ethereum lords to end the curse once and for all . . . or die trying.

ONE PLACE. MANY STORIES

Bold, innovative and
empowering publishing.

FOLLOW US ON:

@HQStories